TENKO KING

Volume 1: A New Leaf

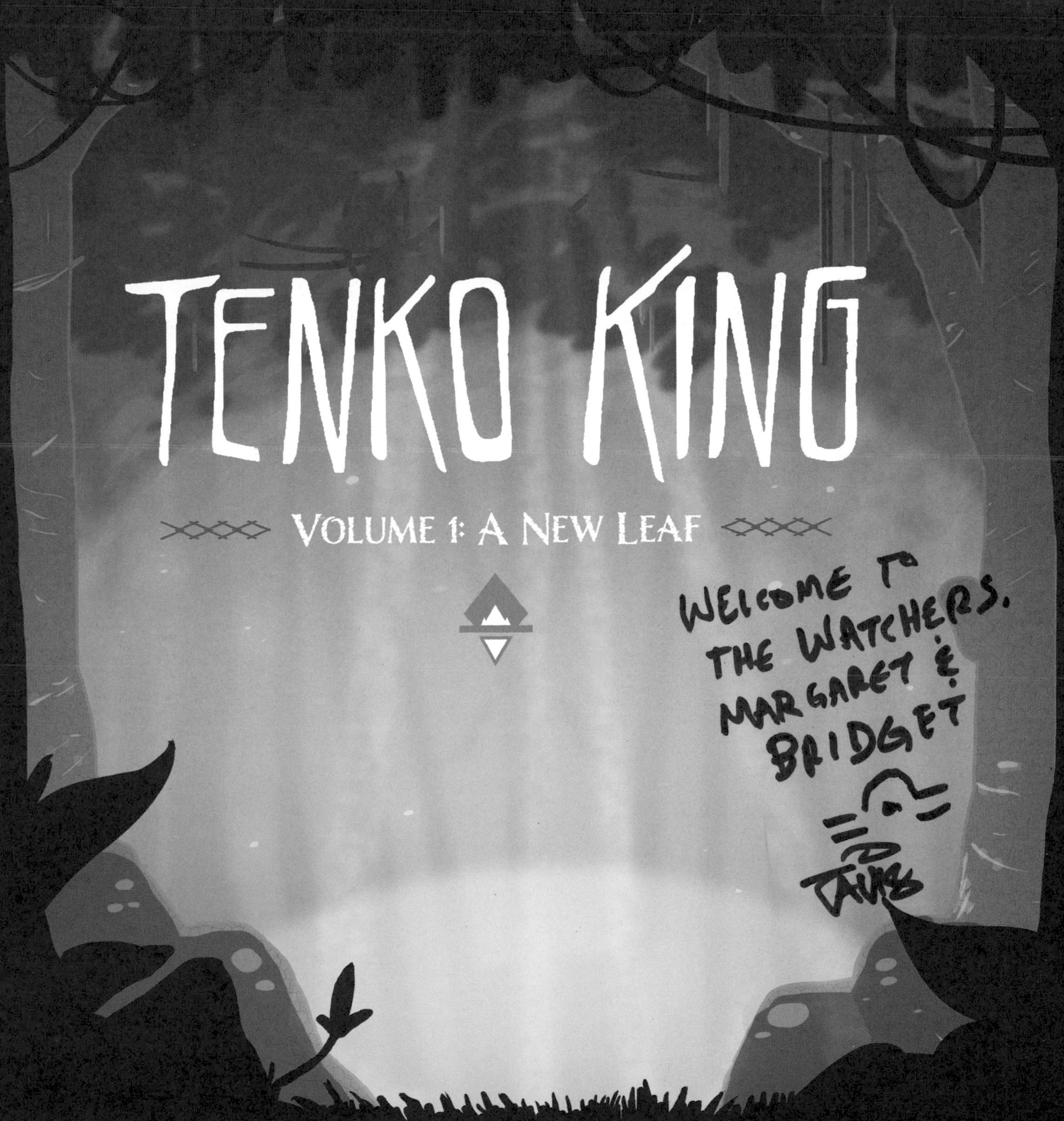

Welcome to the Watchers.
Margaret & Bridget

Toonhound Studios
www.toonhoundstudios.com

TENKO KING

VOLUME 1: A NEW LEAF

~ BY ~

TAVIS MAIDEN

DESIGN BY

KEITH WOOD

TENKO KING

VOLUME ONE: A NEW LEAF

Tenko King™, Volume 1: A New Leaf © 2016 Tavis Maiden. No portion
of this publication may be reproduced or transmitted, in any form or by
any means, without the express written permission of Tavis Maiden.
Names, characters, places, and incidents featured in this publication
either are the product of the author's imagination or are used fictitiously.
Any resemblance to actual persons (living or dead), events, institutions,
or locales, without satiric intent, is coincidental.

PUBLISHED BY TOONHOUND STUDIOS, LLC
4110 SE HAWTHORNE BLVD
#244
PORTLAND, OR 97214

THIS VOLUME COLLECTS THE FIRST YEAR OF TENKO KING.

 FACEBOOK.COM/TENKOKINGCOMIC
 TWITTER.COM/TAVISMAIDEN
 TAVISMAIDEN.TUMBLR.COM

FIRST EDITION: AUGUST 2016
ISBN: 978-0-9972269-0-4

LIBRARY OF CONGRESS CONTROL NUMBER: 2016941170

1 3 5 7 9 10 8 6 4 2

TENKOKING.COM

Printed in China

PROLOGUE

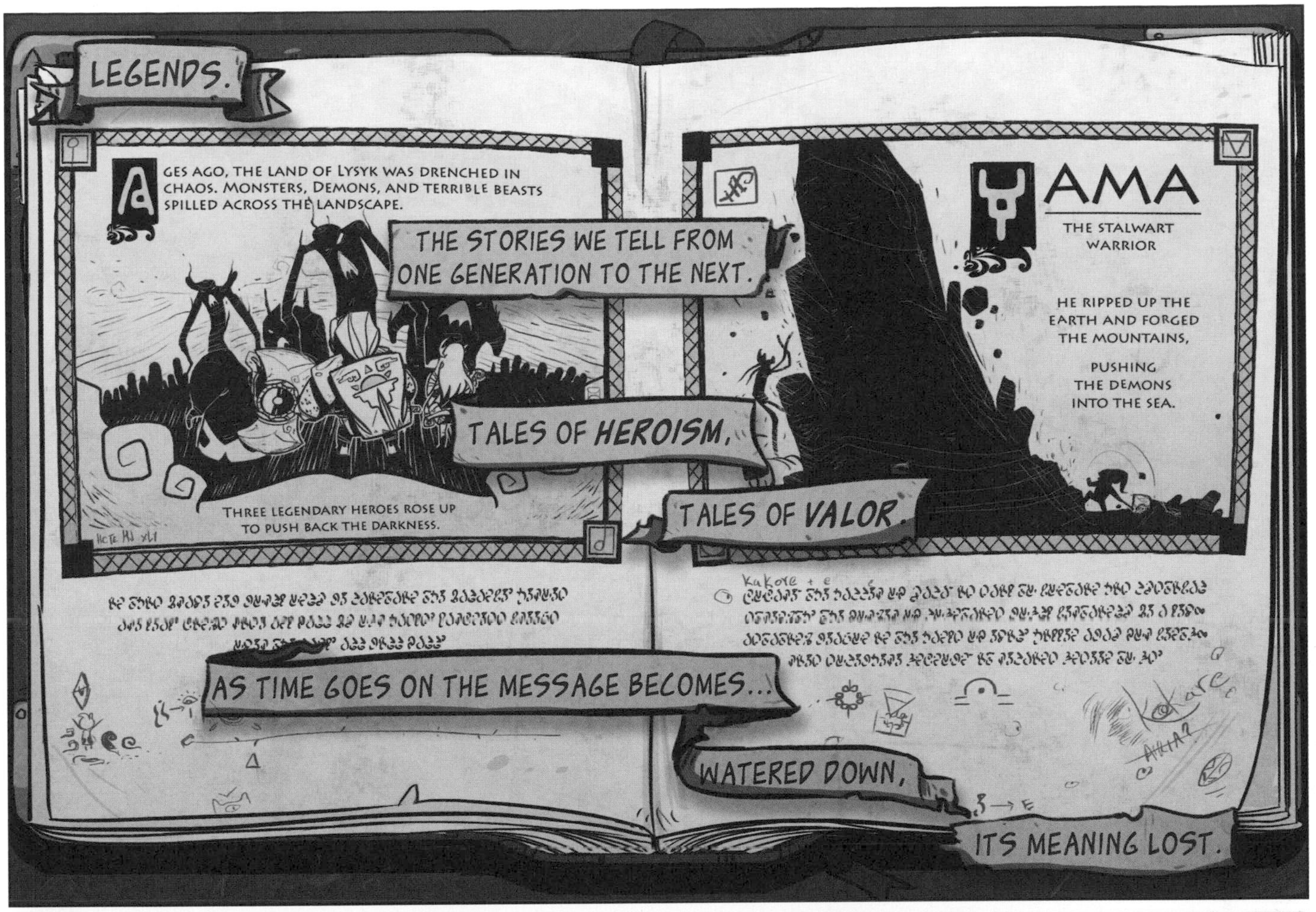
LEGENDS.
Ages ago, the land of Lysyk was drenched in chaos. Monsters, Demons, and terrible beasts spilled across the landscape.
THE STORIES WE TELL FROM ONE GENERATION TO THE NEXT.
YAMA
The Stalwart Warrior
He ripped up the earth and forged the mountains,
Pushing the demons into the sea.
TALES OF HEROISM,
Three legendary heroes rose up to push back the darkness.
TALES OF VALOR.
AS TIME GOES ON THE MESSAGE BECOMES...
WATERED DOWN,
ITS MEANING LOST.

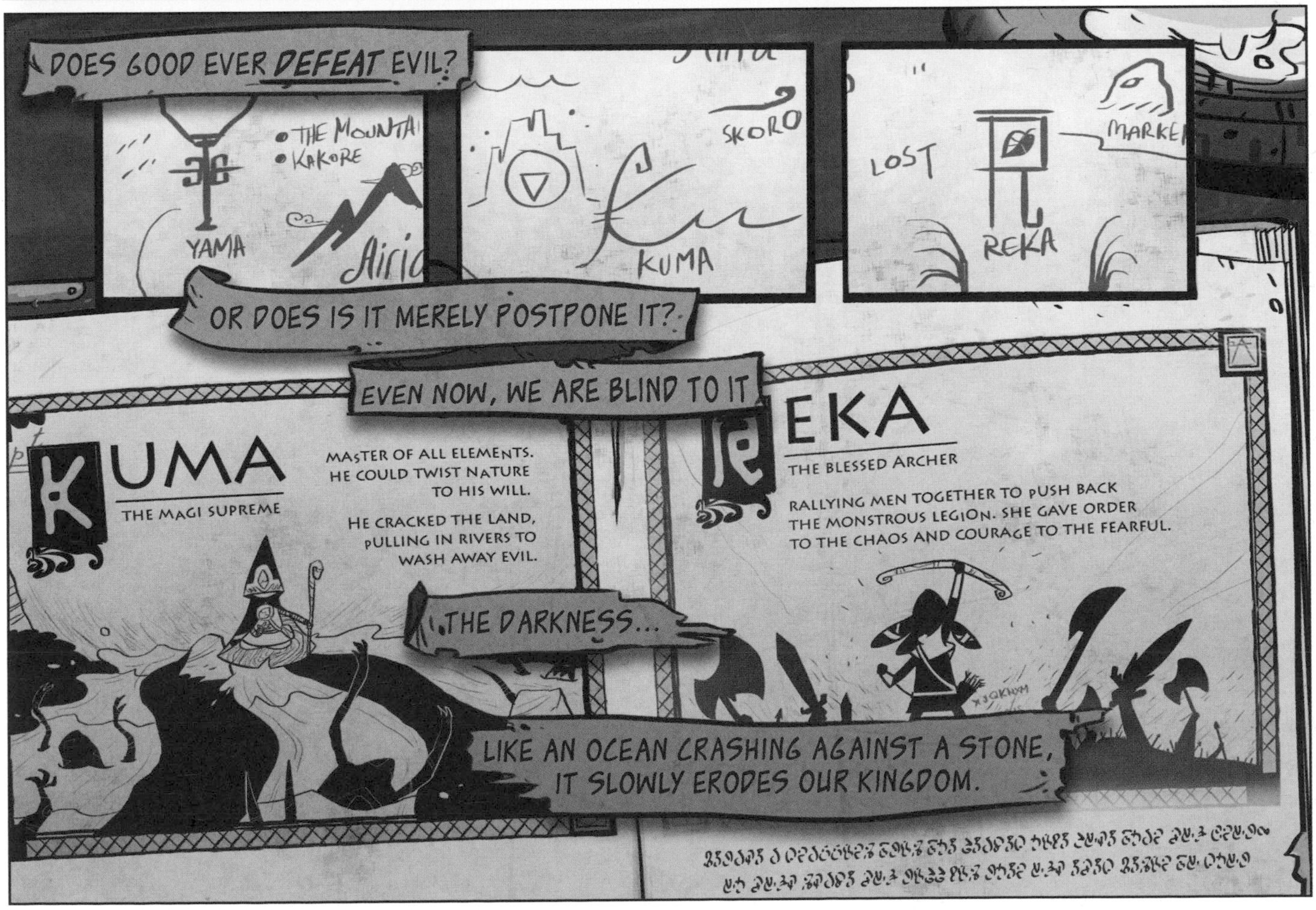
DOES GOOD EVER DEFEAT EVIL?
THE MOUNTA
KAKORE
YAMA
Airia
SKORO
KUMA
LOST
MARKE
REKA
OR DOES IS IT MERELY POSTPONE IT?
EVEN NOW, WE ARE BLIND TO IT
KUMA
The Magi Supreme
Master of all elements. He could twist nature to his will.
He cracked the land, pulling in rivers to wash away evil.
EKA
The Blessed Archer
Rallying men together to push back the monstrous legion. She gave order to the chaos and courage to the fearful.
THE DARKNESS...
LIKE AN OCEAN CRASHING AGAINST A STONE, IT SLOWLY ERODES OUR KINGDOM.

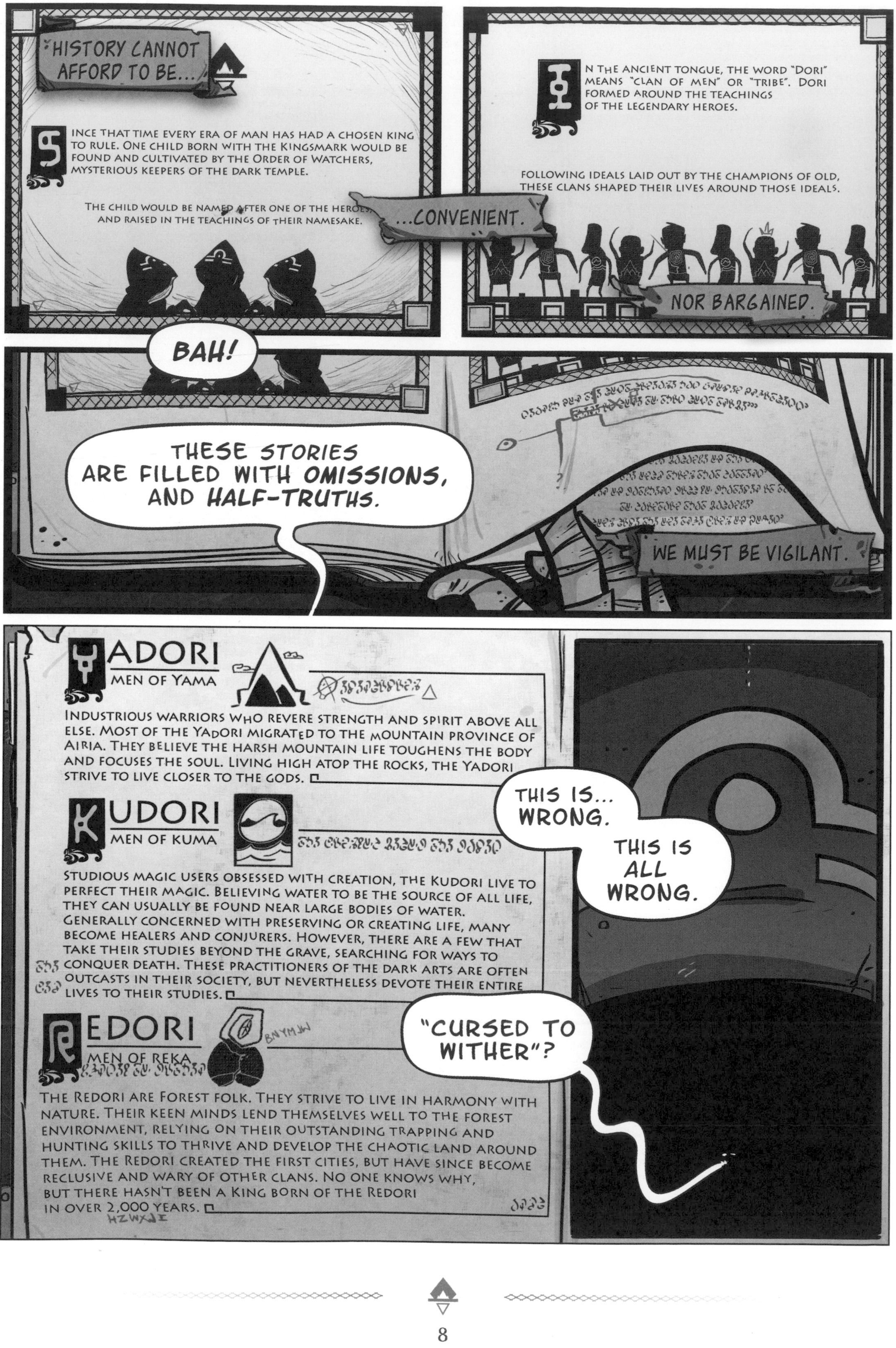
HISTORY CANNOT AFFORD TO BE...
SINCE THAT TIME EVERY ERA OF MAN HAS HAD A CHOSEN KING TO RULE. ONE CHILD BORN WITH THE KINGSMARK WOULD BE FOUND AND CULTIVATED BY THE ORDER OF WATCHERS, MYSTERIOUS KEEPERS OF THE DARK TEMPLE.
THE CHILD WOULD BE NAMED AFTER ONE OF THE HEROES AND RAISED IN THE TEACHINGS OF THEIR NAMESAKE.
...CONVENIENT.
IN THE ANCIENT TONGUE, THE WORD "DORI" MEANS "CLAN OF MEN" OR "TRIBE". DORI FORMED AROUND THE TEACHINGS OF THE LEGENDARY HEROES.
FOLLOWING IDEALS LAID OUT BY THE CHAMPIONS OF OLD, THESE CLANS SHAPED THEIR LIVES AROUND THOSE IDEALS.
NOR BARGAINED.
BAH!
THESE STORIES ARE FILLED WITH OMISSIONS, AND HALF-TRUTHS.
WE MUST BE VIGILANT.
YADORI
MEN OF YAMA
INDUSTRIOUS WARRIORS WHO REVERE STRENGTH AND SPIRIT ABOVE ALL ELSE. MOST OF THE YADORI MIGRATED TO THE MOUNTAIN PROVINCE OF AIRIA. THEY BELIEVE THE HARSH MOUNTAIN LIFE TOUGHENS THE BODY AND FOCUSES THE SOUL. LIVING HIGH ATOP THE ROCKS, THE YADORI STRIVE TO LIVE CLOSER TO THE GODS.
KUDORI
MEN OF KUMA
STUDIOUS MAGIC USERS OBSESSED WITH CREATION, THE KUDORI LIVE TO PERFECT THEIR MAGIC. BELIEVING WATER TO BE THE SOURCE OF ALL LIFE, THEY CAN USUALLY BE FOUND NEAR LARGE BODIES OF WATER. GENERALLY CONCERNED WITH PRESERVING OR CREATING LIFE, MANY BECOME HEALERS AND CONJURERS. HOWEVER, THERE ARE A FEW THAT TAKE THEIR STUDIES BEYOND THE GRAVE, SEARCHING FOR WAYS TO CONQUER DEATH. THESE PRACTITIONERS OF THE DARK ARTS ARE OFTEN OUTCASTS IN THEIR SOCIETY, BUT NEVERTHELESS DEVOTE THEIR ENTIRE LIVES TO THEIR STUDIES.
REDORI
MEN OF REKA
THE REDORI ARE FOREST FOLK. THEY STRIVE TO LIVE IN HARMONY WITH NATURE. THEIR KEEN MINDS LEND THEMSELVES WELL TO THE FOREST ENVIRONMENT, RELYING ON THEIR OUTSTANDING TRAPPING AND HUNTING SKILLS TO THRIVE AND DEVELOP THE CHAOTIC LAND AROUND THEM. THE REDORI CREATED THE FIRST CITIES, BUT HAVE SINCE BECOME RECLUSIVE AND WARY OF OTHER CLANS. NO ONE KNOWS WHY, BUT THERE HASN'T BEEN A KING BORN OF THE REDORI IN OVER 2,000 YEARS.
THIS IS... WRONG.
THIS IS ALL WRONG.
"CURSED TO WITHER"?

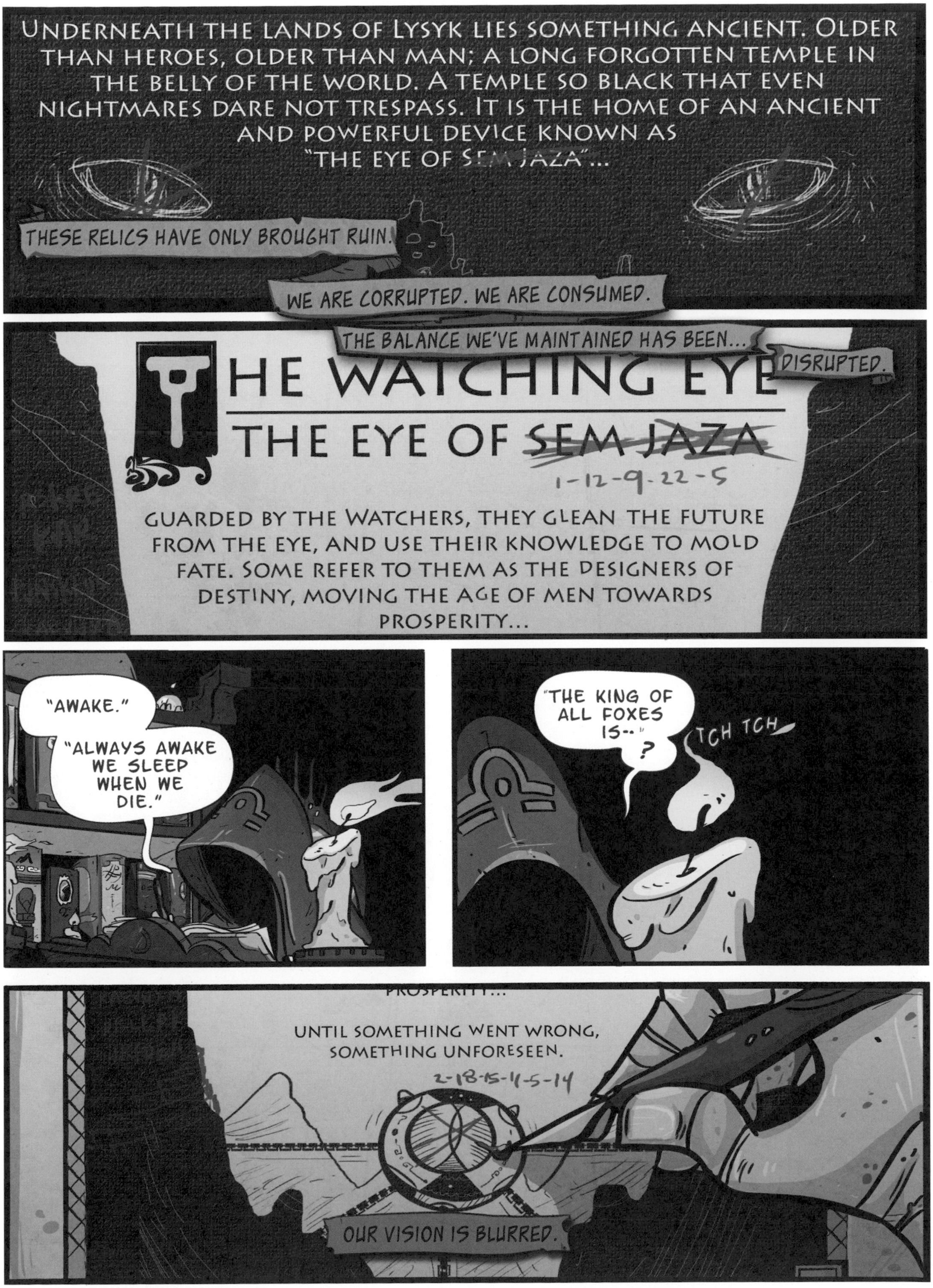
UNDERNEATH THE LANDS OF LYSYK LIES SOMETHING ANCIENT. OLDER THAN HEROES, OLDER THAN MAN; A LONG FORGOTTEN TEMPLE IN THE BELLY OF THE WORLD. A TEMPLE SO BLACK THAT EVEN NIGHTMARES DARE NOT TRESPASS. IT IS THE HOME OF AN ANCIENT AND POWERFUL DEVICE KNOWN AS "THE EYE OF SEM JAZA"...
THESE RELICS HAVE ONLY BROUGHT RUIN.
WE ARE CORRUPTED. WE ARE CONSUMED.
THE BALANCE WE'VE MAINTAINED HAS BEEN...
DISRUPTED.
THE WATCHING EYE
THE EYE OF SEM JAZA
1-12-9-22-5
GUARDED BY THE WATCHERS, THEY GLEAN THE FUTURE FROM THE EYE, AND USE THEIR KNOWLEDGE TO MOLD FATE. SOME REFER TO THEM AS THE DESIGNERS OF DESTINY, MOVING THE AGE OF MEN TOWARDS PROSPERITY...
"AWAKE."
"ALWAYS AWAKE WE SLEEP WHEN WE DIE."
"THE KING OF ALL FOXES IS-- "
?
TCH TCH
UNTIL SOMETHING WENT WRONG, SOMETHING UNFORESEEN.
2-18-15-11-5-14
OUR VISION IS BLURRED.

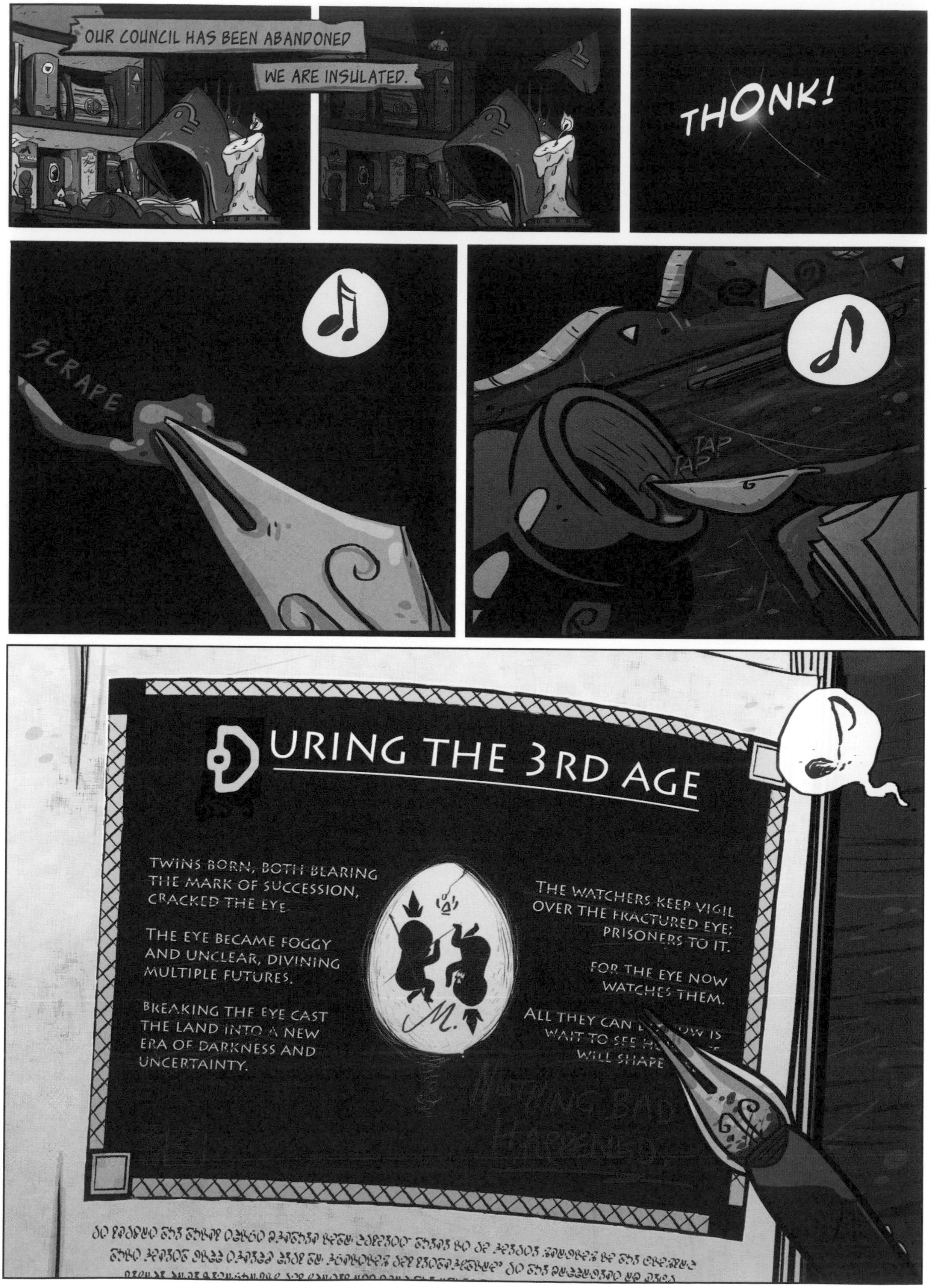
OUR COUNCIL HAS BEEN ABANDONED
WE ARE INSULATED.
THONK!
SCRAPE
TAP TAP
DURING THE 3RD AGE
TWINS BORN, BOTH BLARING THE MARK OF SUCCESSION, CRACKED THE EYE.
THE EYE BECAME FOGGY AND UNCLEAR, DIVINING MULTIPLE FUTURES.
BREAKING THE EYE CAST THE LAND INTO A NEW ERA OF DARKNESS AND UNCERTAINTY.
THE WATCHERS KEEP VIGIL OVER THE FRACTURED EYE; PRISONERS TO IT.
FOR THE EYE NOW WATCHES THEM.

CHAPTER 1

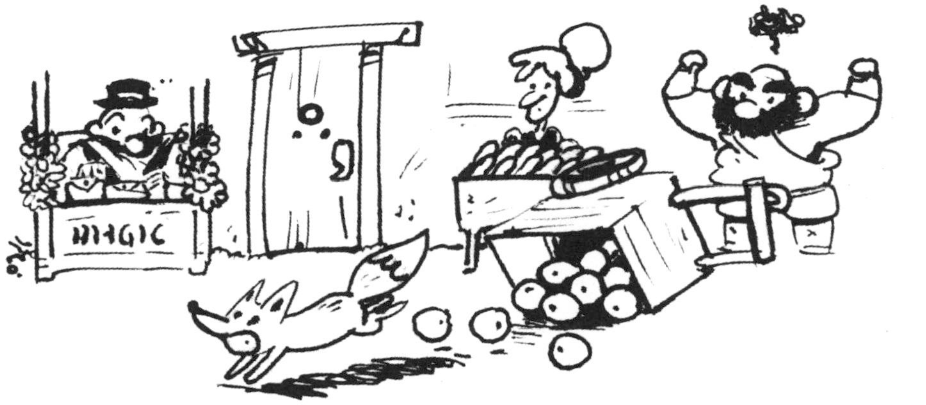
MAGIC

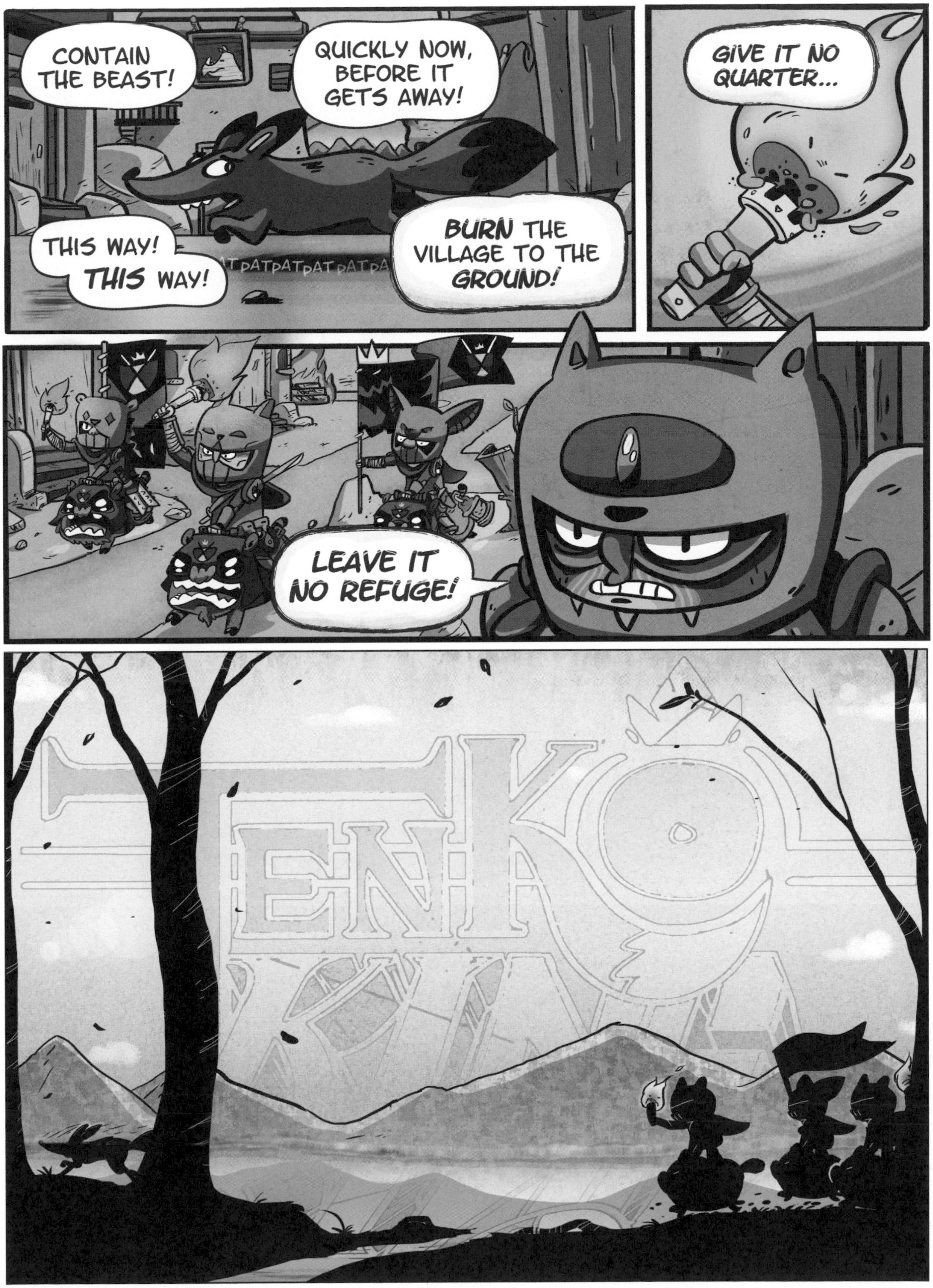
CONTAIN THE BEAST!
QUICKLY NOW, BEFORE IT GETS AWAY!
THIS WAY! THIS WAY!
BURN THE VILLAGE TO THE GROUND!
GIVE IT NO QUARTER...
LEAVE IT NO REFUGE!

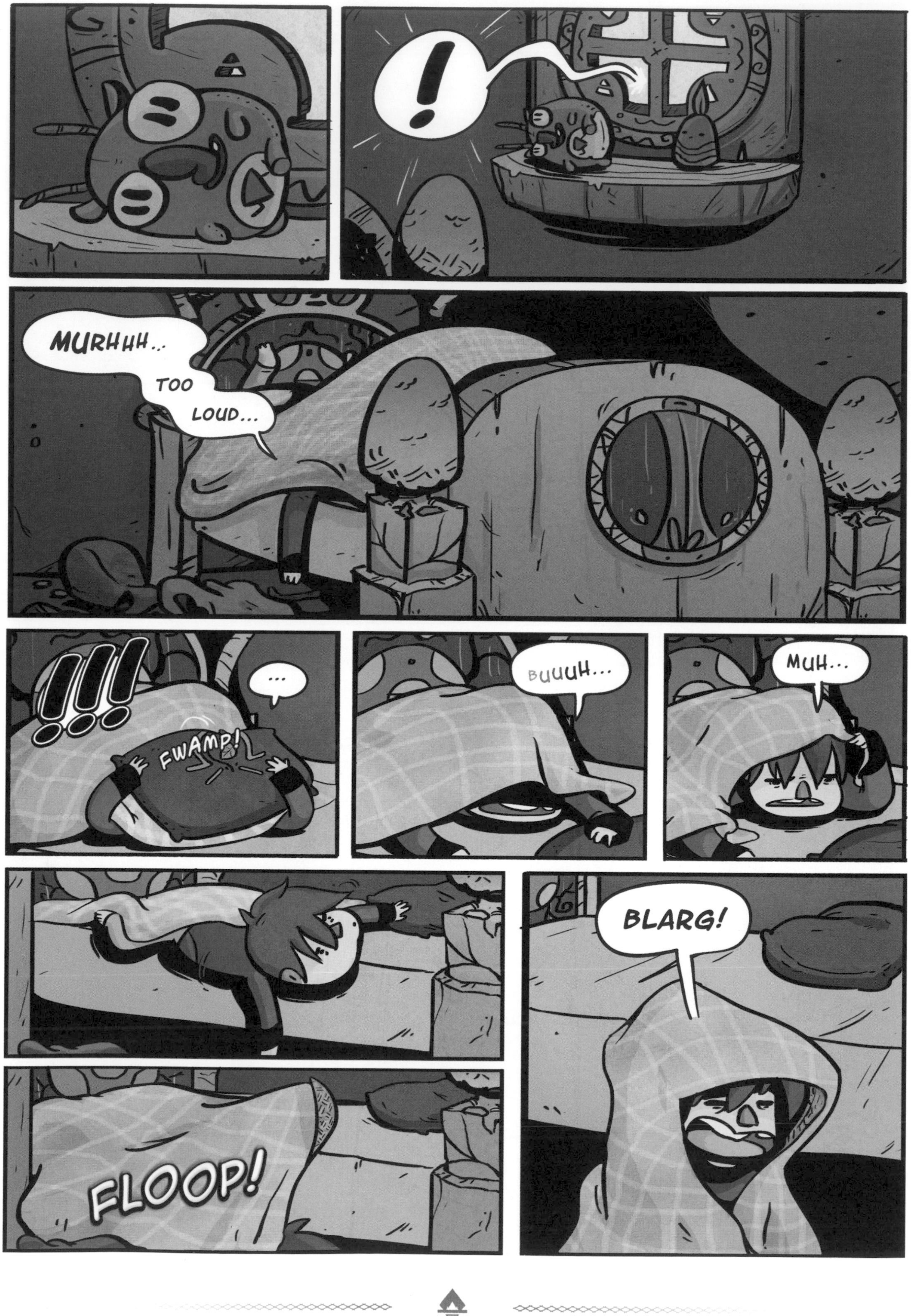
!
MURHHH...
TOO
LOUD...
!!!
...
FWAMP!
BUUUH...
MUH...
FLOOP!
BLARG!

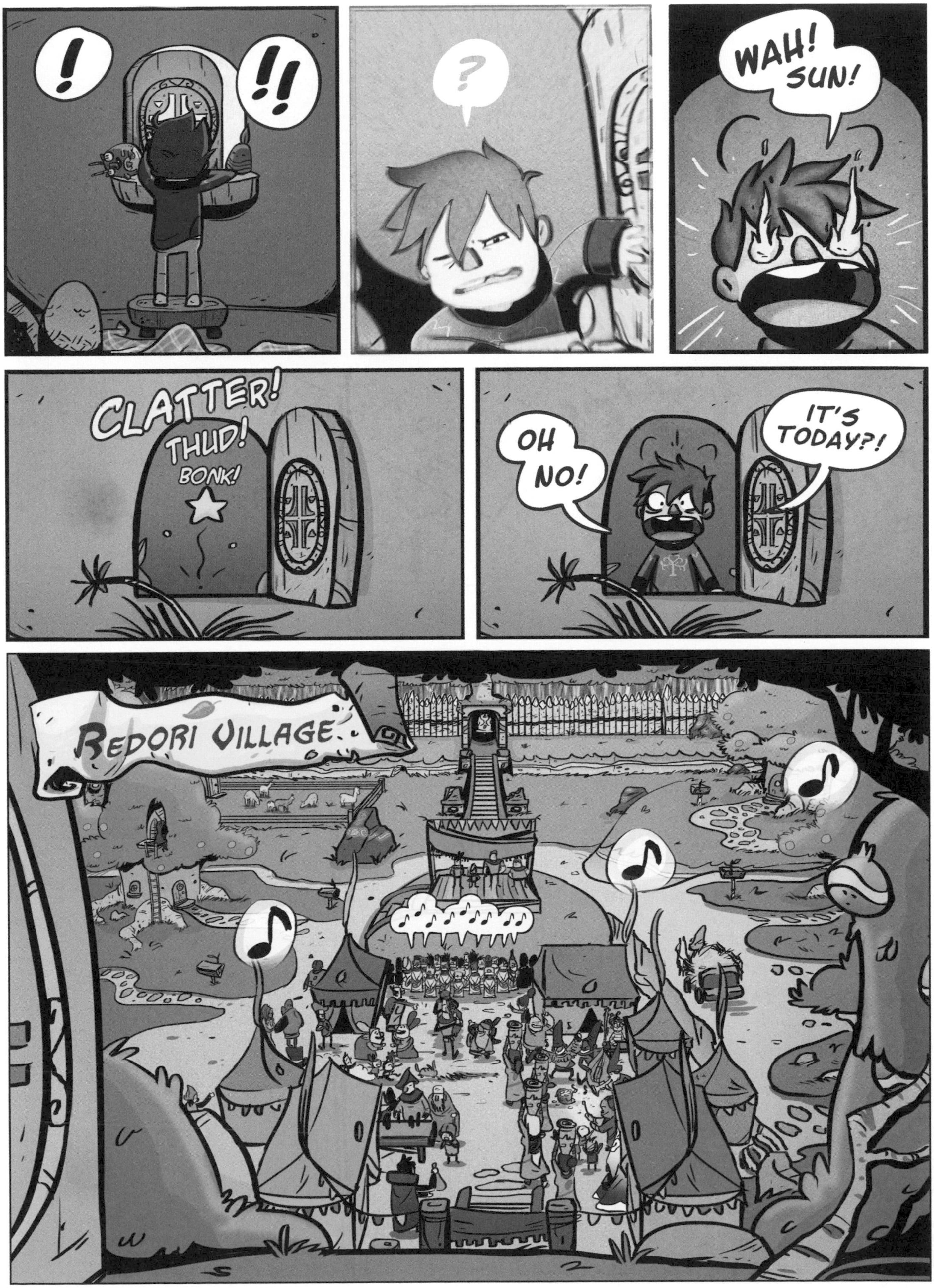
!
!!
?
WAH! SUN!
CLATTER!
THUD!
BONK!
OH NO!
IT'S TODAY?!
REDORI VILLAGE

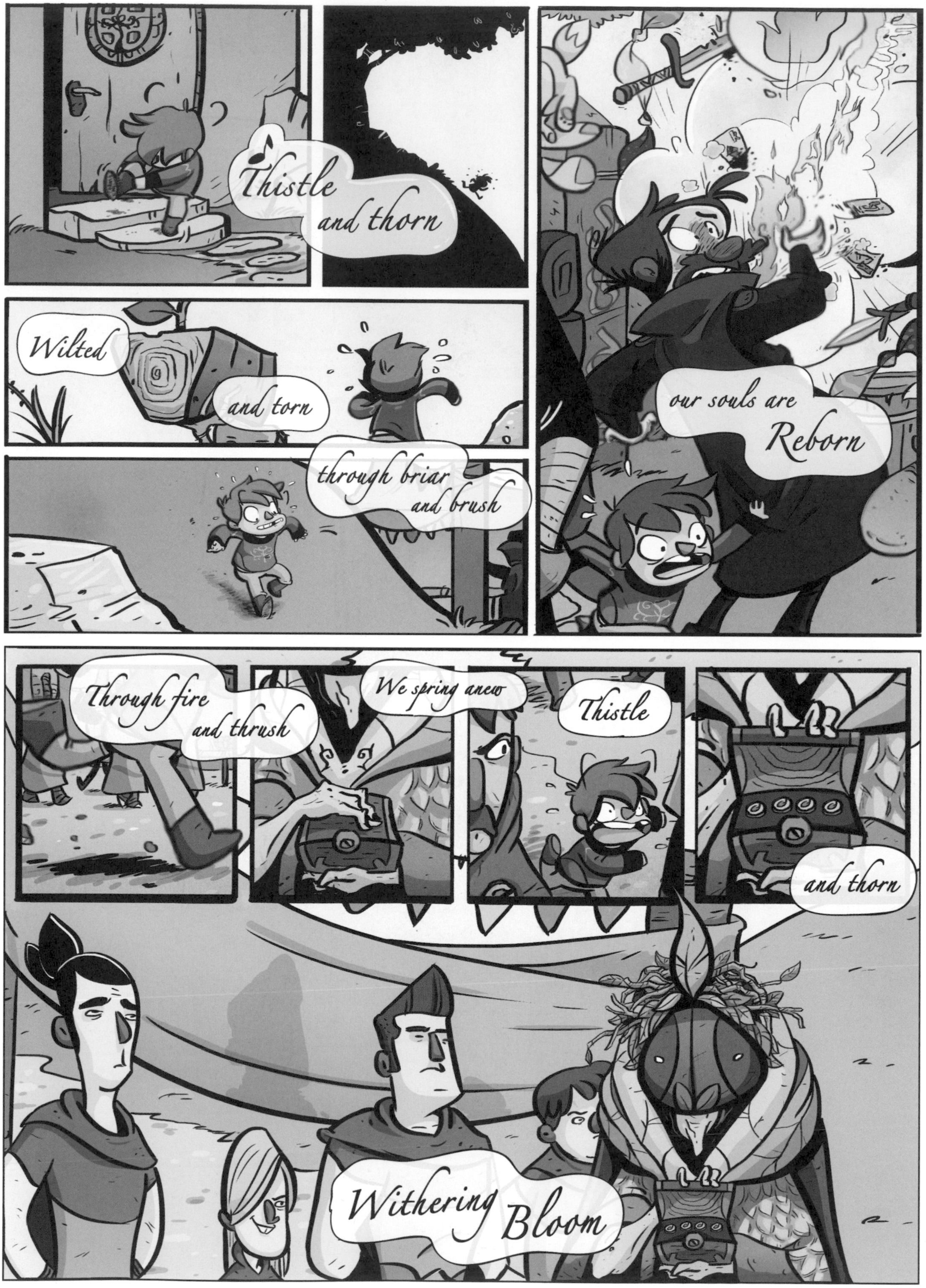
Thistle
and thorn
Wilted
and torn
through briar
and brush
our souls are
Reborn
Through fire
and thrush
We spring anew
Thistle
and thorn
Withering Bloom

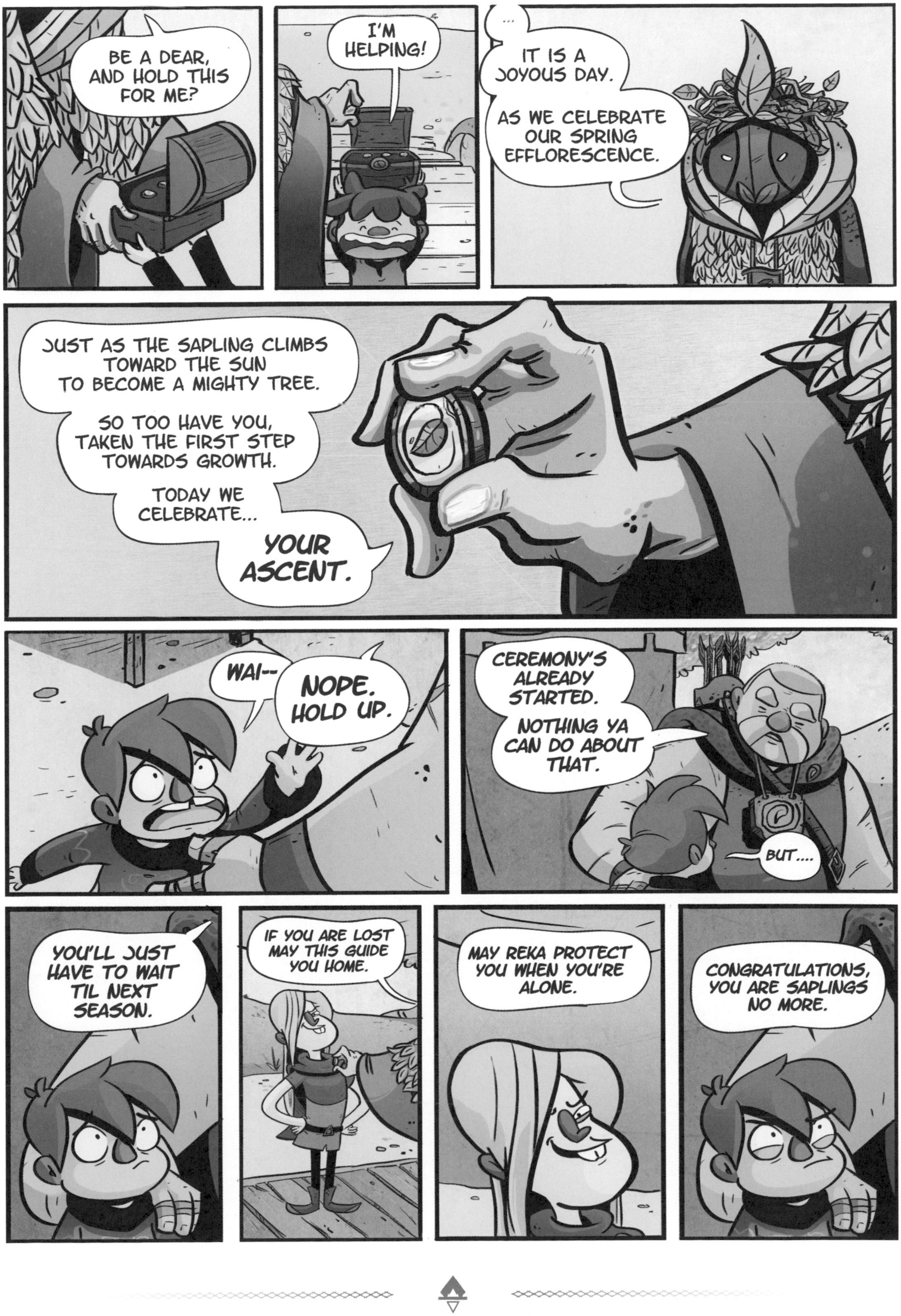
BE A DEAR, AND HOLD THIS FOR ME?
I'M HELPING!
...
IT IS A JOYOUS DAY.
AS WE CELEBRATE OUR SPRING EFFLORESCENCE.
JUST AS THE SAPLING CLIMBS TOWARD THE SUN TO BECOME A MIGHTY TREE.
SO TOO HAVE YOU, TAKEN THE FIRST STEP TOWARDS GROWTH.
TODAY WE CELEBRATE...
YOUR ASCENT.
WAI--
NOPE. HOLD UP.
CEREMONY'S ALREADY STARTED.
NOTHING YA CAN DO ABOUT THAT.
BUT....
YOU'LL JUST HAVE TO WAIT TIL NEXT SEASON.
IF YOU ARE LOST MAY THIS GUIDE YOU HOME.
MAY REKA PROTECT YOU WHEN YOU'RE ALONE.
CONGRATULATIONS, YOU ARE SAPLINGS NO MORE.

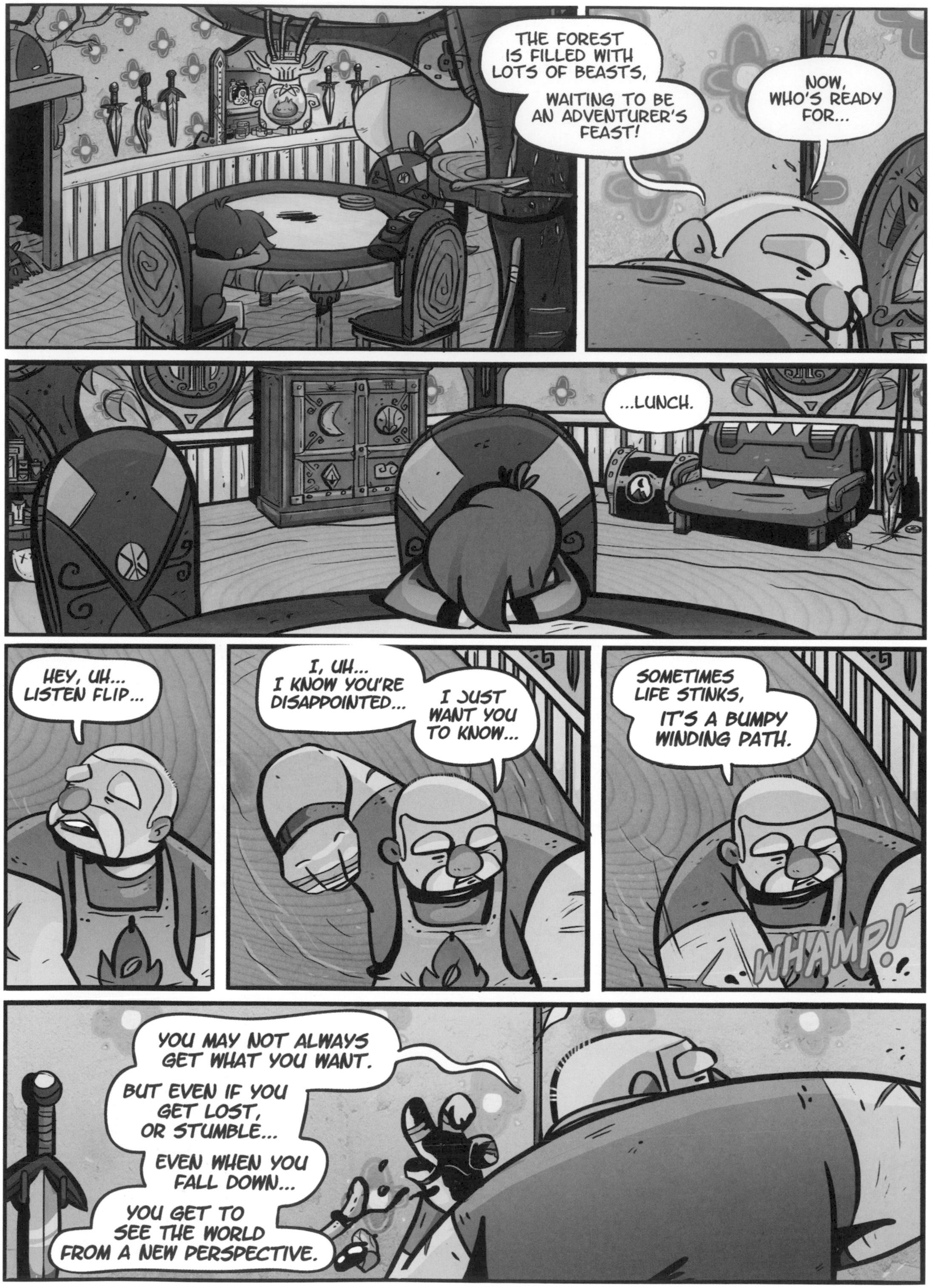
THE FOREST IS FILLED WITH LOTS OF BEASTS,
WAITING TO BE AN ADVENTURER'S FEAST!
NOW, WHO'S READY FOR...
...LUNCH.
HEY, UH... LISTEN FLIP...
I, UH... I KNOW YOU'RE DISAPPOINTED...
I JUST WANT YOU TO KNOW...
SOMETIMES LIFE STINKS,
IT'S A BUMPY WINDING PATH.
WHAMP!
YOU MAY NOT ALWAYS GET WHAT YOU WANT.
BUT EVEN IF YOU GET LOST, OR STUMBLE...
EVEN WHEN YOU FALL DOWN...
YOU GET TO SEE THE WORLD FROM A NEW PERSPECTIVE.

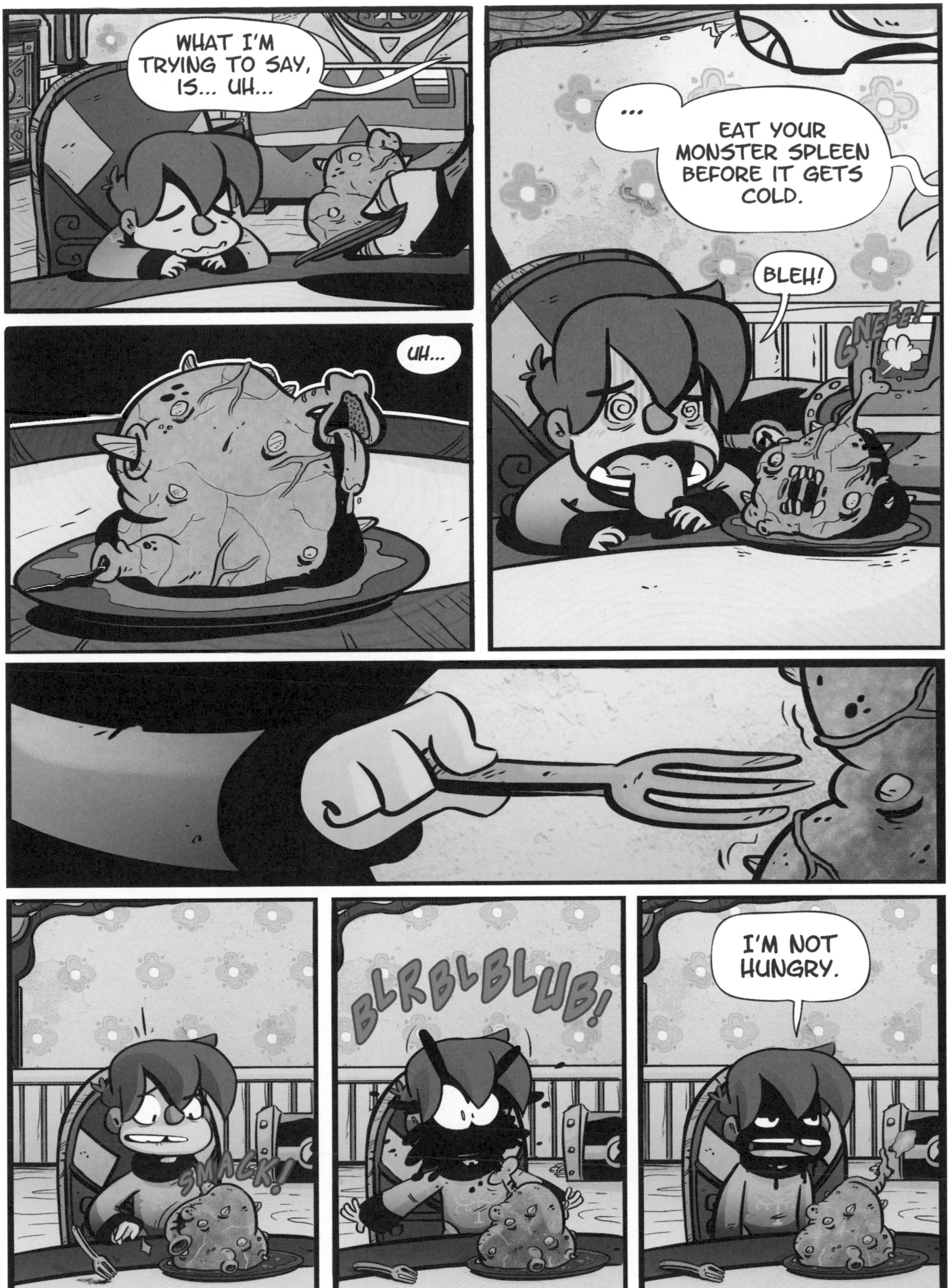

WHAT I'M TRYING TO SAY, IS... UH...
...
EAT YOUR MONSTER SPLEEN BEFORE IT GETS COLD.
UH...
BLEH!
GNEEE!
SMACK!
BLRBLBLUB!
I'M NOT HUNGRY.

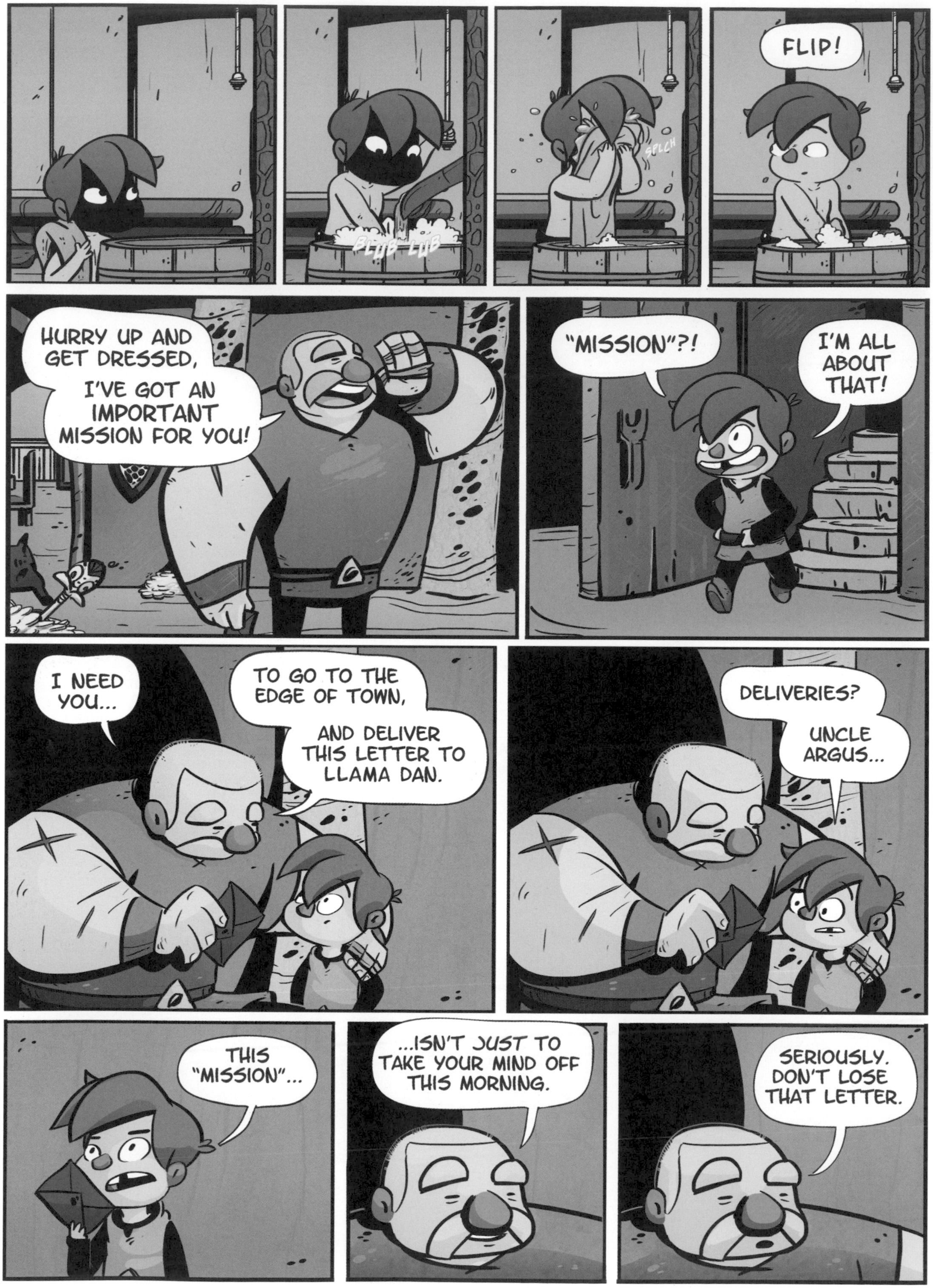
BLUB LUB
SPLCH
FLIP!
HURRY UP AND GET DRESSED,
I'VE GOT AN IMPORTANT MISSION FOR YOU!
"MISSION"?!
I'M ALL ABOUT THAT!
I NEED YOU...
TO GO TO THE EDGE OF TOWN,
AND DELIVER THIS LETTER TO LLAMA DAN.
DELIVERIES?
UNCLE ARGUS...
THIS "MISSION"...
...ISN'T JUST TO TAKE YOUR MIND OFF THIS MORNING.
SERIOUSLY. DON'T LOSE THAT LETTER.

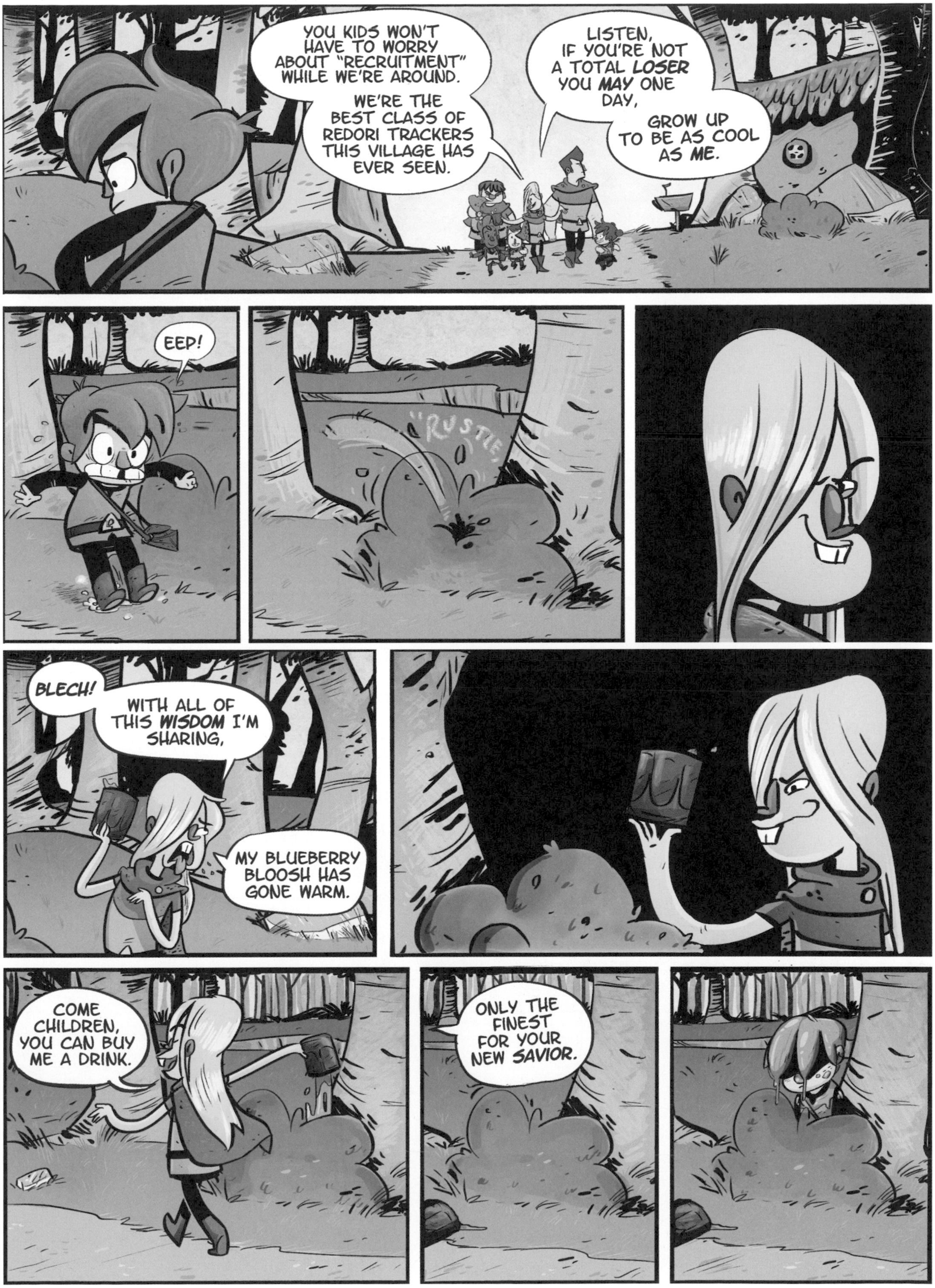
YOU KIDS WON'T HAVE TO WORRY ABOUT "RECRUITMENT" WHILE WE'RE AROUND.
WE'RE THE BEST CLASS OF REDORI TRACKERS THIS VILLAGE HAS EVER SEEN.
LISTEN, IF YOU'RE NOT A TOTAL LOSER YOU MAY ONE DAY,
GROW UP TO BE AS COOL AS ME.
EEP!
"RUSTLE"
BLECH!
WITH ALL OF THIS WISDOM I'M SHARING,
MY BLUEBERRY BLOOSH HAS GONE WARM.
COME CHILDREN, YOU CAN BUY ME A DRINK.
ONLY THE FINEST FOR YOUR NEW SAVIOR.

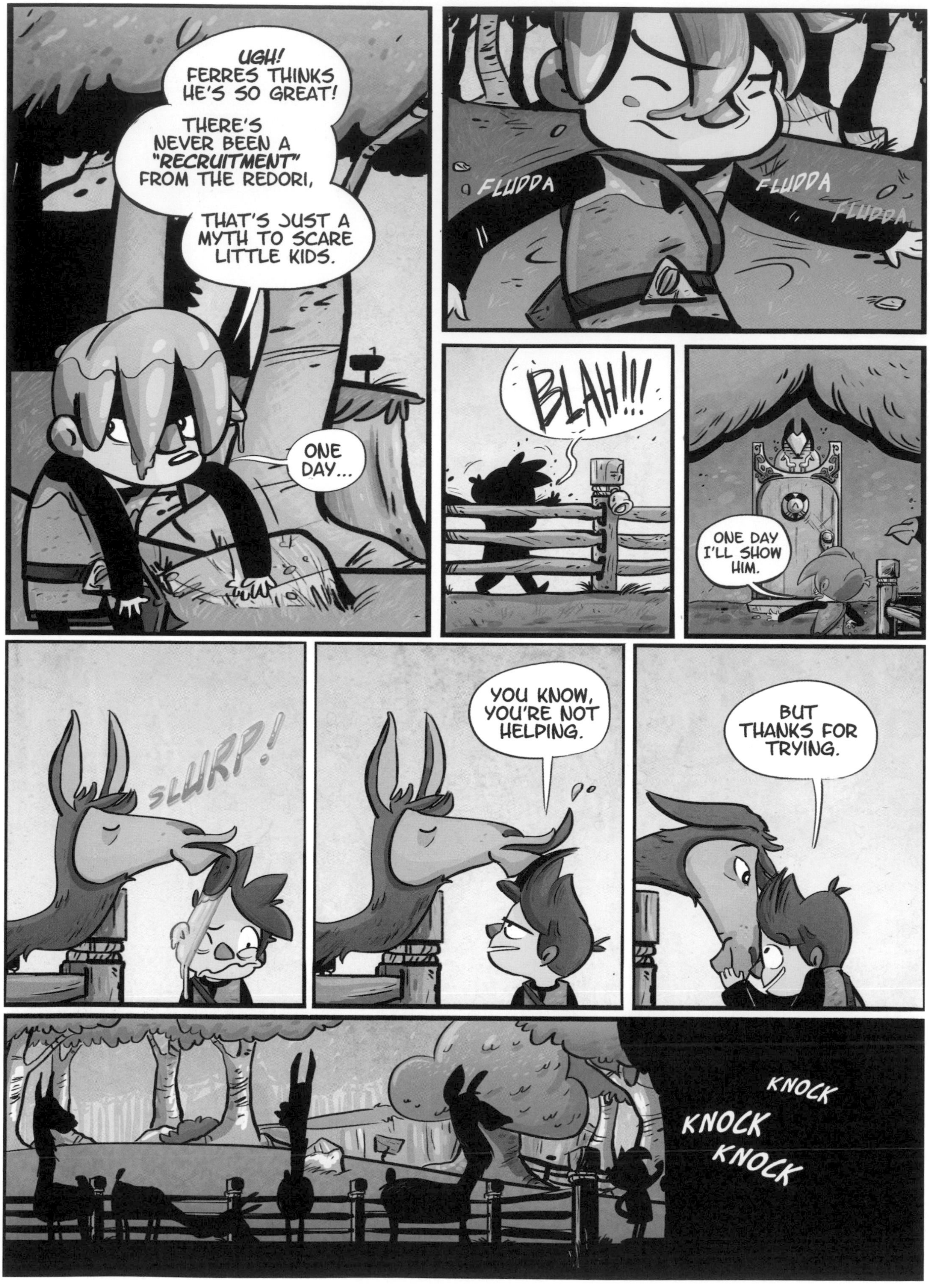
UGH! FERRES THINKS HE'S SO GREAT!
THERE'S NEVER BEEN A "RECRUITMENT" FROM THE REDORI,
THAT'S JUST A MYTH TO SCARE LITTLE KIDS.
ONE DAY...
FLUDDA
FLUDDA
FLUDDA
BLAH!!!
ONE DAY I'LL SHOW HIM.
SLURP!
YOU KNOW, YOU'RE NOT HELPING.
BUT THANKS FOR TRYING.
KNOCK
KNOCK
KNOCK

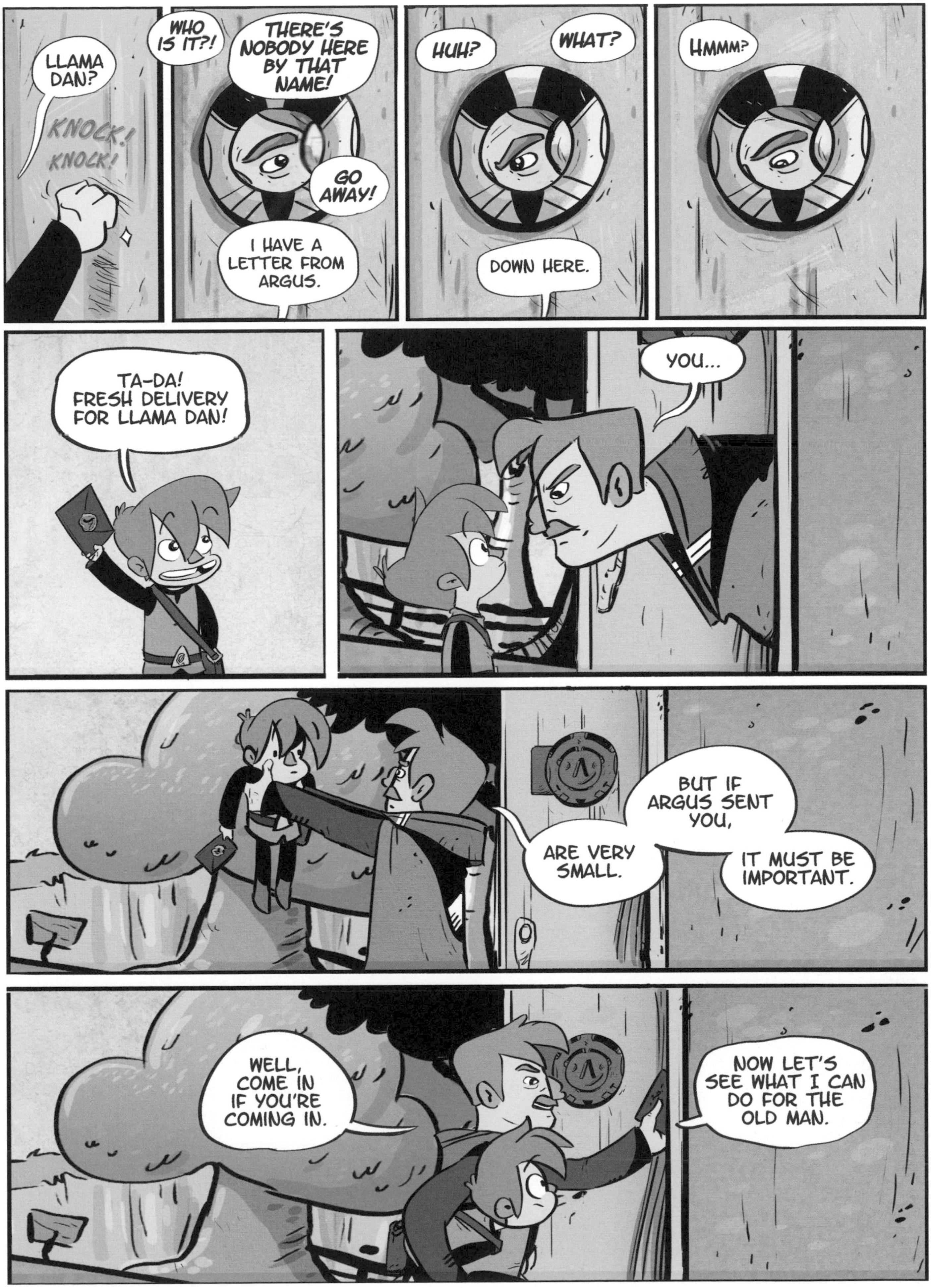
LLAMA DAN?
KNOCK! KNOCK!
WHO IS IT?!
THERE'S NOBODY HERE BY THAT NAME!
GO AWAY!
I HAVE A LETTER FROM ARGUS.
HUH?
WHAT?
DOWN HERE.
HMMM?
TA-DA! FRESH DELIVERY FOR LLAMA DAN!
YOU...
ARE VERY SMALL.
BUT IF ARGUS SENT YOU,
IT MUST BE IMPORTANT.
WELL, COME IN IF YOU'RE COMING IN.
NOW LET'S SEE WHAT I CAN DO FOR THE OLD MAN.

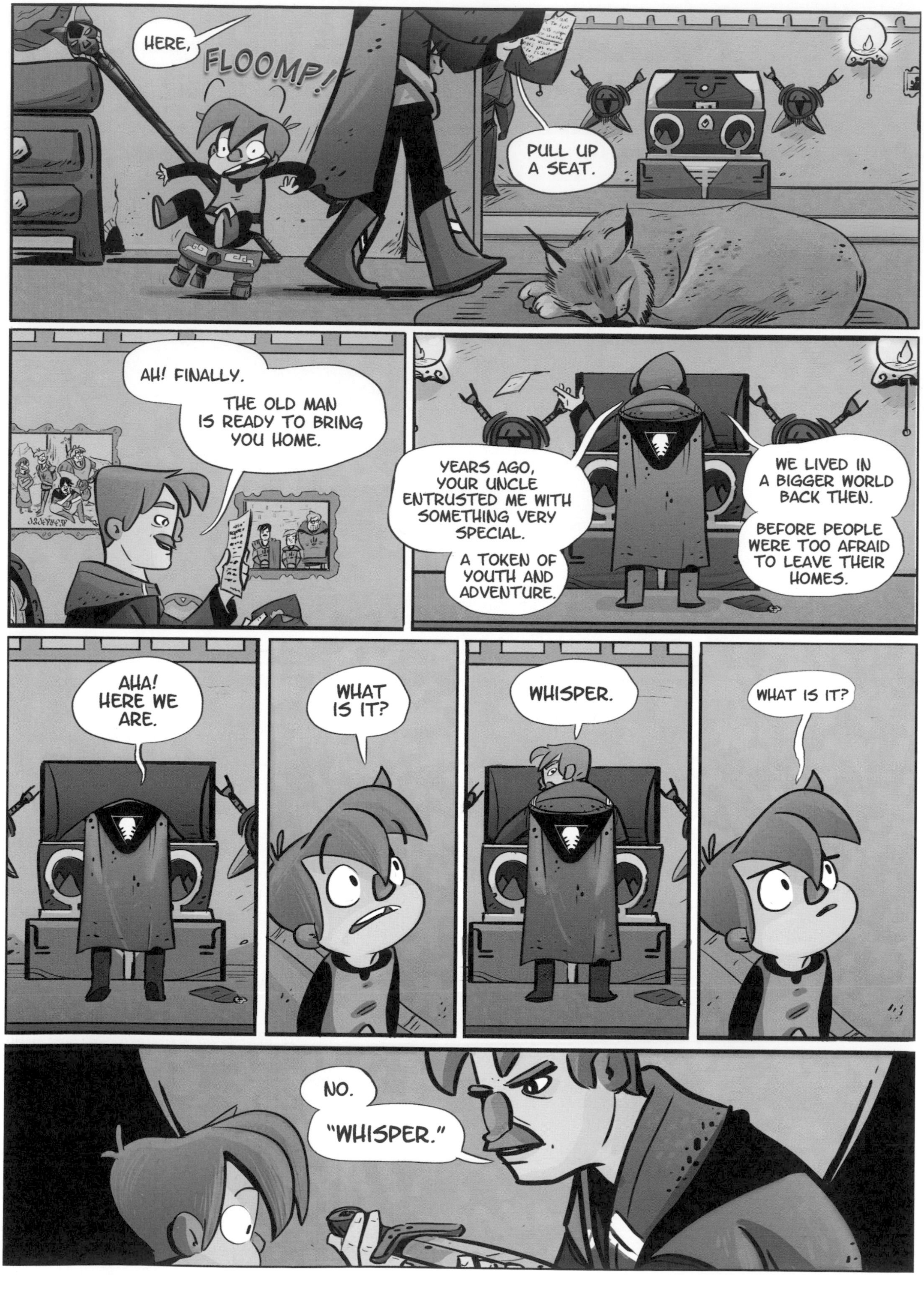
HERE,
FLOOMP!
PULL UP A SEAT.
AH! FINALLY.
THE OLD MAN IS READY TO BRING YOU HOME.
YEARS AGO, YOUR UNCLE ENTRUSTED ME WITH SOMETHING VERY SPECIAL.
A TOKEN OF YOUTH AND ADVENTURE.
WE LIVED IN A BIGGER WORLD BACK THEN.
BEFORE PEOPLE WERE TOO AFRAID TO LEAVE THEIR HOMES.
AHA! HERE WE ARE.
WHAT IS IT?
WHISPER.
WHAT IS IT?
NO.
"WHISPER."

CHAPTER 2

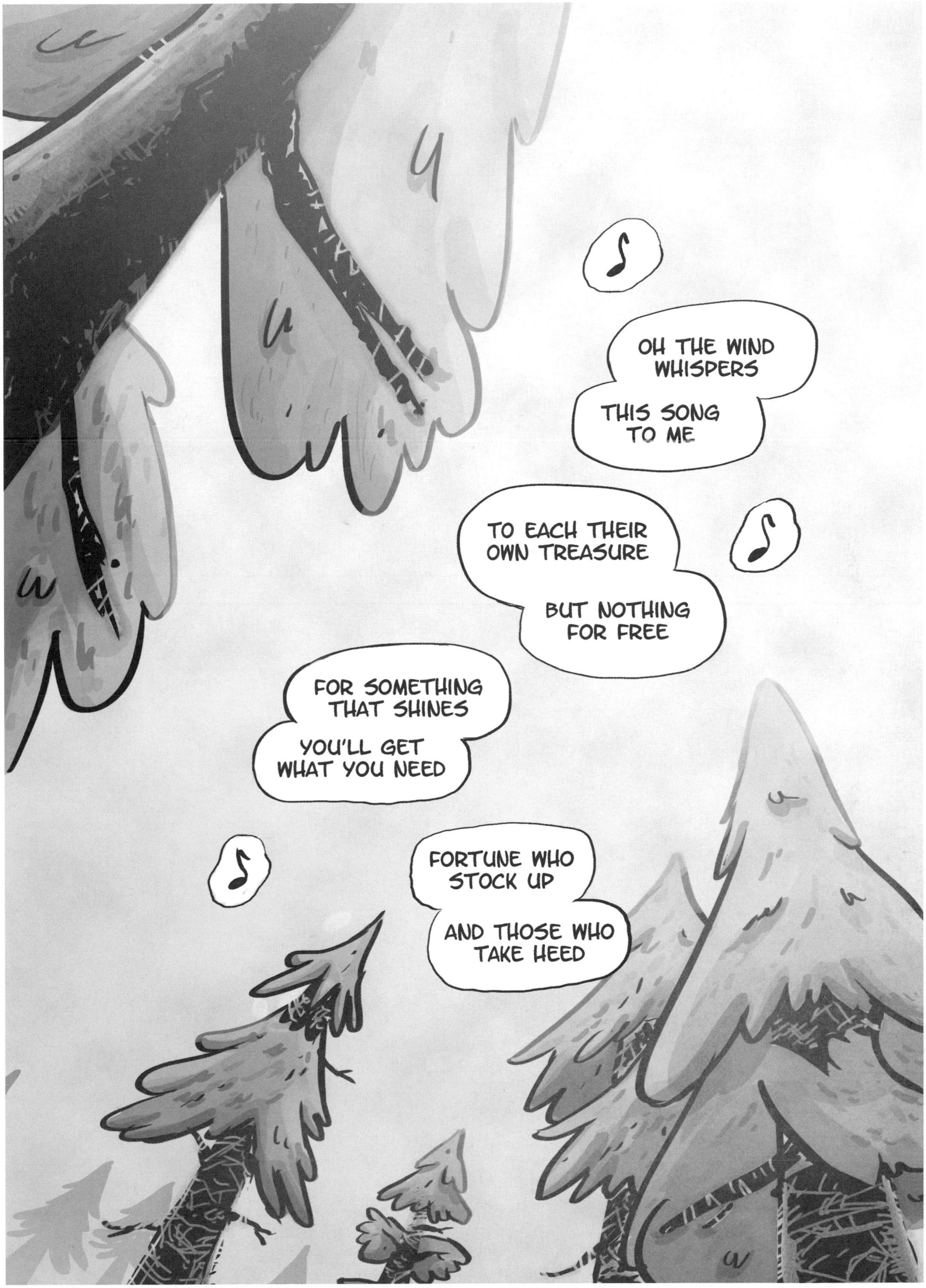
OH THE WIND WHISPERS
THIS SONG TO ME
TO EACH THEIR OWN TREASURE
BUT NOTHING FOR FREE
FOR SOMETHING THAT SHINES
YOU'LL GET WHAT YOU NEED
FORTUNE WHO STOCK UP
AND THOSE WHO TAKE HEED

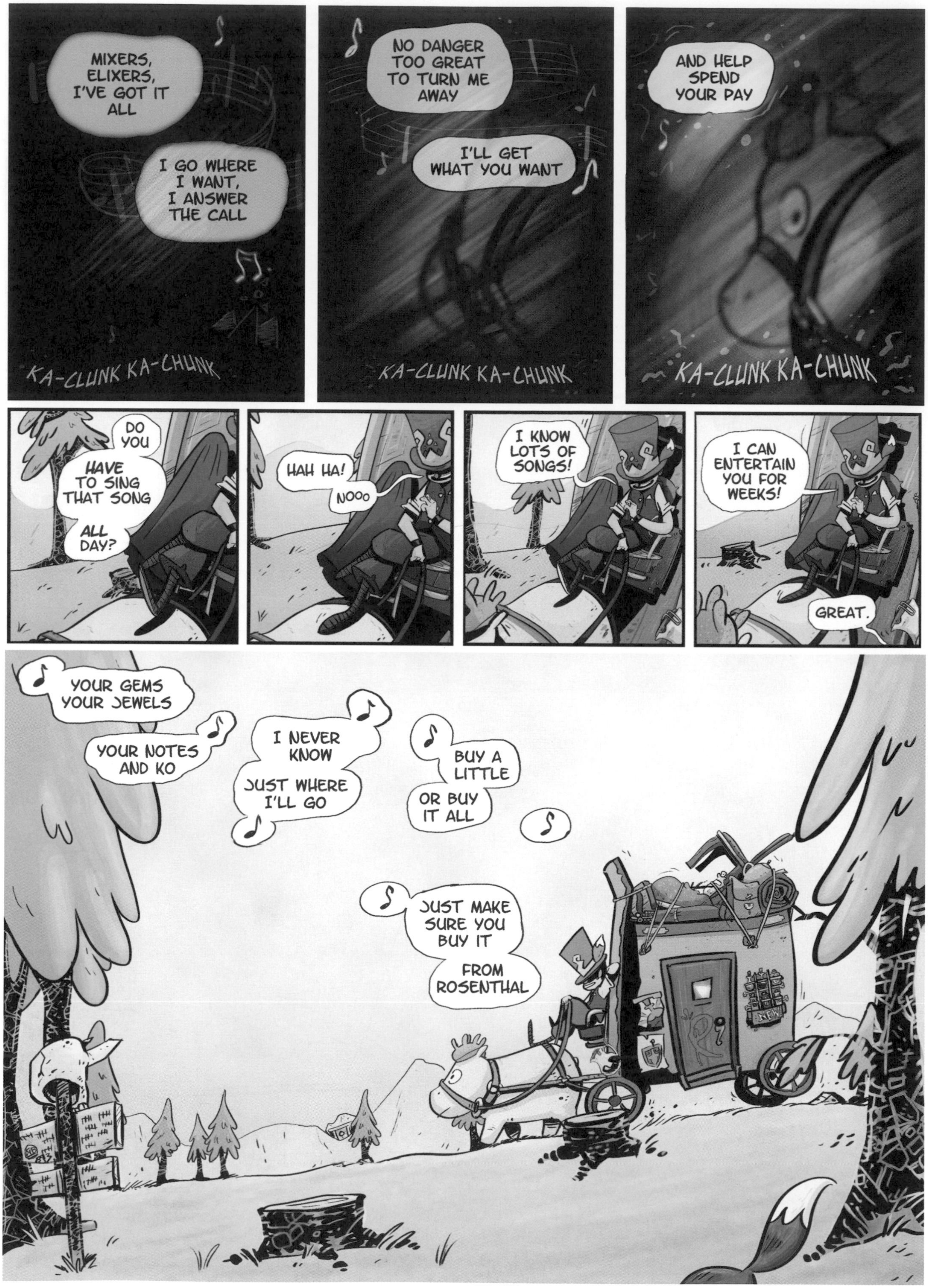

MIXERS, ELIXERS, I'VE GOT IT ALL
I GO WHERE I WANT, I ANSWER THE CALL
KA-CLUNK KA-CHUNK
NO DANGER TOO GREAT TO TURN ME AWAY
I'LL GET WHAT YOU WANT
KA-CLUNK KA-CHUNK
AND HELP SPEND YOUR PAY
KA-CLUNK KA-CHUNK
DO YOU HAVE TO SING THAT SONG ALL DAY?
HAH HA!
NOOO
I KNOW LOTS OF SONGS!
I CAN ENTERTAIN YOU FOR WEEKS!
GREAT.
YOUR GEMS YOUR JEWELS
YOUR NOTES AND KO
I NEVER KNOW
JUST WHERE I'LL GO
BUY A LITTLE
OR BUY IT ALL
JUST MAKE SURE YOU BUY IT
FROM ROSENTHAL
NEW

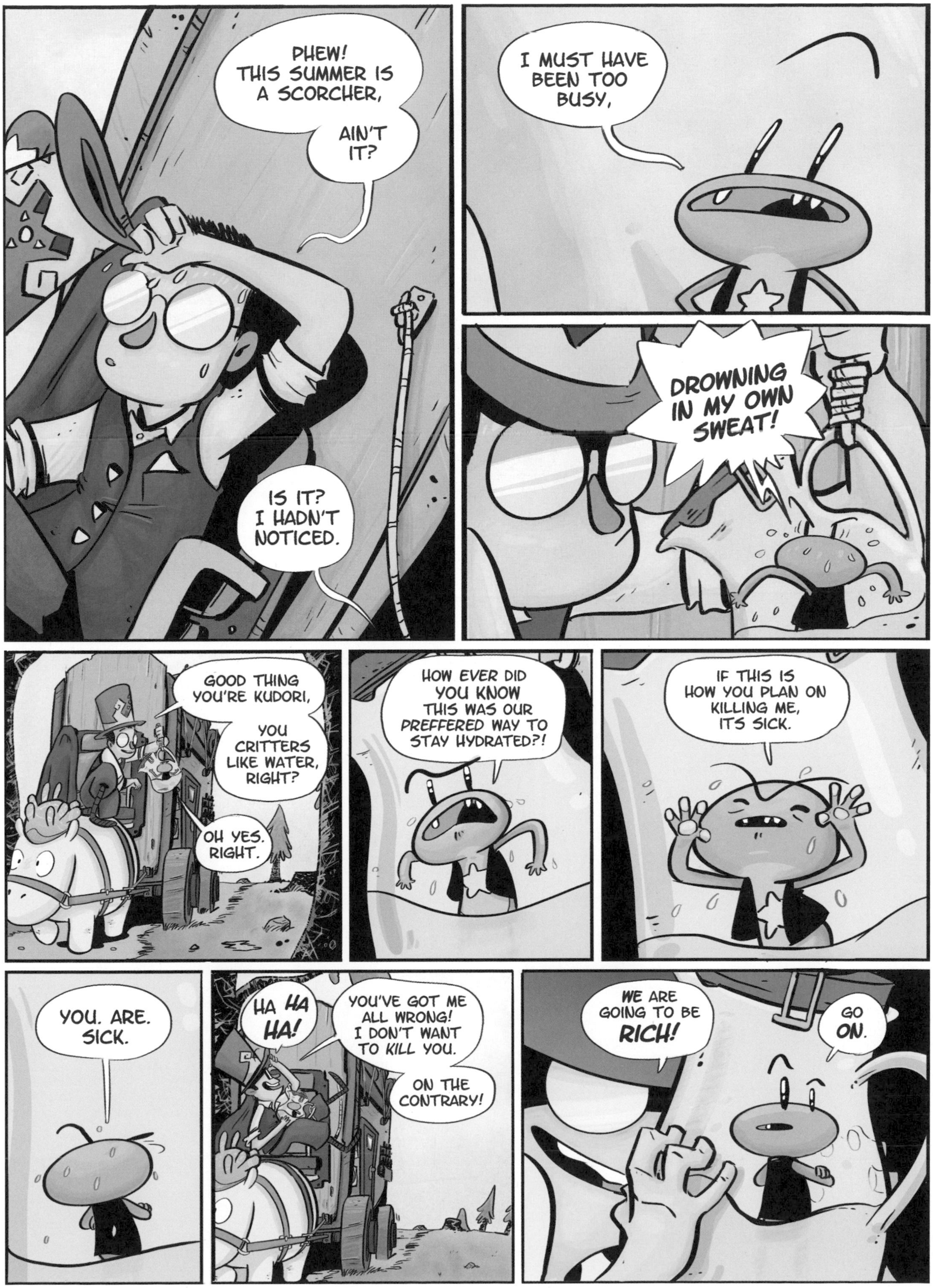
PHEW! THIS SUMMER IS A SCORCHER,
AIN'T IT?
I MUST HAVE BEEN TOO BUSY,
IS IT? I HADN'T NOTICED.
DROWNING IN MY OWN SWEAT!
GOOD THING YOU'RE KUDORI,
YOU CRITTERS LIKE WATER, RIGHT?
OH YES. RIGHT.
HOW EVER DID YOU KNOW THIS WAS OUR PREFFERED WAY TO STAY HYDRATED?!
IF THIS IS HOW YOU PLAN ON KILLING ME, ITS SICK.
YOU. ARE. SICK.
HA HA HA!
YOU'VE GOT ME ALL WRONG! I DON'T WANT TO KILL YOU.
ON THE CONTRARY!
WE ARE GOING TO BE RICH!
GO ON.

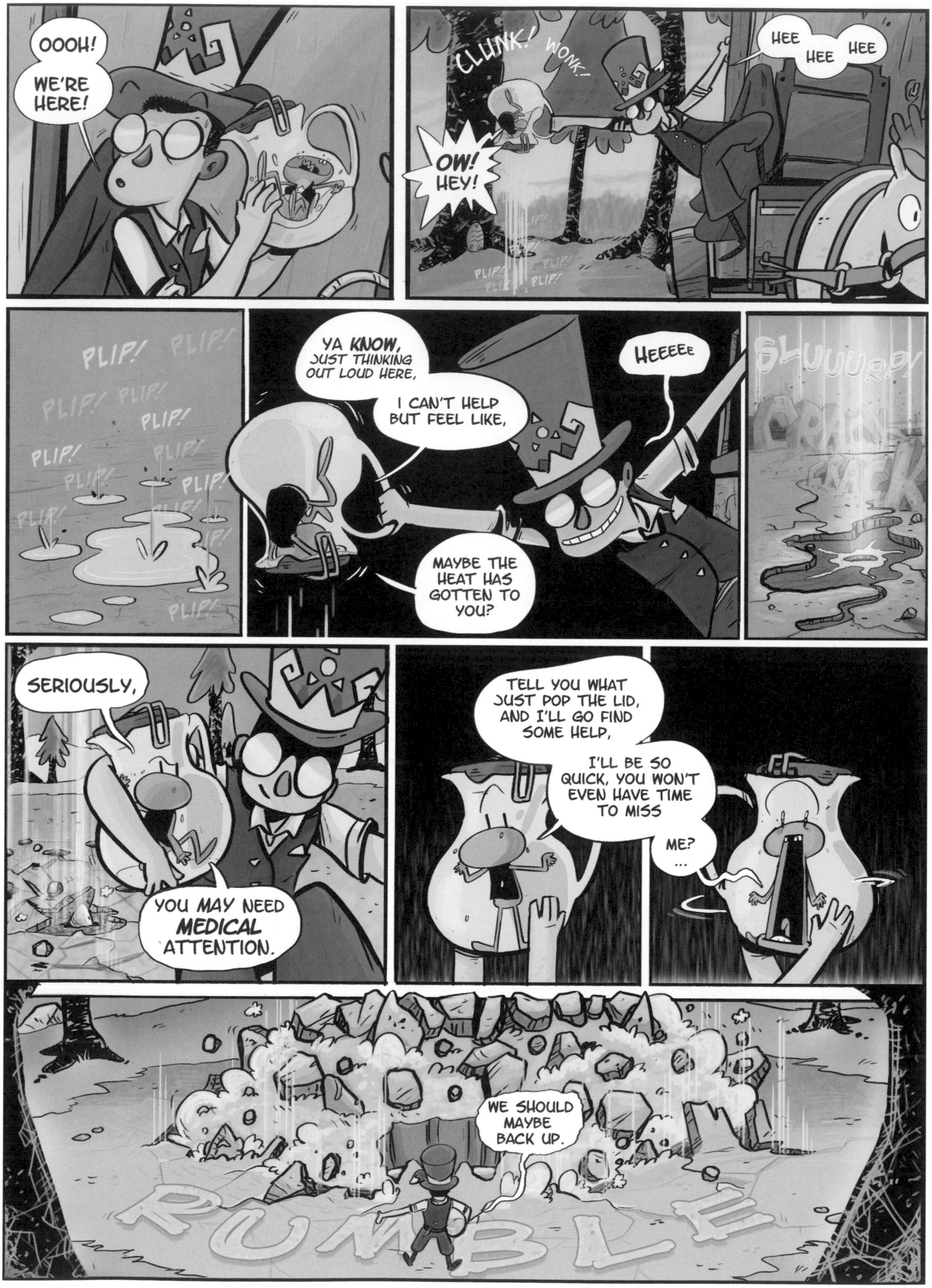
OOOH!
WE'RE HERE!
CLUNK! WONK!
HEE HEE HEE
OW! HEY!
PLIP! PLIP! PLIP!
PLIP! PLIP! PLIP! PLIP! PLIP! PLIP! PLIP! PLIP! PLIP!
YA KNOW, JUST THINKING OUT LOUD HERE,
I CAN'T HELP BUT FEEL LIKE,
HEEEEE
MAYBE THE HEAT HAS GOTTEN TO YOU?
SLUUURP!
SERIOUSLY,
YOU MAY NEED MEDICAL ATTENTION.
TELL YOU WHAT JUST POP THE LID, AND I'LL GO FIND SOME HELP,
I'LL BE SO QUICK, YOU WON'T EVEN HAVE TIME TO MISS
ME? ...
WE SHOULD MAYBE BACK UP.
RUMBLE

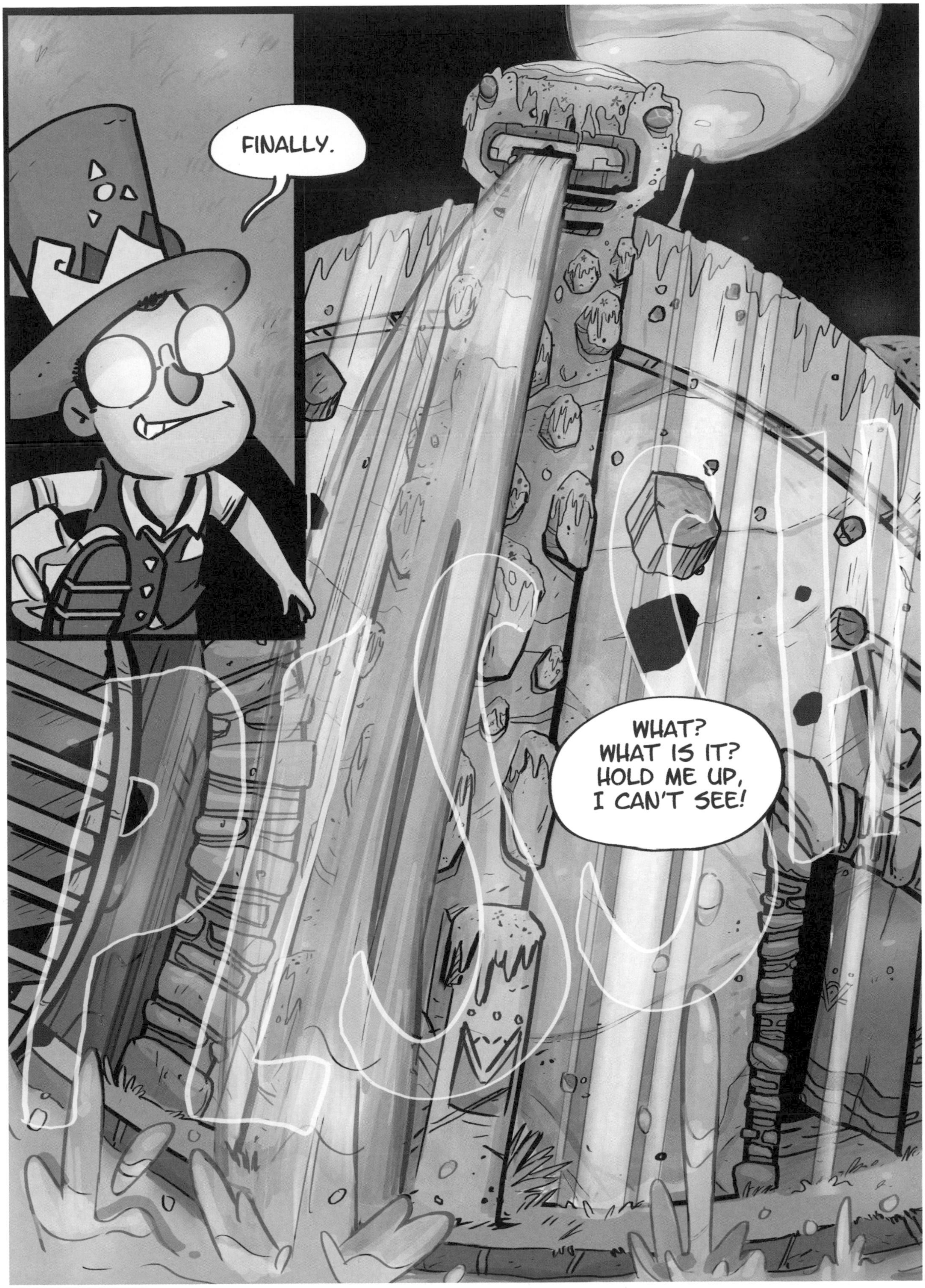
FINALLY.
WHAT? WHAT IS IT? HOLD ME UP, I CAN'T SEE!

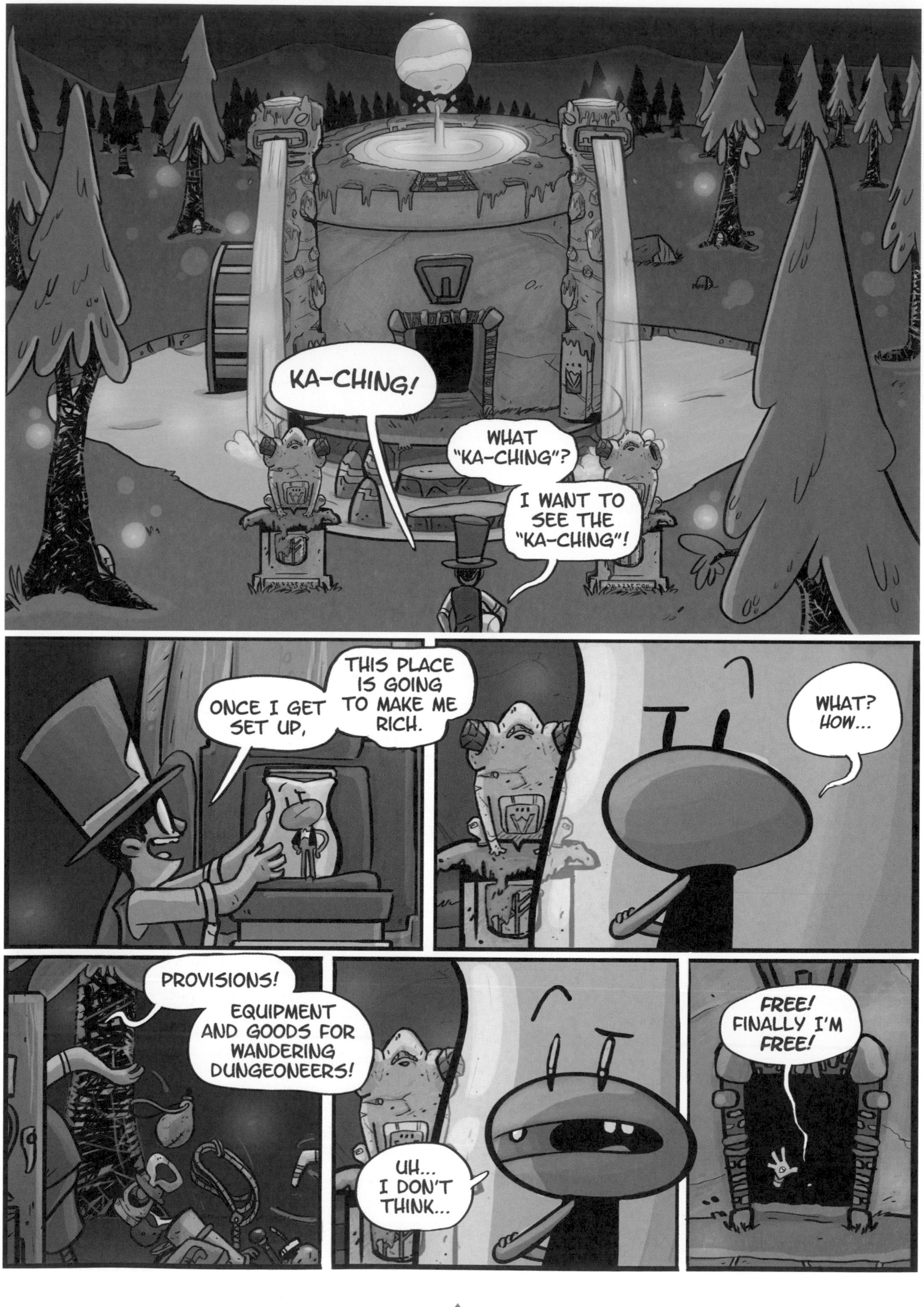
KA-CHING!
WHAT "KA-CHING"?
I WANT TO SEE THE "KA-CHING"!
ONCE I GET SET UP,
THIS PLACE IS GOING TO MAKE ME RICH.
WHAT? HOW...
PROVISIONS!
EQUIPMENT AND GOODS FOR WANDERING DUNGEONEERS!
UH... I DON'T THINK...
FREE! FINALLY I'M FREE!

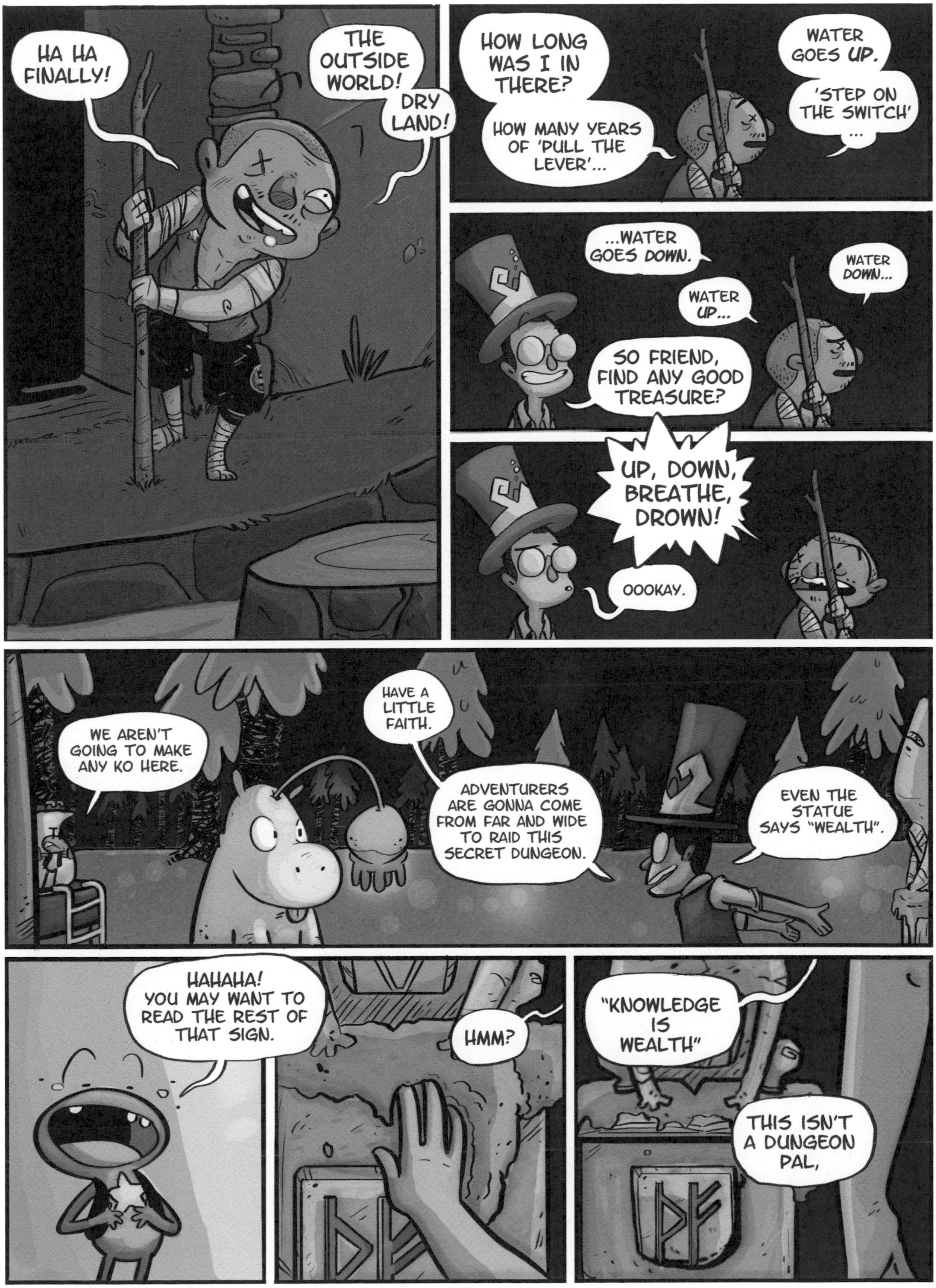
HA HA FINALLY!
THE OUTSIDE WORLD!
DRY LAND!
HOW LONG WAS I IN THERE?
HOW MANY YEARS OF 'PULL THE LEVER'...
WATER GOES UP.
'STEP ON THE SWITCH' ...
...WATER GOES DOWN.
WATER UP...
WATER DOWN...
SO FRIEND, FIND ANY GOOD TREASURE?
UP, DOWN, BREATHE, DROWN!
OOOKAY.
WE AREN'T GOING TO MAKE ANY KO HERE.
HAVE A LITTLE FAITH.
ADVENTURERS ARE GONNA COME FROM FAR AND WIDE TO RAID THIS SECRET DUNGEON.
EVEN THE STATUE SAYS "WEALTH".
HAHAHA! YOU MAY WANT TO READ THE REST OF THAT SIGN.
HMM?
"KNOWLEDGE IS WEALTH"
THIS ISN'T A DUNGEON PAL,

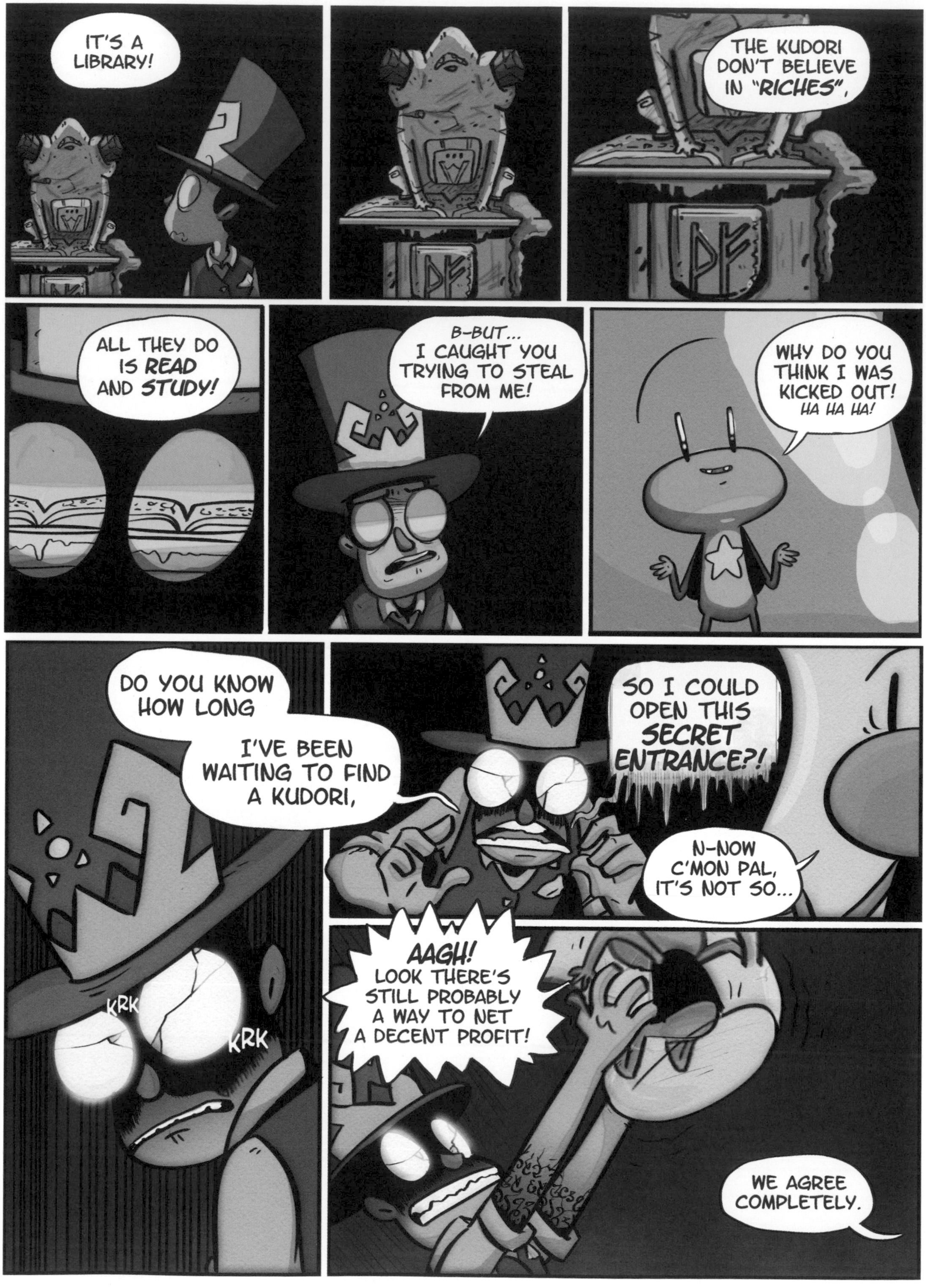
IT'S A LIBRARY!
THE KUDORI DON'T BELIEVE IN "RICHES",
ALL THEY DO IS READ AND STUDY!
B-BUT... I CAUGHT YOU TRYING TO STEAL FROM ME!
WHY DO YOU THINK I WAS KICKED OUT! HA HA HA!
DO YOU KNOW HOW LONG
I'VE BEEN WAITING TO FIND A KUDORI,
KRK
KRK
SO I COULD OPEN THIS SECRET ENTRANCE?!
N-NOW C'MON PAL, IT'S NOT SO...
AAGH! LOOK THERE'S STILL PROBABLY A WAY TO NET A DECENT PROFIT!
WE AGREE COMPLETELY.

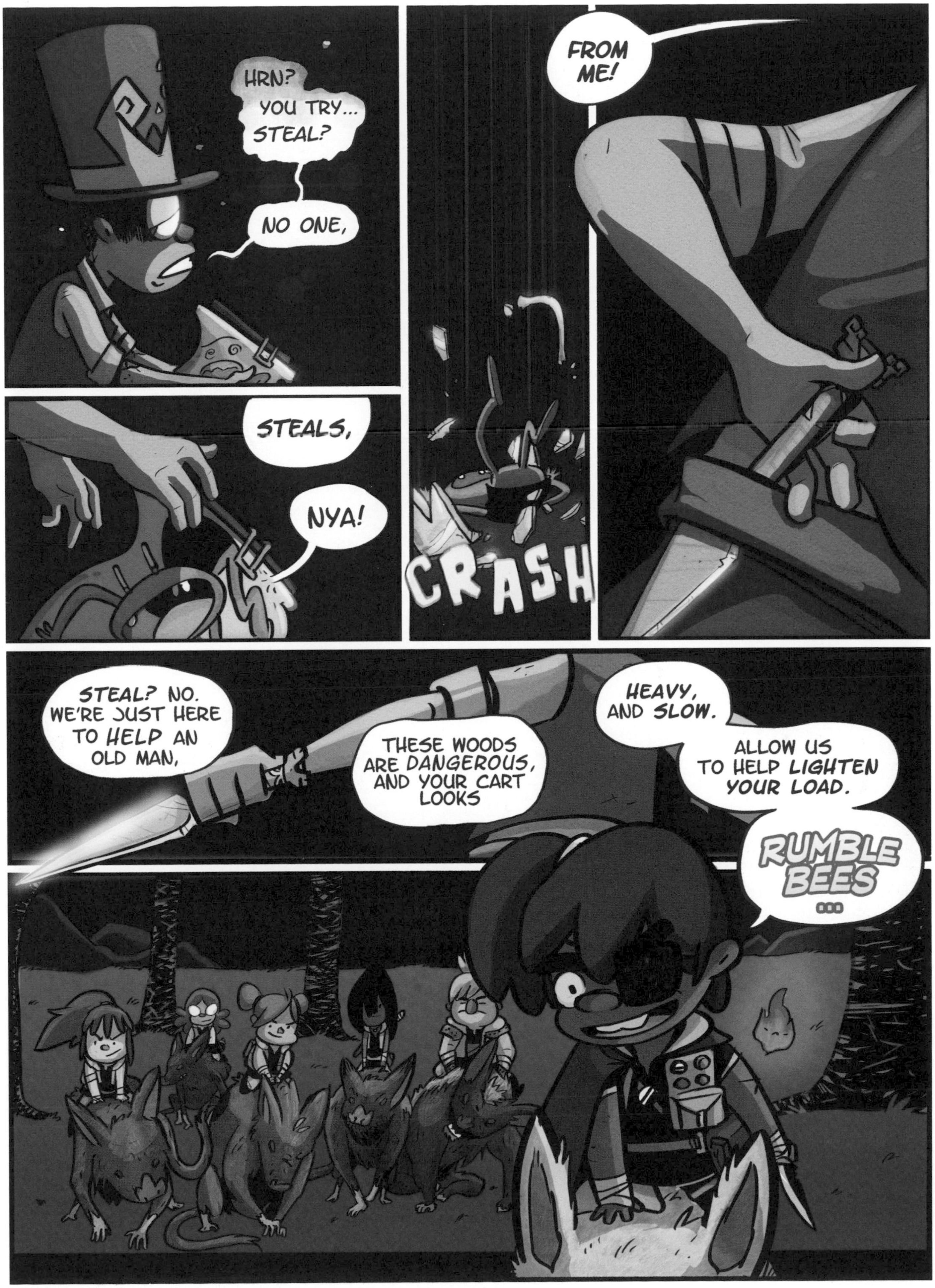

HRN? YOU TRY... STEAL?
NO ONE,
STEALS,
NYA!
CRASH
FROM ME!
STEAL? NO. WE'RE JUST HERE TO HELP AN OLD MAN,
THESE WOODS ARE DANGEROUS, AND YOUR CART LOOKS
HEAVY, AND SLOW.
ALLOW US TO HELP LIGHTEN YOUR LOAD.
RUMBLE BEES ...

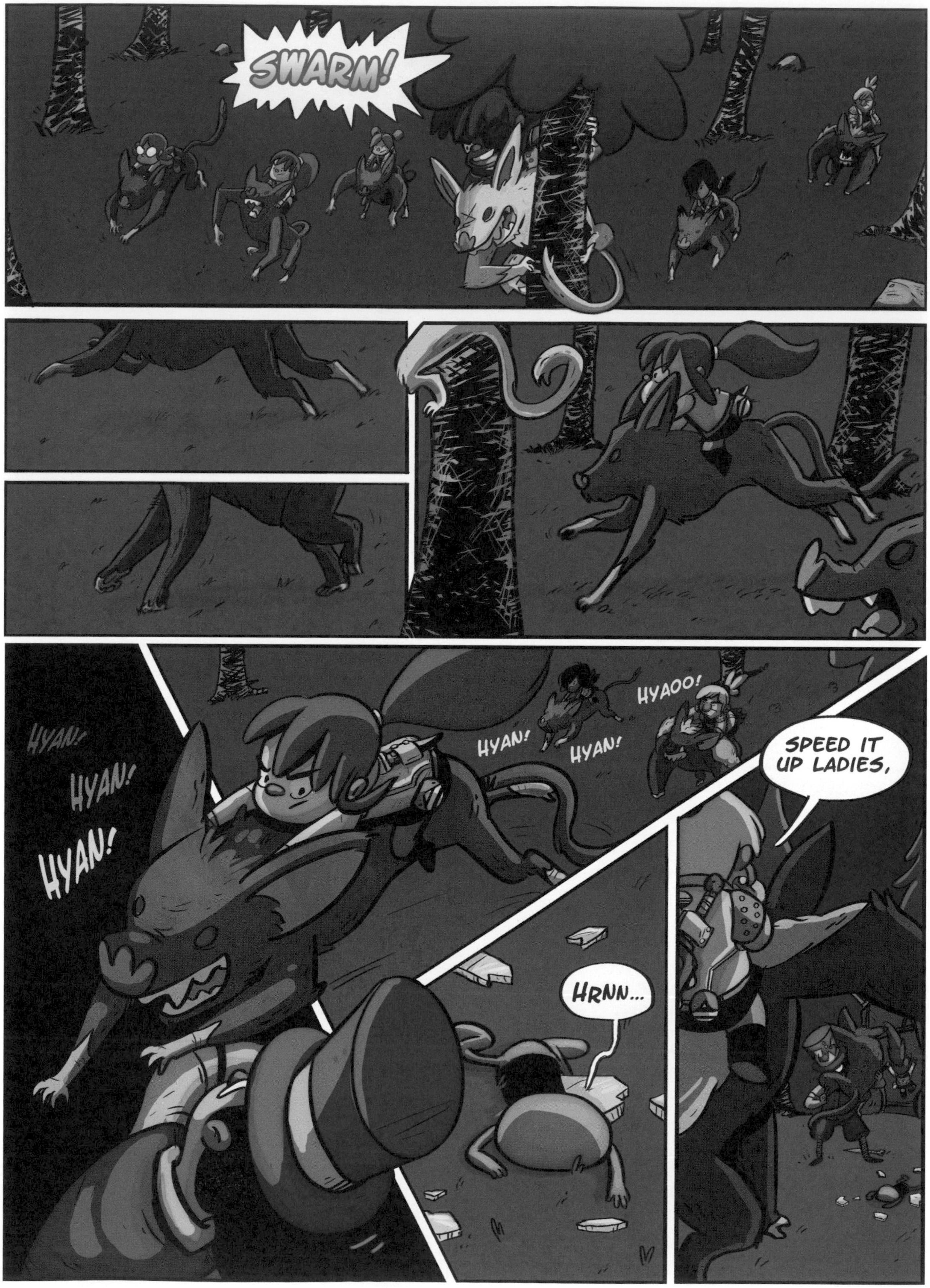
SWARM!
HYAN!
HYAN!
HYAN!
HYAN!
HYAN!
HYAOO!
SPEED IT UP LADIES,
HRNN...

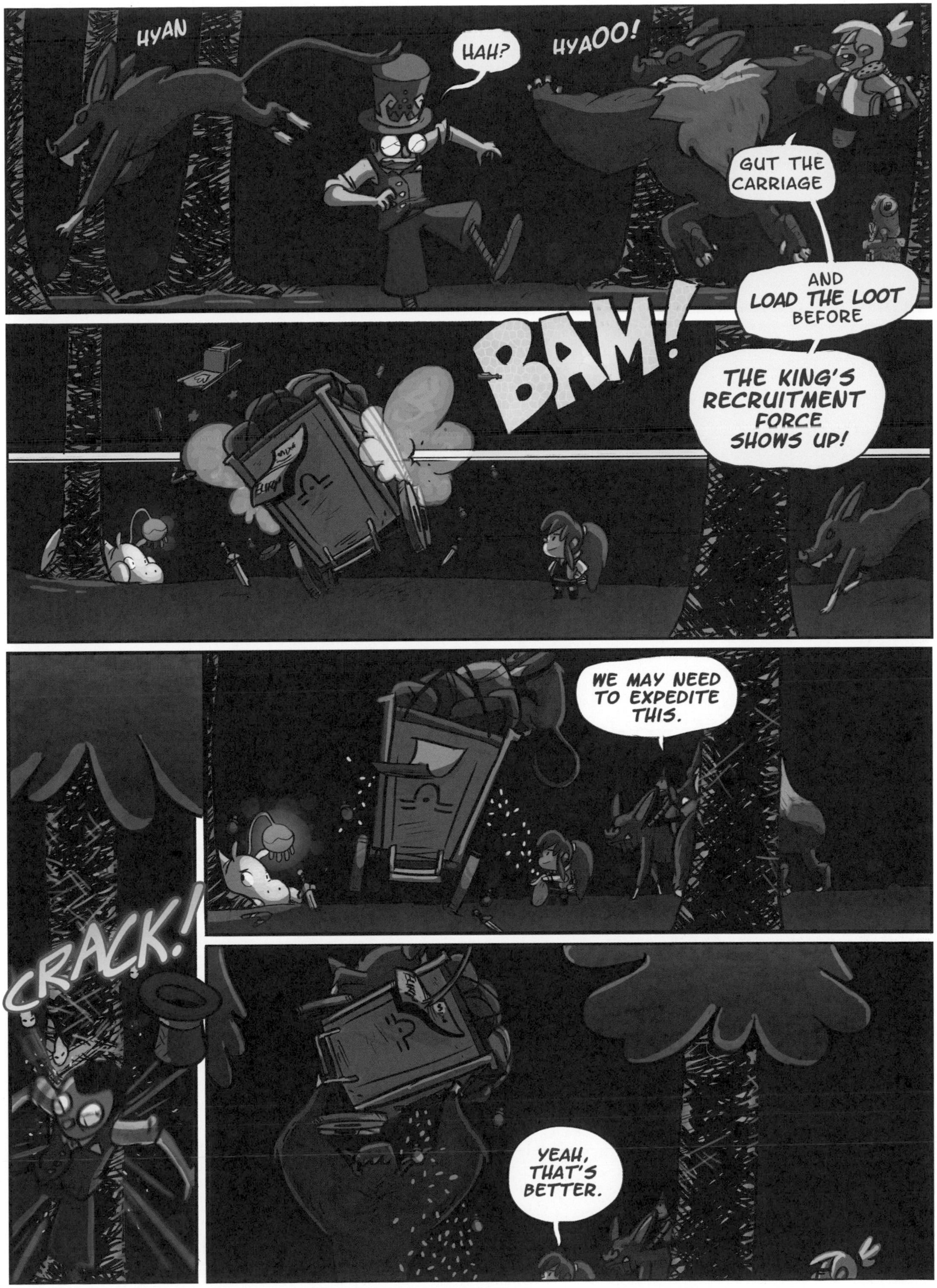
HYAN
HAH?
HYAOO!
GUT THE CARRIAGE
AND LOAD THE LOOT BEFORE
BAM!
THE KING'S RECRUITMENT FORCE SHOWS UP!
WE MAY NEED TO EXPEDITE THIS.
CRACK!
YEAH, THAT'S BETTER.

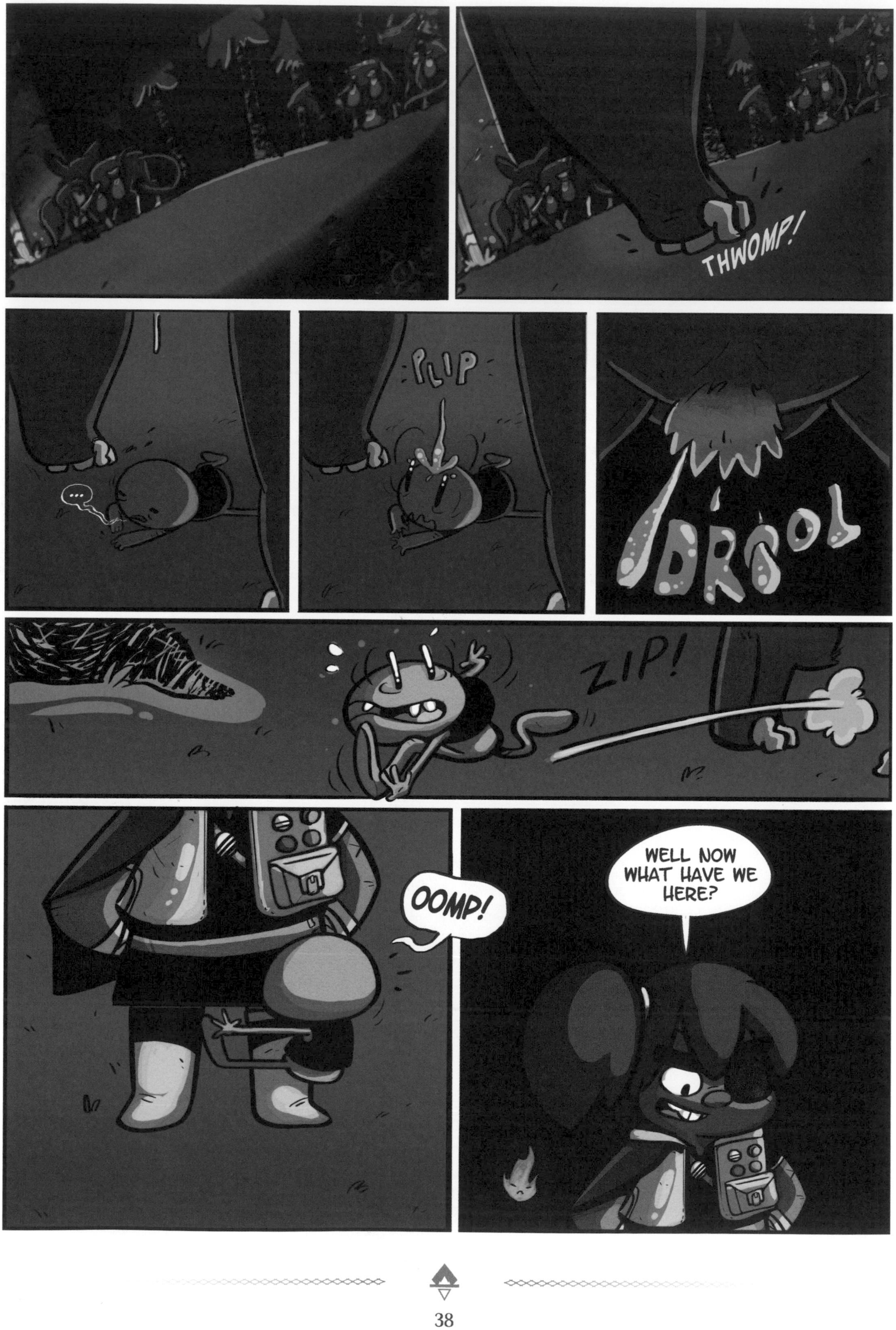
THWOMP!
...
PLIP
DROOL
ZIP!
OOMP!
WELL NOW WHAT HAVE WE HERE?

CHAPTER 3

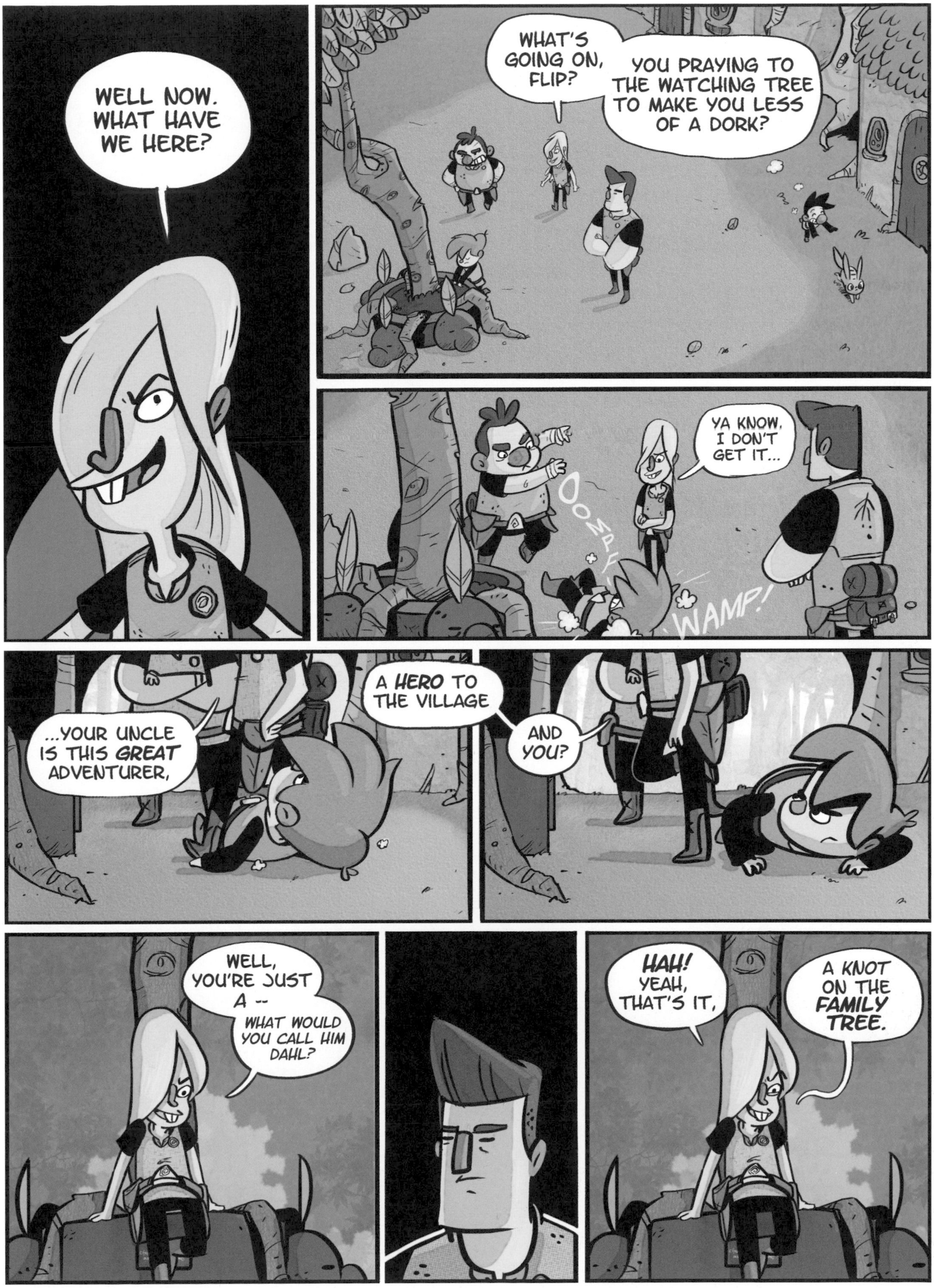
WELL NOW. WHAT HAVE WE HERE?
WHAT'S GOING ON, FLIP?
YOU PRAYING TO THE WATCHING TREE TO MAKE YOU LESS OF A DORK?
OOMPF
WAMP!
YA KNOW, I DON'T GET IT...
...YOUR UNCLE IS THIS GREAT ADVENTURER,
A HERO TO THE VILLAGE
AND YOU?
WELL, YOU'RE JUST A --
WHAT WOULD YOU CALL HIM DAHL?
HAH! YEAH, THAT'S IT,
A KNOT ON THE FAMILY TREE.

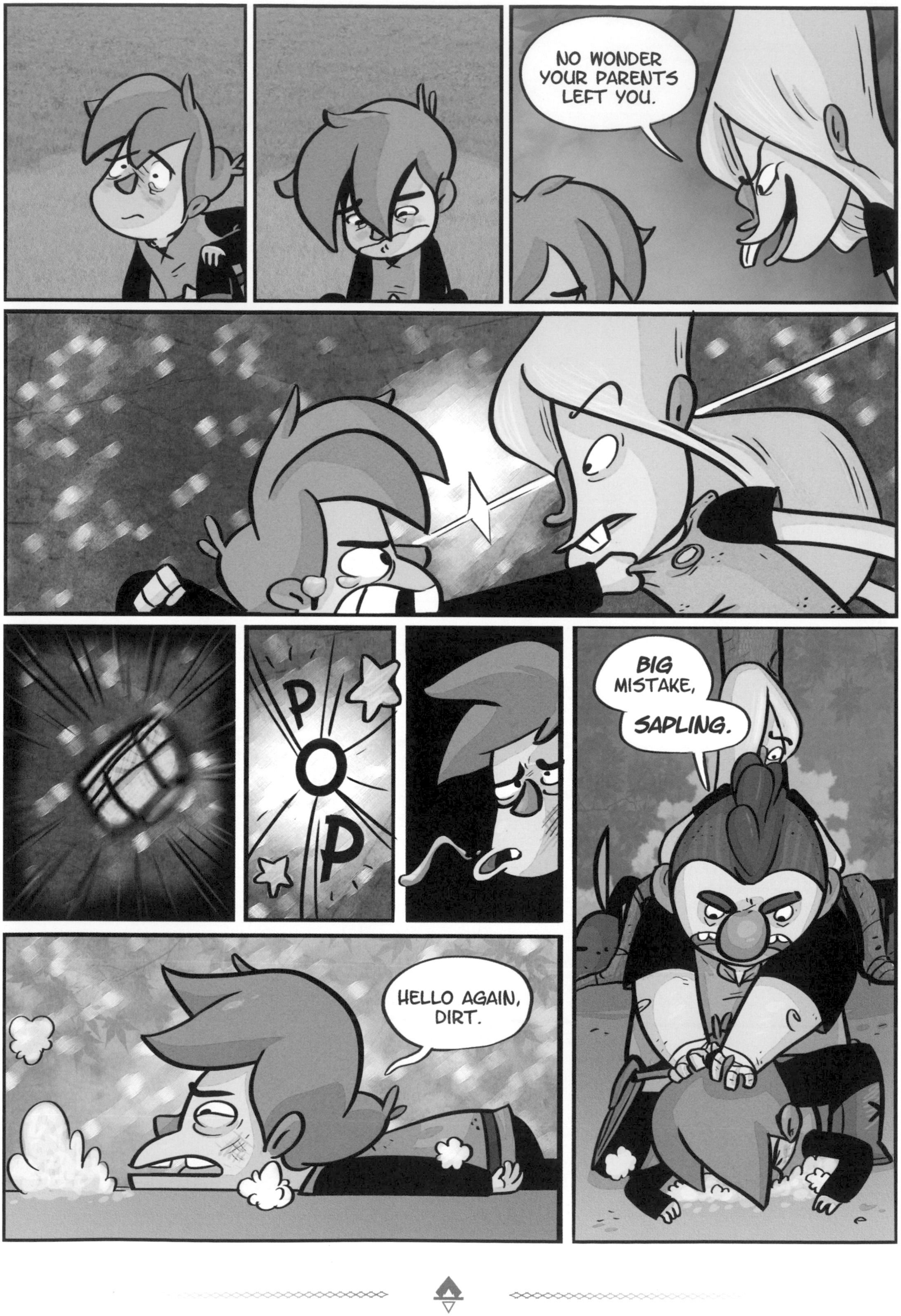
NO WONDER YOUR PARENTS LEFT YOU.
POP
BIG MISTAKE, SAPLING.
HELLO AGAIN, DIRT.

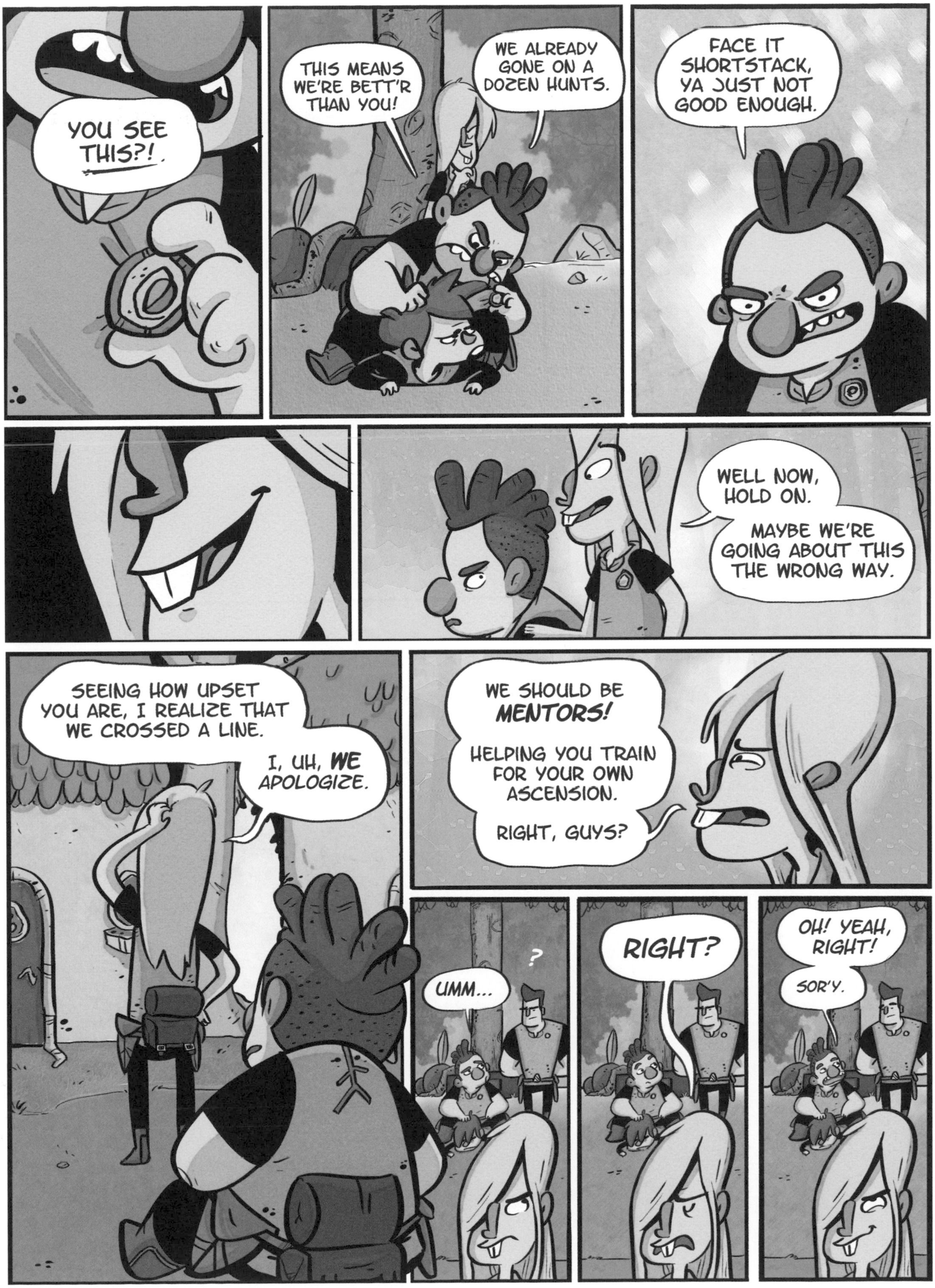
YOU SEE THIS?!
THIS MEANS WE'RE BETT'R THAN YOU!
WE ALREADY GONE ON A DOZEN HUNTS.
FACE IT SHORTSTACK, YA JUST NOT GOOD ENOUGH.
WELL NOW, HOLD ON.
MAYBE WE'RE GOING ABOUT THIS THE WRONG WAY.
SEEING HOW UPSET YOU ARE, I REALIZE THAT WE CROSSED A LINE.
I, UH, WE APOLOGIZE.
WE SHOULD BE MENTORS!
HELPING YOU TRAIN FOR YOUR OWN ASCENSION.
RIGHT, GUYS?
UMM...
?
RIGHT?
OH! YEAH, RIGHT!
SOR'Y.

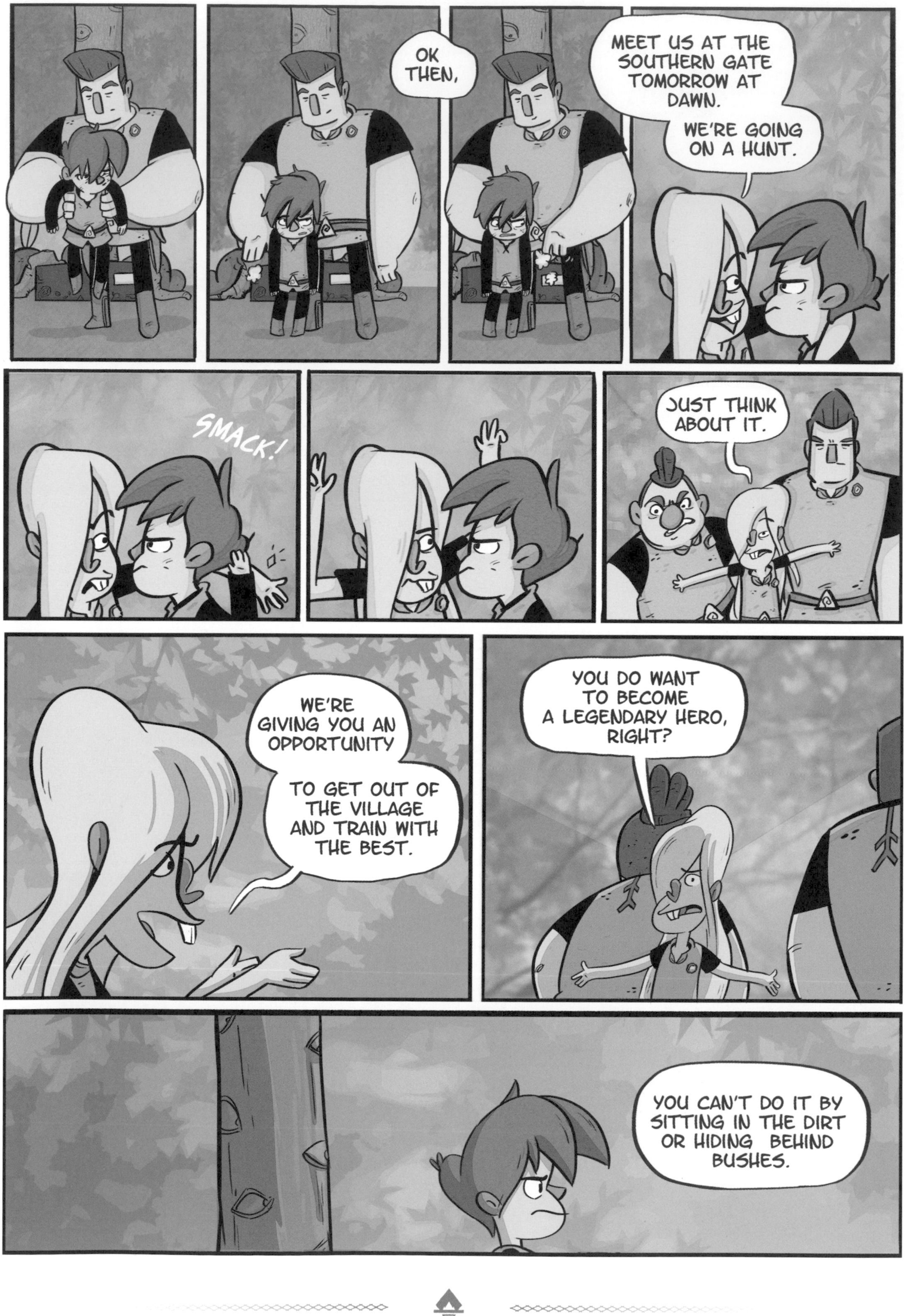
OK THEN,
MEET US AT THE SOUTHERN GATE TOMORROW AT DAWN.
WE'RE GOING ON A HUNT.
SMACK!
JUST THINK ABOUT IT.
WE'RE GIVING YOU AN OPPORTUNITY
TO GET OUT OF THE VILLAGE AND TRAIN WITH THE BEST.
YOU DO WANT TO BECOME A LEGENDARY HERO, RIGHT?
YOU CAN'T DO IT BY SITTING IN THE DIRT OR HIDING BEHIND BUSHES.

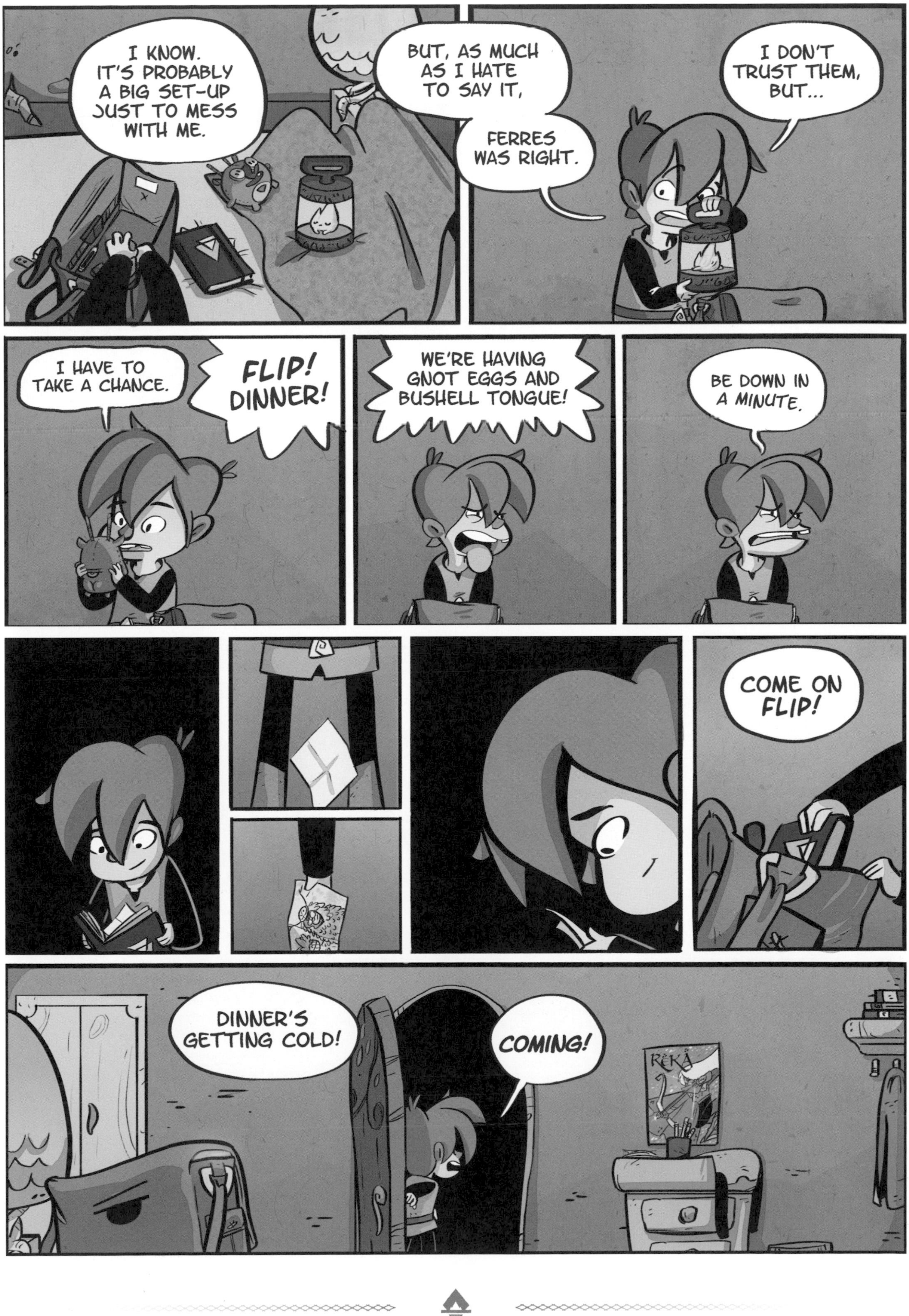
I KNOW. IT'S PROBABLY A BIG SET-UP JUST TO MESS WITH ME.
BUT, AS MUCH AS I HATE TO SAY IT,
FERRES WAS RIGHT.
I DON'T TRUST THEM, BUT...
I HAVE TO TAKE A CHANCE.
FLIP! DINNER!
WE'RE HAVING GNOT EGGS AND BUSHELL TONGUE!
BE DOWN IN A MINUTE.
COME ON FLIP!
DINNER'S GETTING COLD!
COMING!
REKA

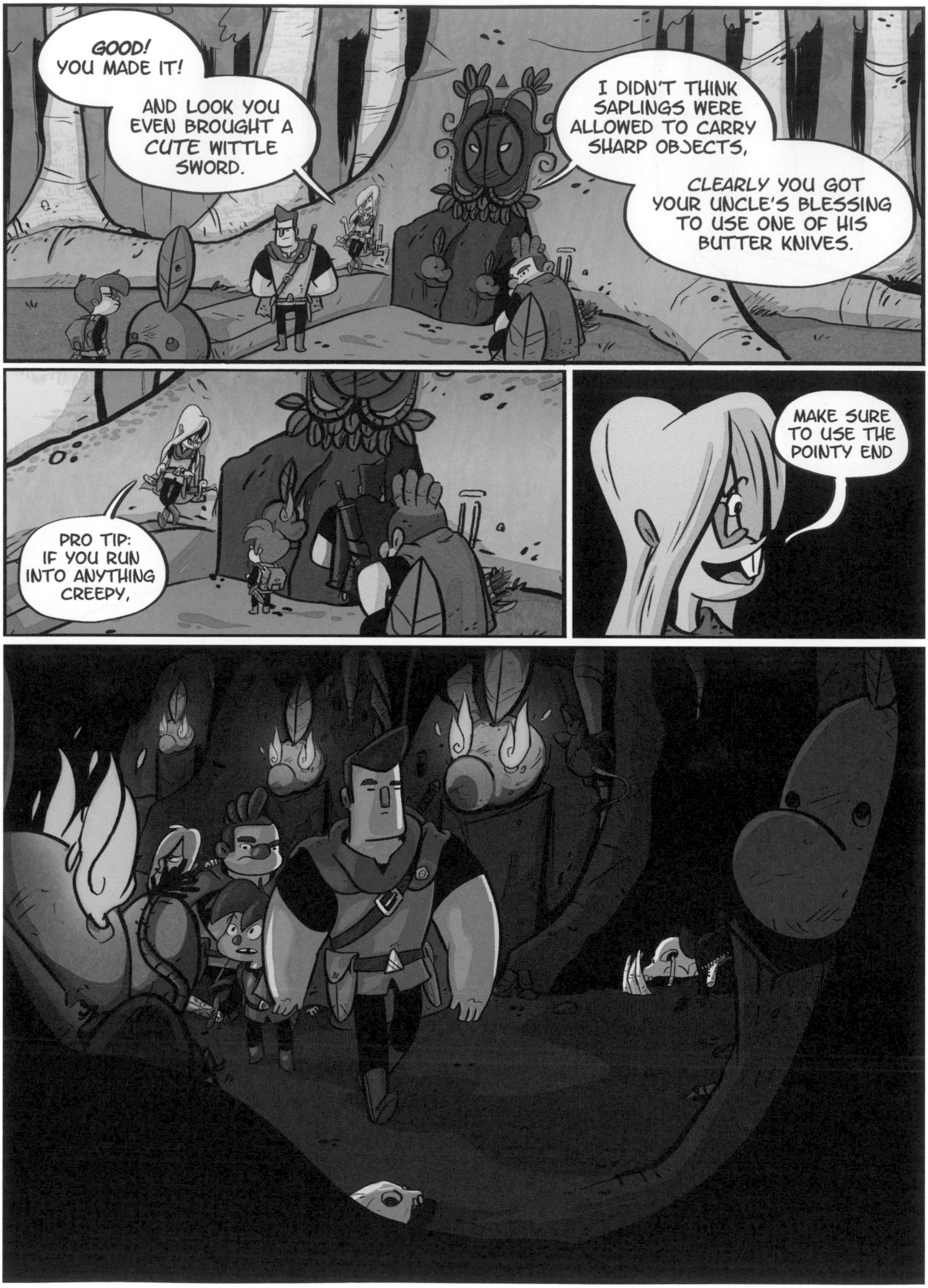
GOOD! YOU MADE IT!
AND LOOK YOU EVEN BROUGHT A CUTE WITTLE SWORD.
I DIDN'T THINK SAPLINGS WERE ALLOWED TO CARRY SHARP OBJECTS,
CLEARLY YOU GOT YOUR UNCLE'S BLESSING TO USE ONE OF HIS BUTTER KNIVES.
PRO TIP: IF YOU RUN INTO ANYTHING CREEPY,
MAKE SURE TO USE THE POINTY END

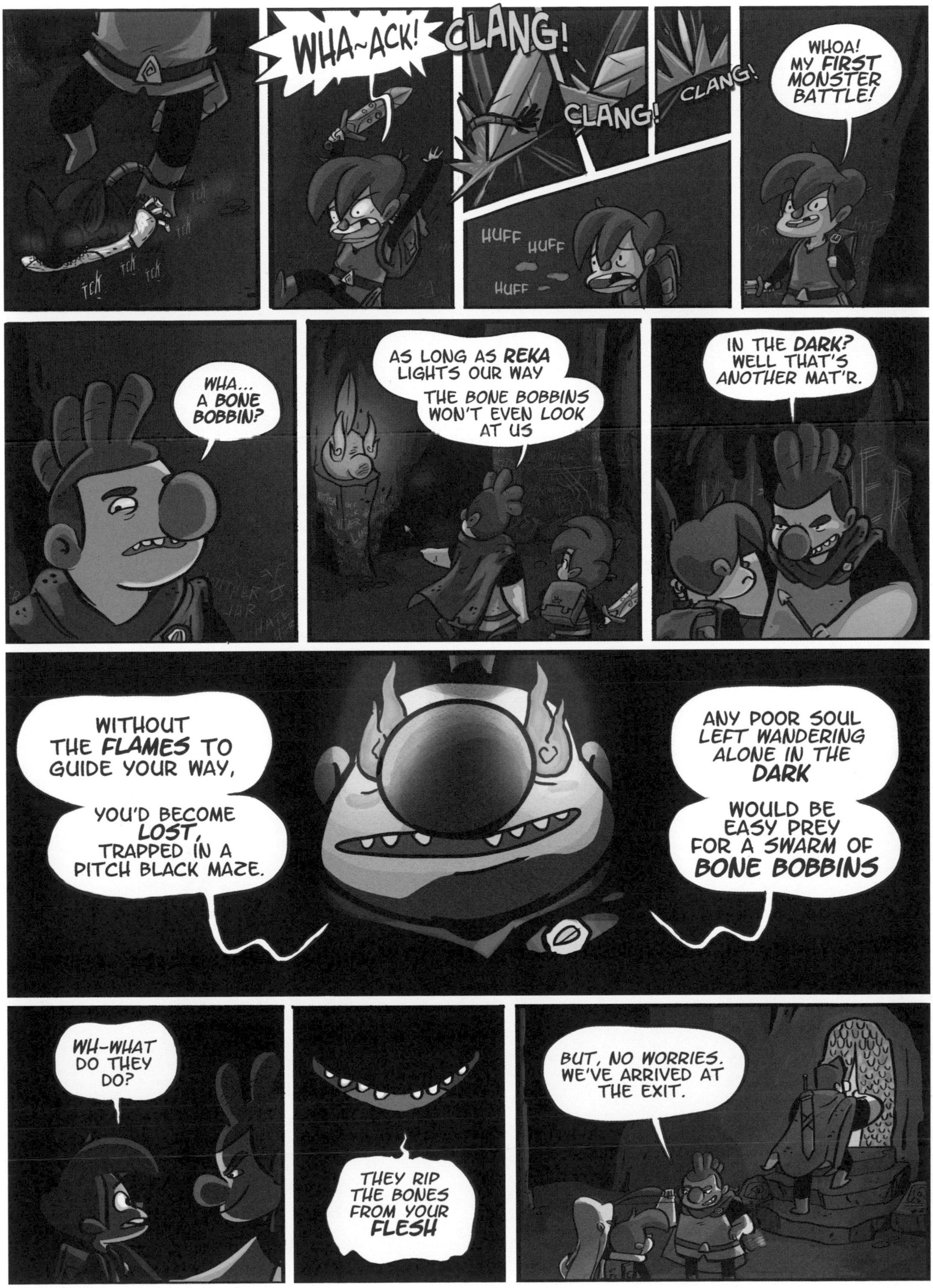
TCK TCK TCK TCK TCK
WHA~ACK!
CLANG!
CLANG!
CLANG!
HUFF HUFF HUFF
WHOA! MY FIRST MONSTER BATTLE!
WHA... A BONE BOBBIN?
AS LONG AS REKA LIGHTS OUR WAY
THE BONE BOBBINS WON'T EVEN LOOK AT US
IN THE DARK? WELL THAT'S ANOTHER MAT'R.
WITHOUT THE FLAMES TO GUIDE YOUR WAY,
YOU'D BECOME LOST, TRAPPED IN A PITCH BLACK MAZE.
ANY POOR SOUL LEFT WANDERING ALONE IN THE DARK
WOULD BE EASY PREY FOR A SWARM OF BONE BOBBINS
WH-WHAT DO THEY DO?
THEY RIP THE BONES FROM YOUR FLESH
BUT, NO WORRIES. WE'VE ARRIVED AT THE EXIT.

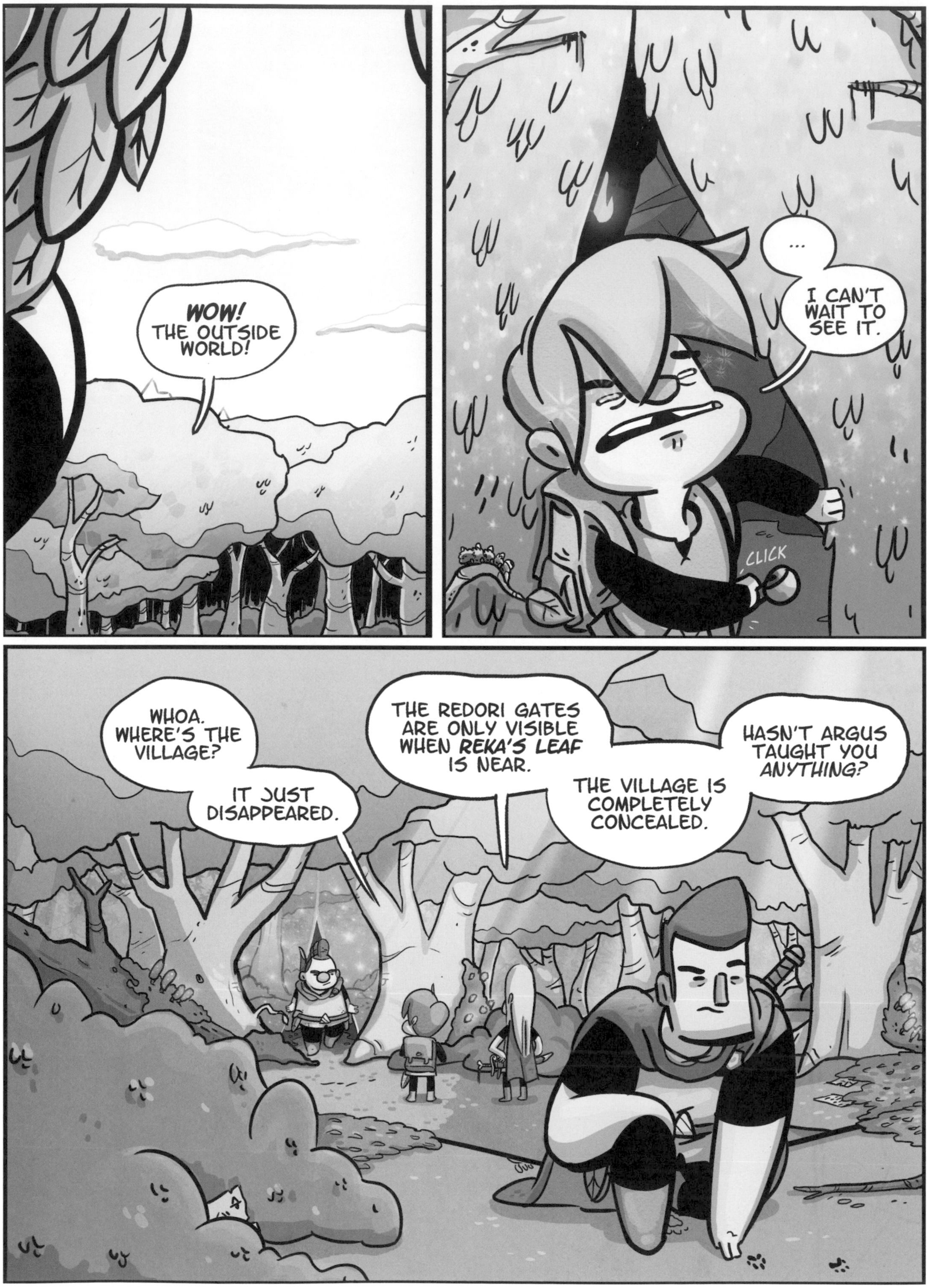
WOW! THE OUTSIDE WORLD!
...
I CAN'T WAIT TO SEE IT.
CLICK
WHOA. WHERE'S THE VILLAGE?
IT JUST DISAPPEARED.
THE REDORI GATES ARE ONLY VISIBLE WHEN REKA'S LEAF IS NEAR.
THE VILLAGE IS COMPLETELY CONCEALED.
HASN'T ARGUS TAUGHT YOU ANYTHING?

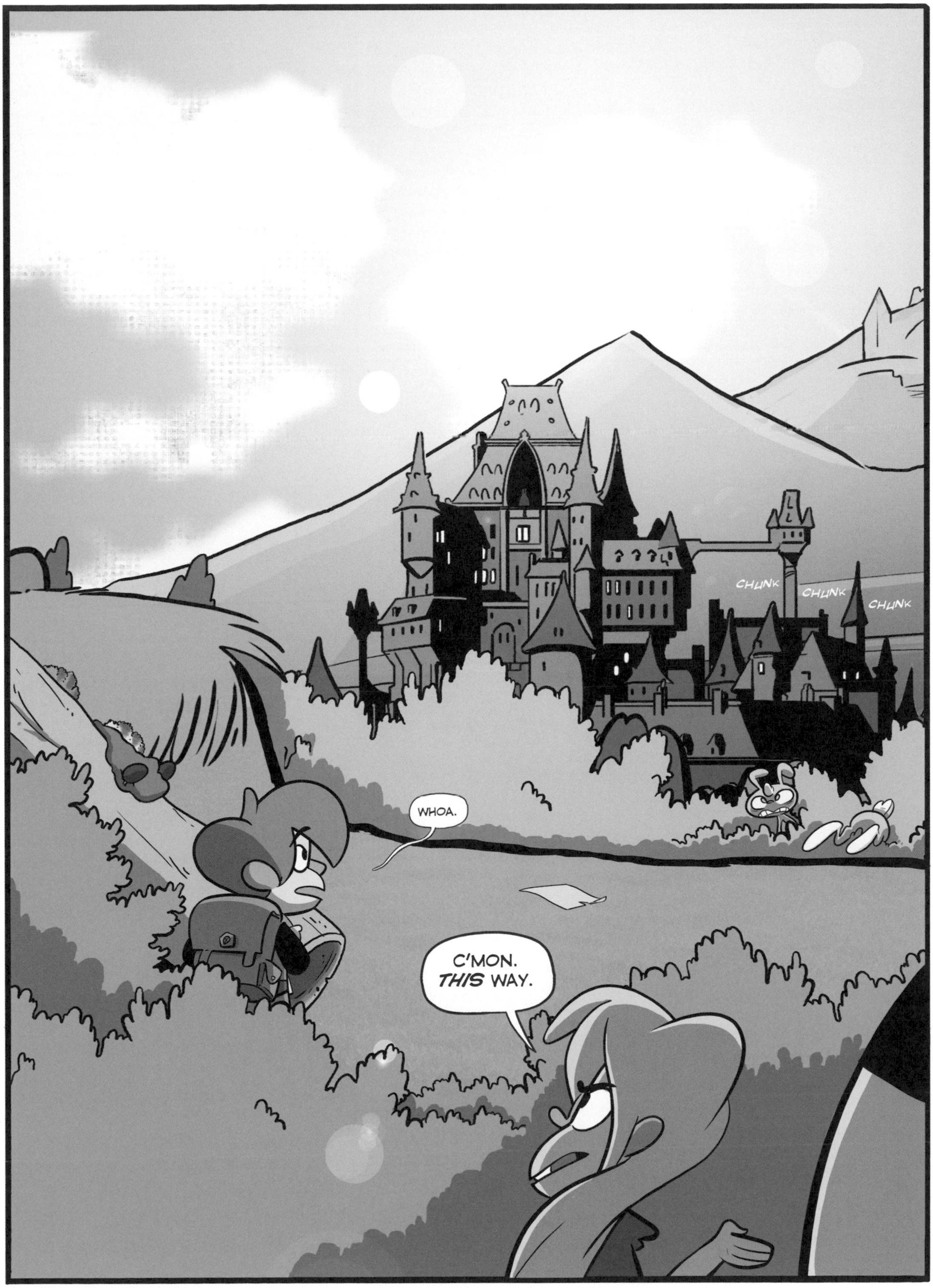
CHUNK
CHUNK
CHUNK
WHOA.
C'MON. *THIS* WAY.

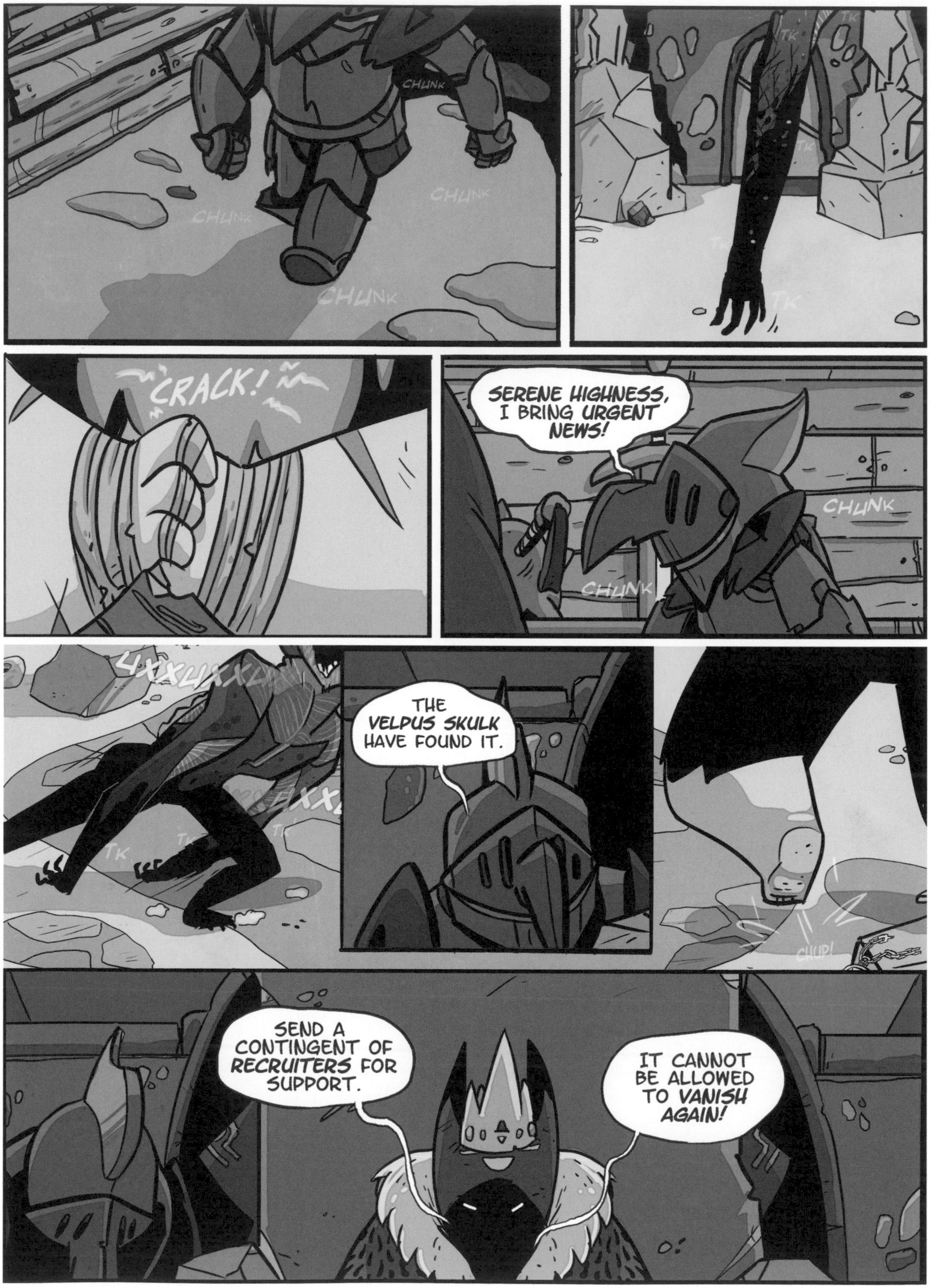
CHUNK
CHUNK
CHUNK
CHUNK
TK
TK
TK
TK
TK
CRACK!
SERENE HIGHNESS, I BRING URGENT NEWS!
CHUNK
CHUNK
TK
TK
THE VELPUS SKULK HAVE FOUND IT.
CHUP!
SEND A CONTINGENT OF RECRUITERS FOR SUPPORT.
IT CANNOT BE ALLOWED TO VANISH AGAIN!

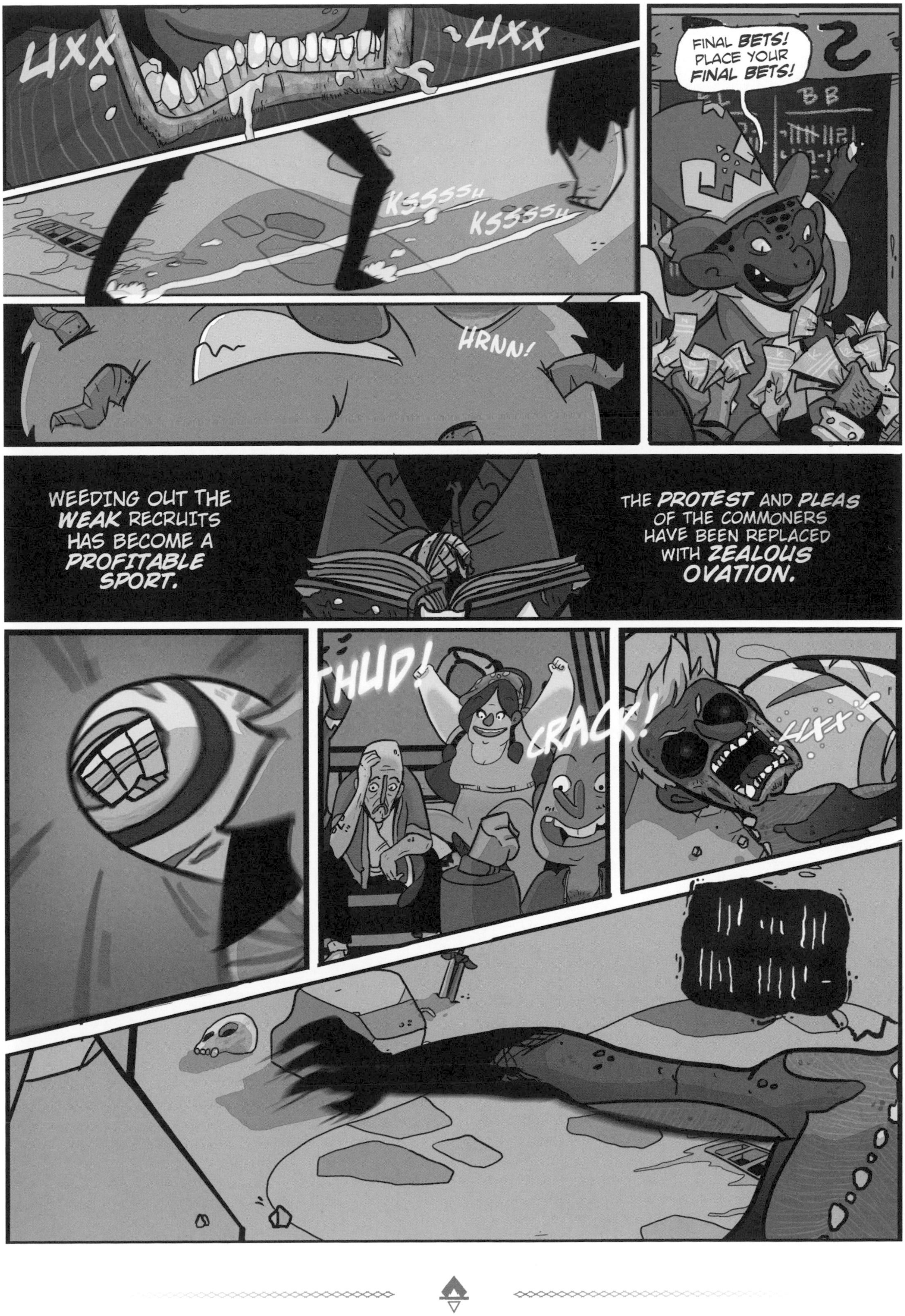

UXX
UXX
KSSSSu
KSSSSu
FINAL BETS! PLACE YOUR FINAL BETS!
HRNN!
WEEDING OUT THE WEAK RECRUITS HAS BECOME A PROFITABLE SPORT.
THE PROTEST AND PLEAS OF THE COMMONERS HAVE BEEN REPLACED WITH ZEALOUS OVATION.
THUD!
CRACK!
UXX

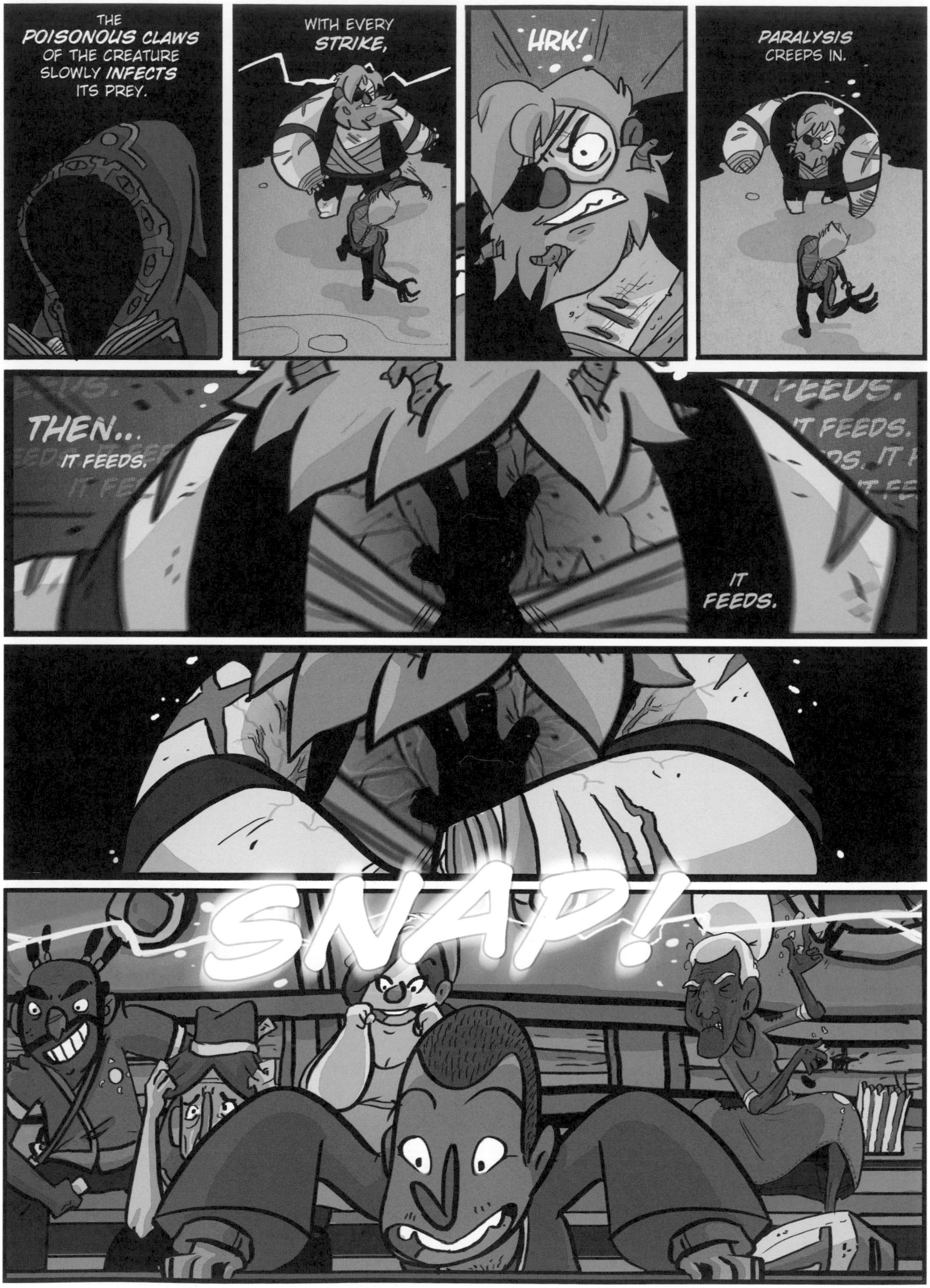
THE POISONOUS CLAWS OF THE CREATURE SLOWLY INFECTS ITS PREY.
WITH EVERY STRIKE,
HRK!
PARALYSIS CREEPS IN.
THEN... IT FEEDS.
IT FEEDS.
IT FEEDS.
IT FEEDS.
SNAP!

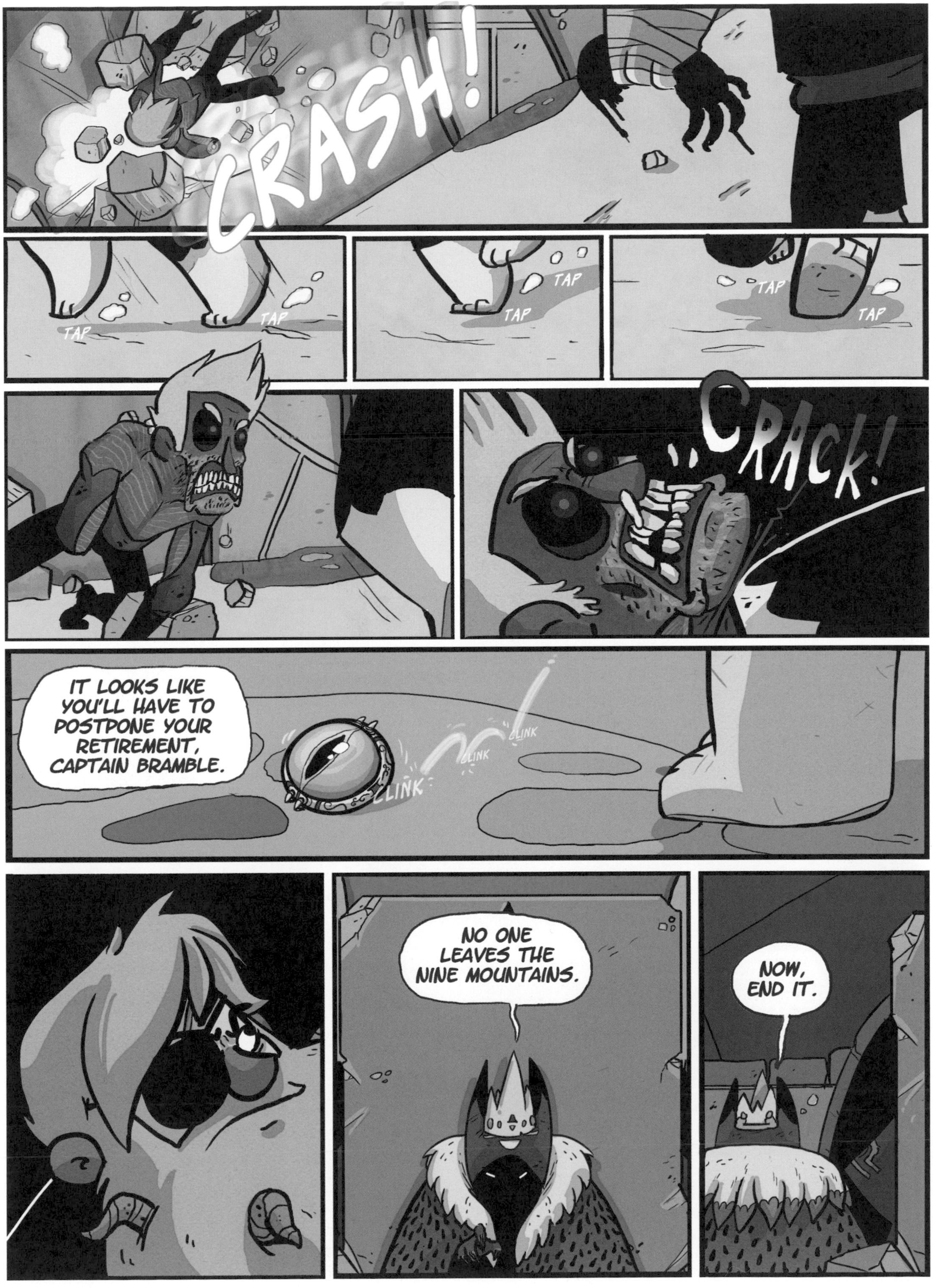
CRASH!
TAP
TAP
TAP
TAP
TAP
TAP
CRACK!
IT LOOKS LIKE YOU'LL HAVE TO POSTPONE YOUR RETIREMENT, CAPTAIN BRAMBLE.
CLINK
CLINK
CLINK
NO ONE LEAVES THE NINE MOUNTAINS.
NOW, END IT.

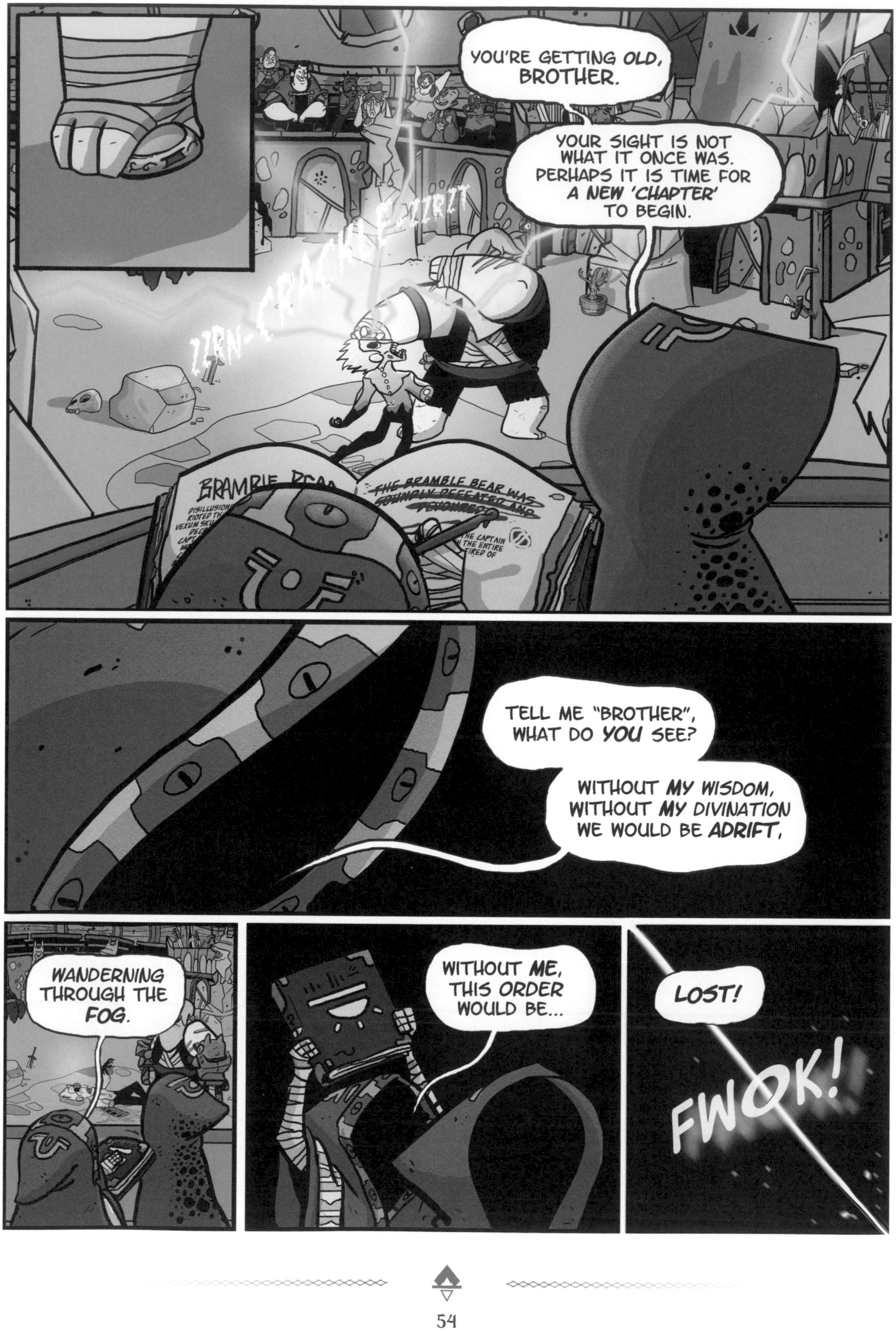
YOU'RE GETTING OLD, BROTHER.
YOUR SIGHT IS NOT WHAT IT ONCE WAS. PERHAPS IT IS TIME FOR A NEW 'CHAPTER' TO BEGIN.
ZZRN-CRACKLE-ZZRZT
TELL ME "BROTHER", WHAT DO YOU SEE?
WITHOUT MY WISDOM, WITHOUT MY DIVINATION WE WOULD BE ADRIFT,
WANDERNING THROUGH THE FOG.
WITHOUT ME, THIS ORDER WOULD BE...
LOST!
FWOK!

CHAPTER 4

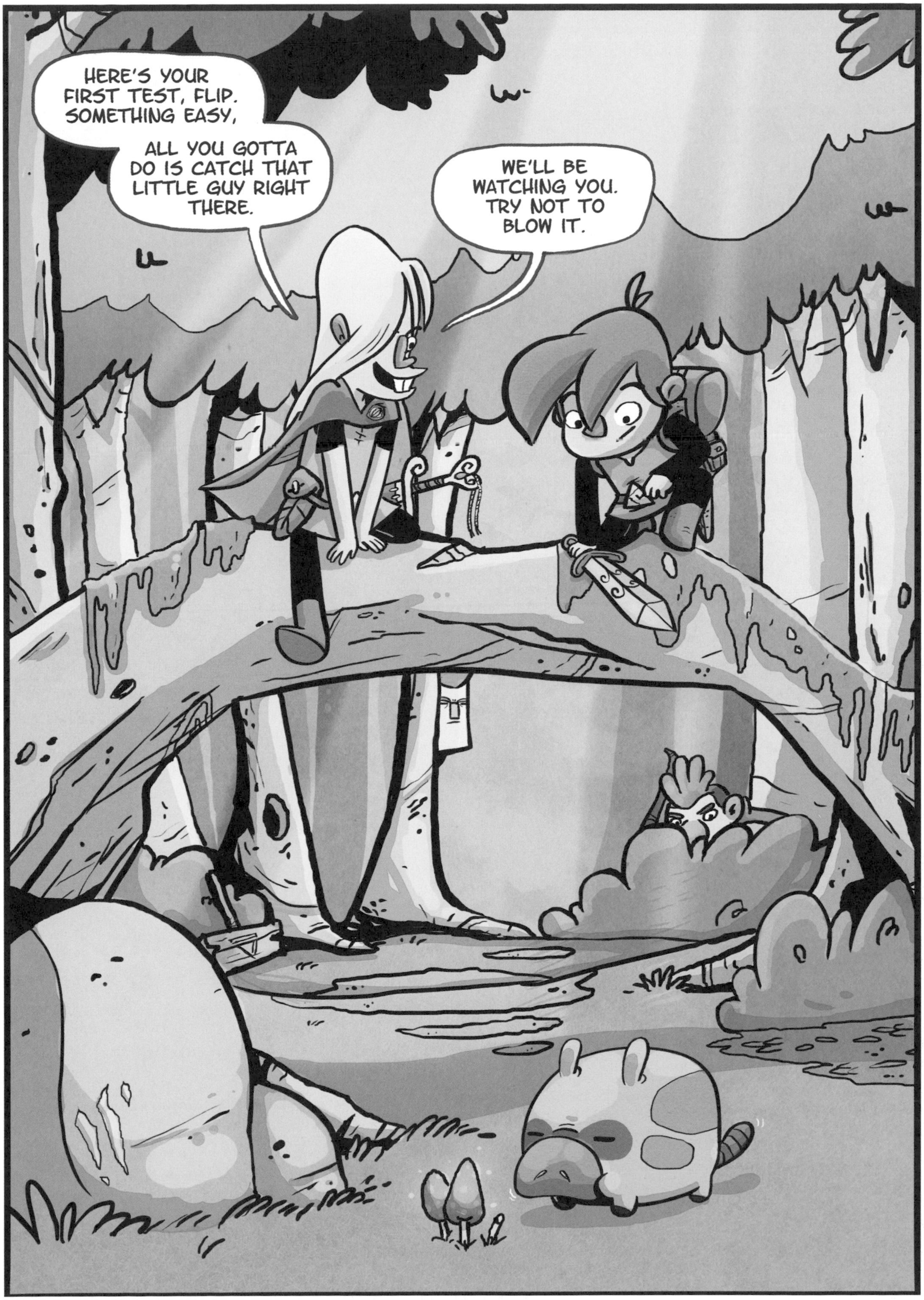
HERE'S YOUR FIRST TEST, FLIP. SOMETHING EASY,
ALL YOU GOTTA DO IS CATCH THAT LITTLE GUY RIGHT THERE.
WE'LL BE WATCHING YOU. TRY NOT TO BLOW IT.

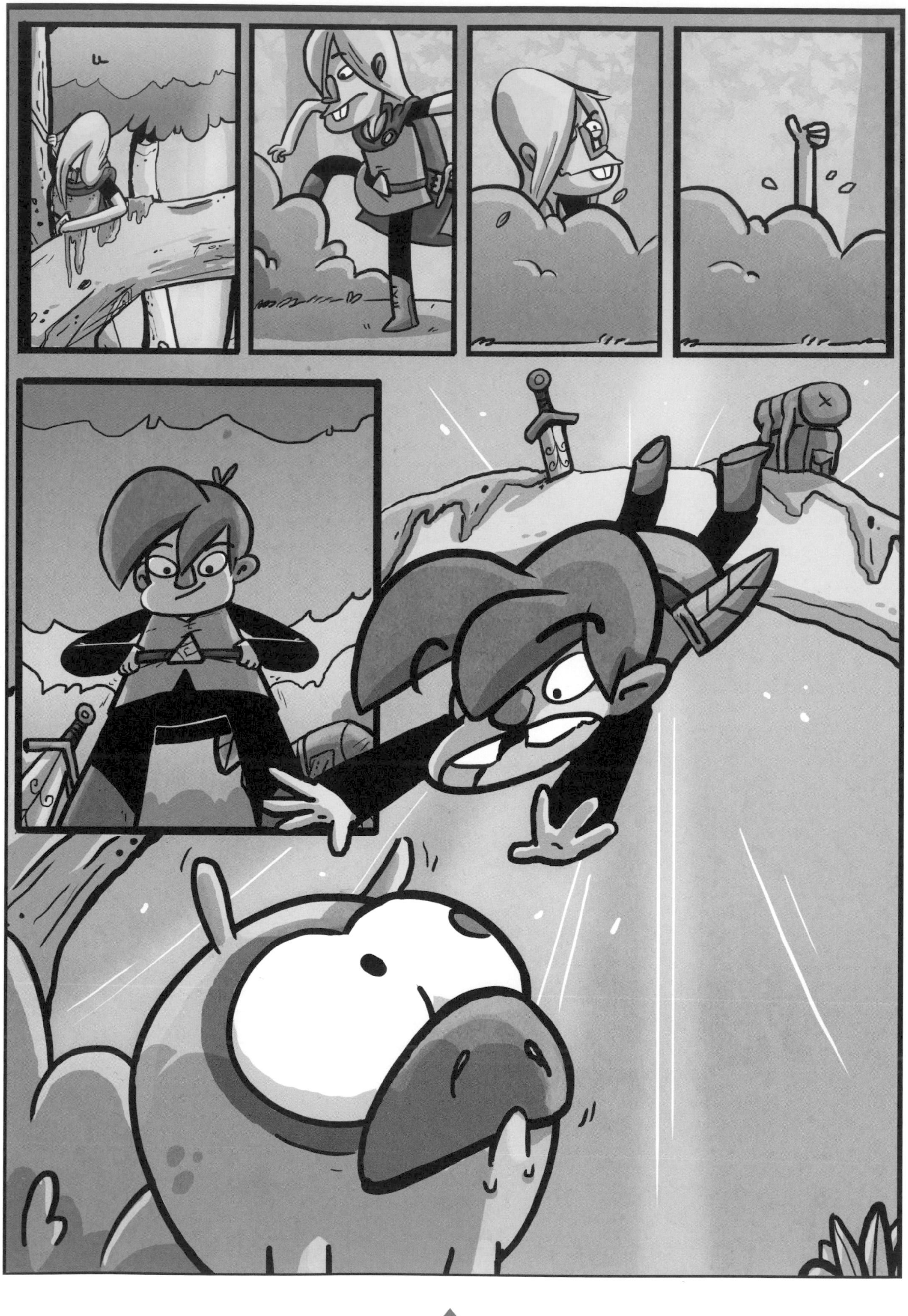

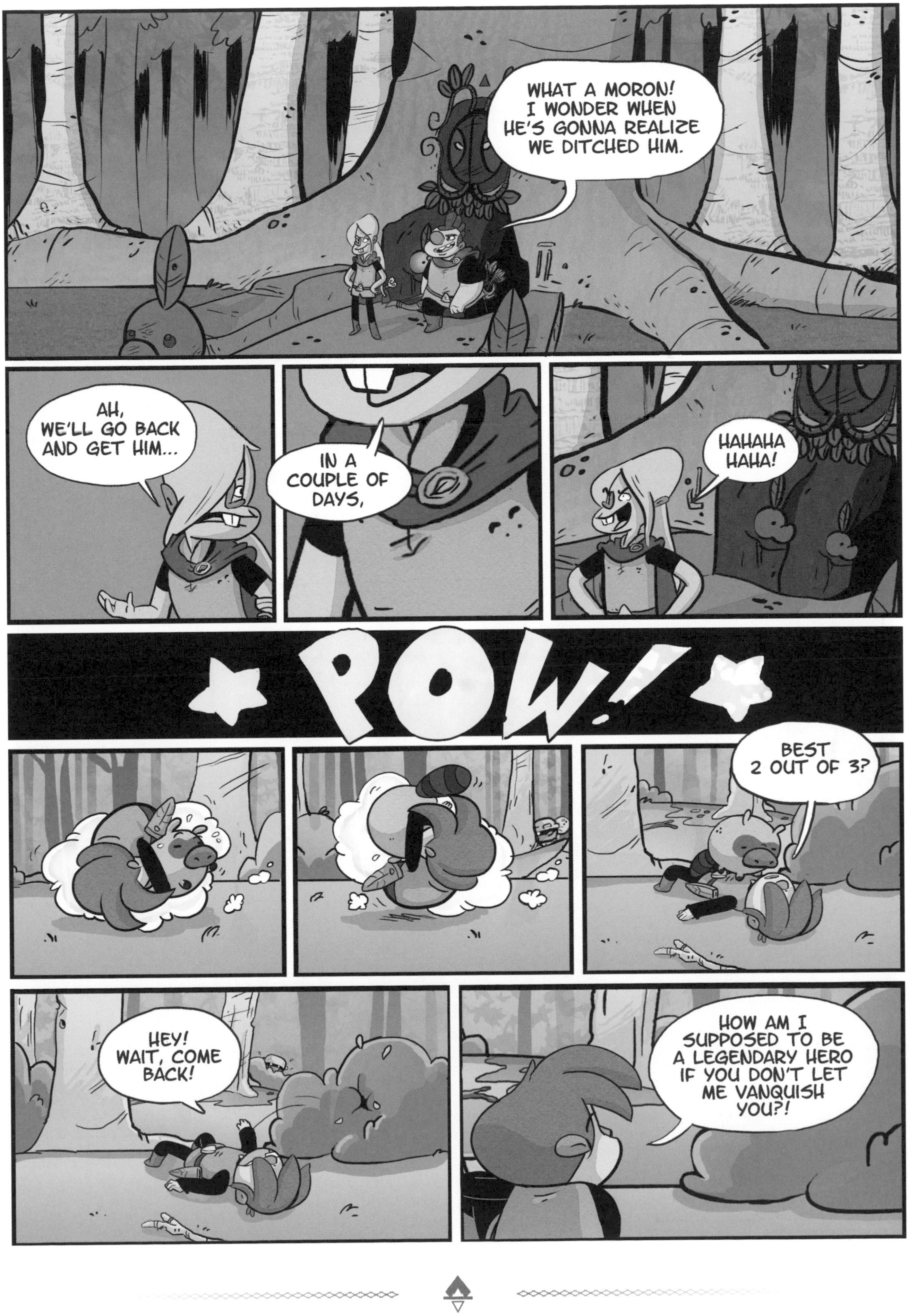
WHAT A MORON! I WONDER WHEN HE'S GONNA REALIZE WE DITCHED HIM.
AH, WE'LL GO BACK AND GET HIM...
IN A COUPLE OF DAYS,
HAHAHA HAHA!
POW!
BEST 2 OUT OF 3?
HEY! WAIT, COME BACK!
HOW AM I SUPPOSED TO BE A LEGENDARY HERO IF YOU DON'T LET ME VANQUISH YOU?!

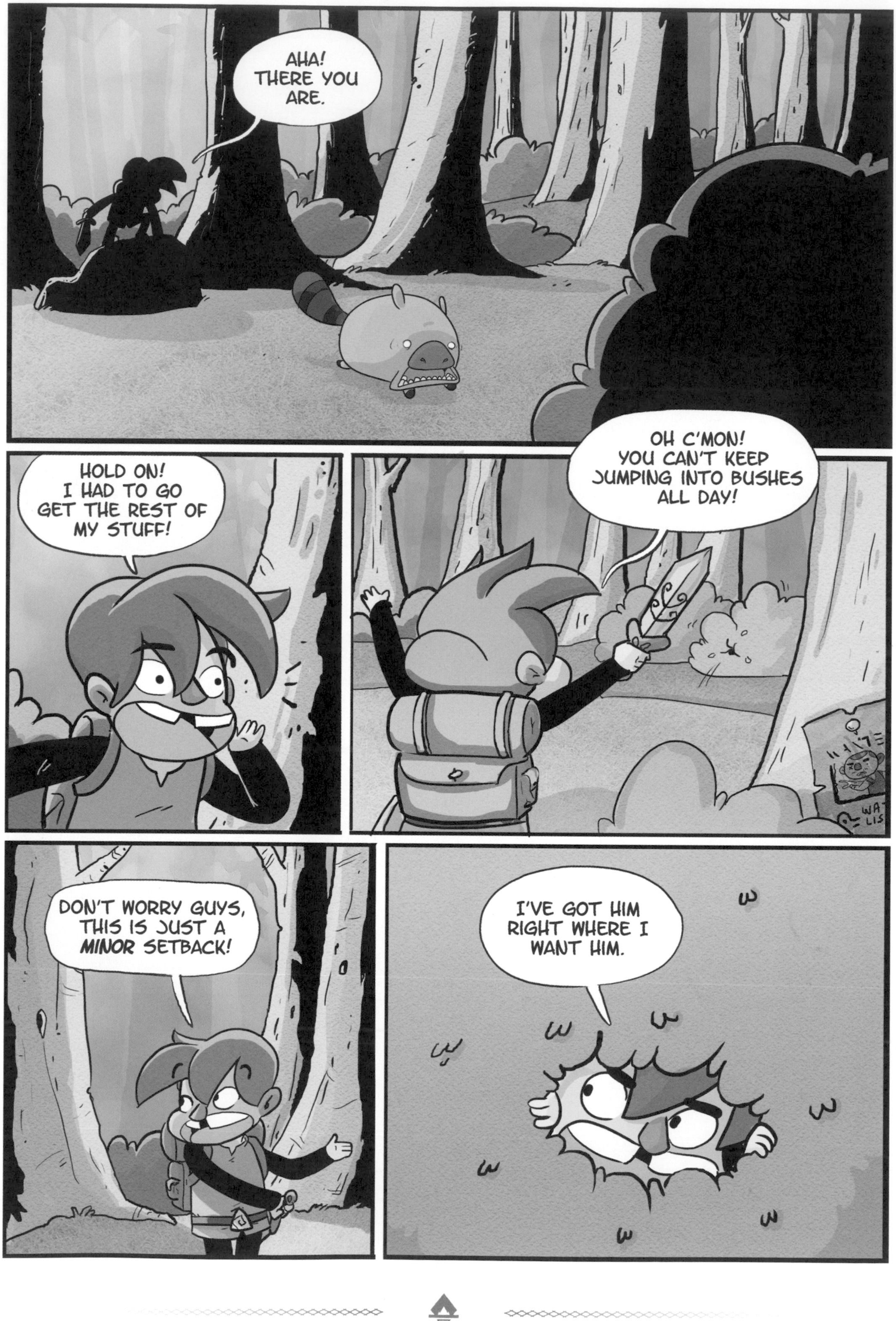
AHA! THERE YOU ARE.
HOLD ON! I HAD TO GO GET THE REST OF MY STUFF!
OH C'MON! YOU CAN'T KEEP JUMPING INTO BUSHES ALL DAY!
DON'T WORRY GUYS, THIS IS JUST A MINOR SETBACK!
I'VE GOT HIM RIGHT WHERE I WANT HIM.

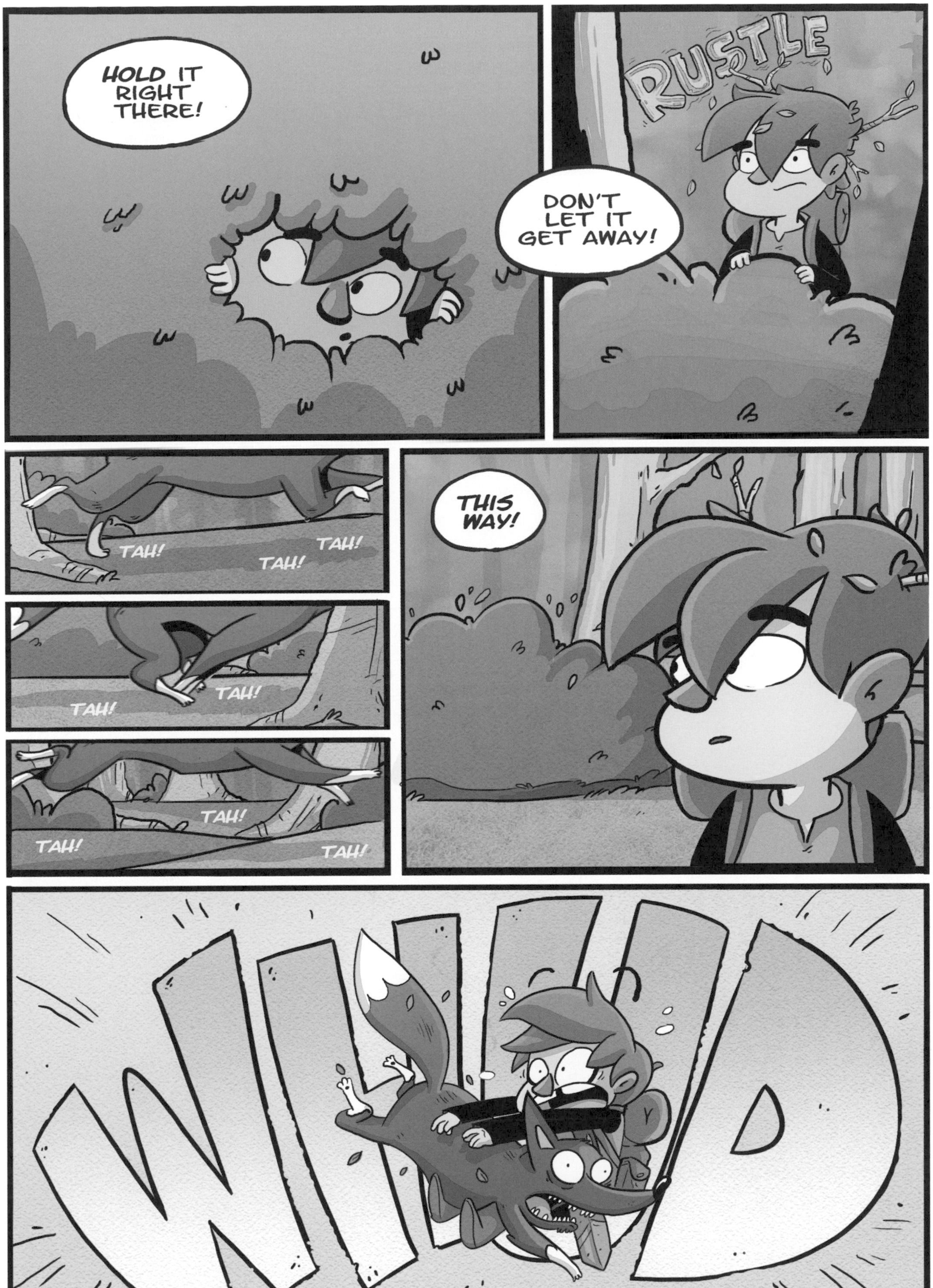
HOLD IT RIGHT THERE!
RUSTLE
DON'T LET IT GET AWAY!
TAH!
TAH!
TAH!
TAH!
TAH!
TAH!
TAH!
TAH!
THIS WAY!
WHUD

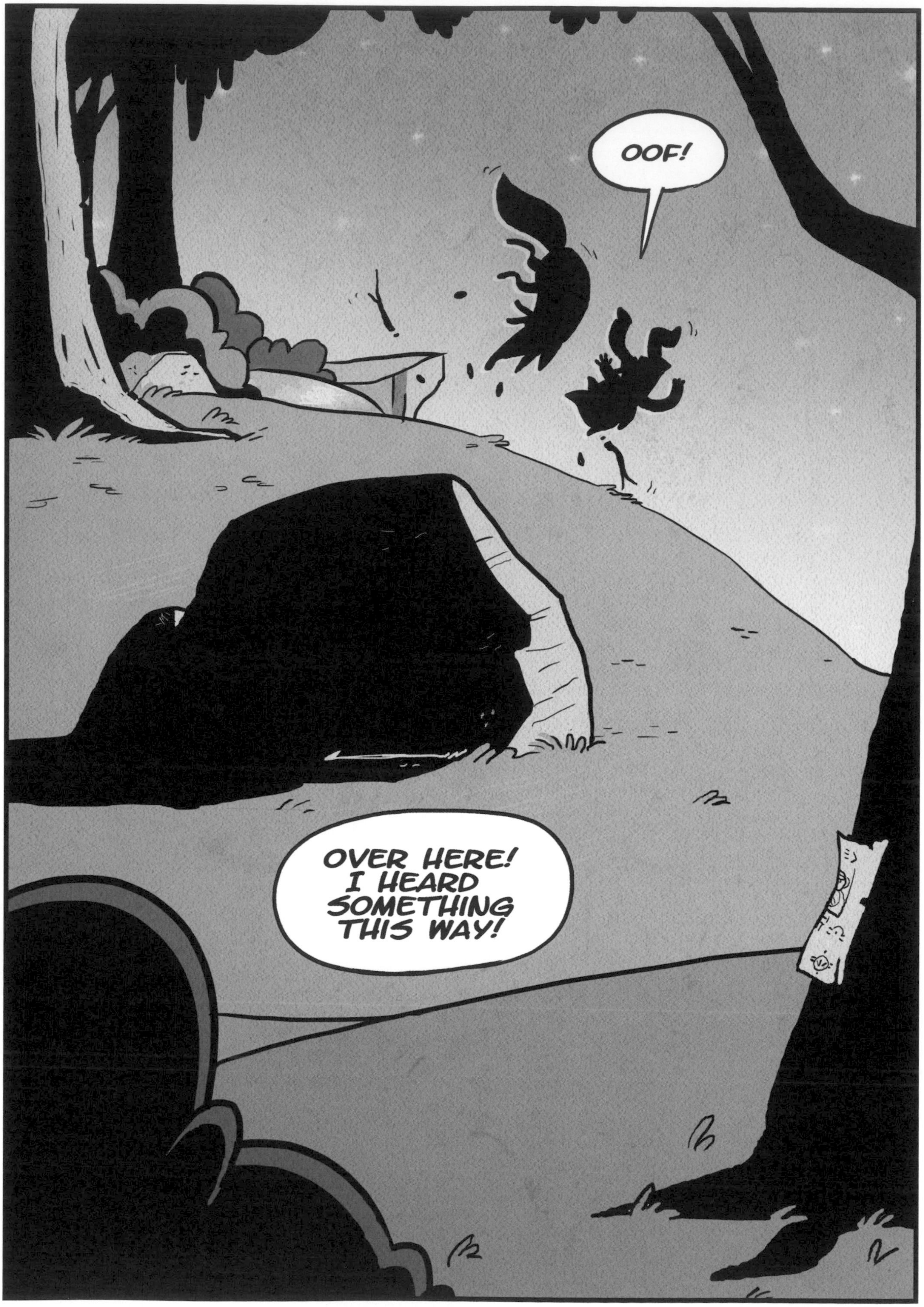
OOF!
OVER HERE! I HEARD SOMETHING THIS WAY!

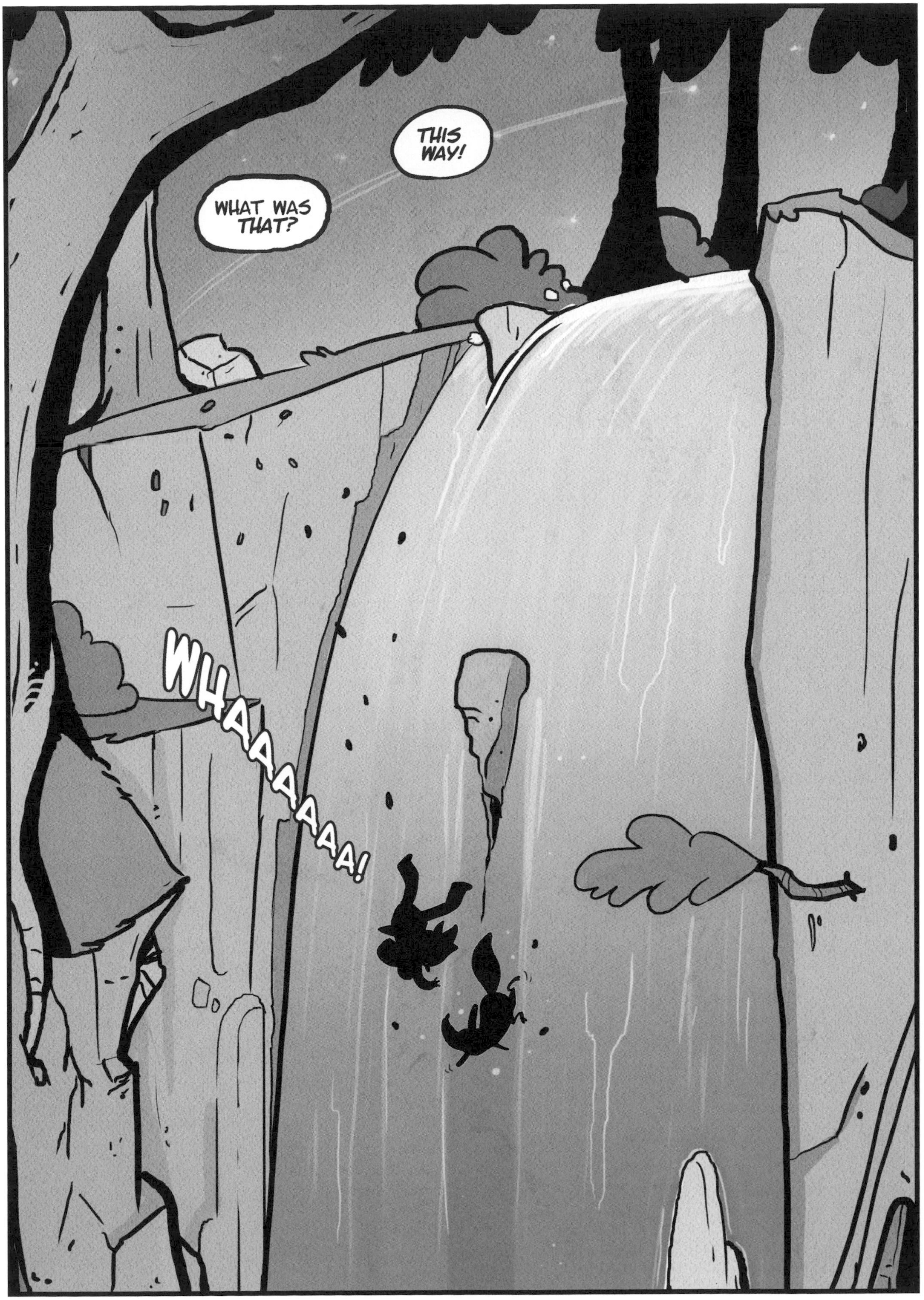
WHAT WAS THAT?
THIS WAY!
WHAAAAAAAA!

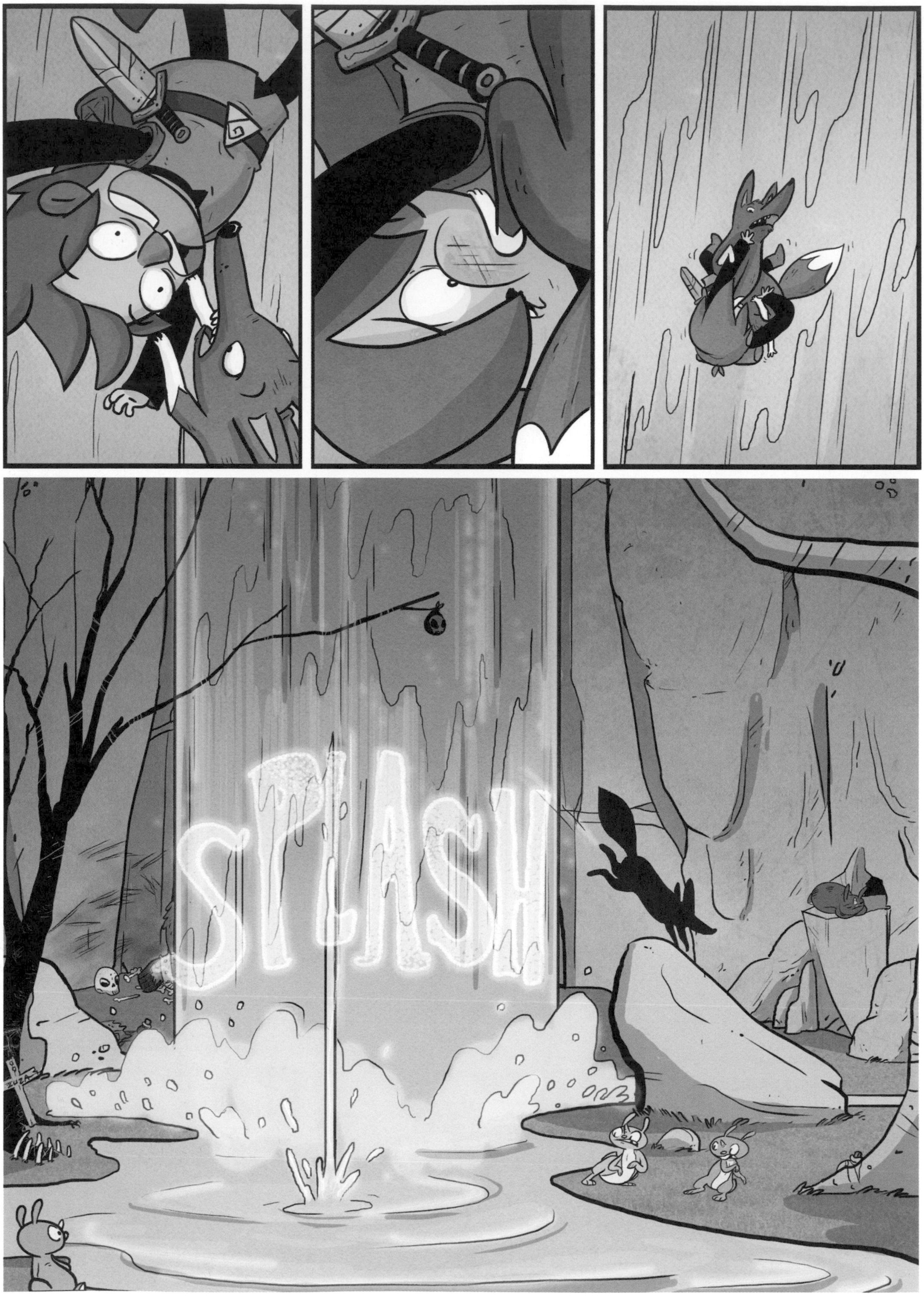
SPLASH

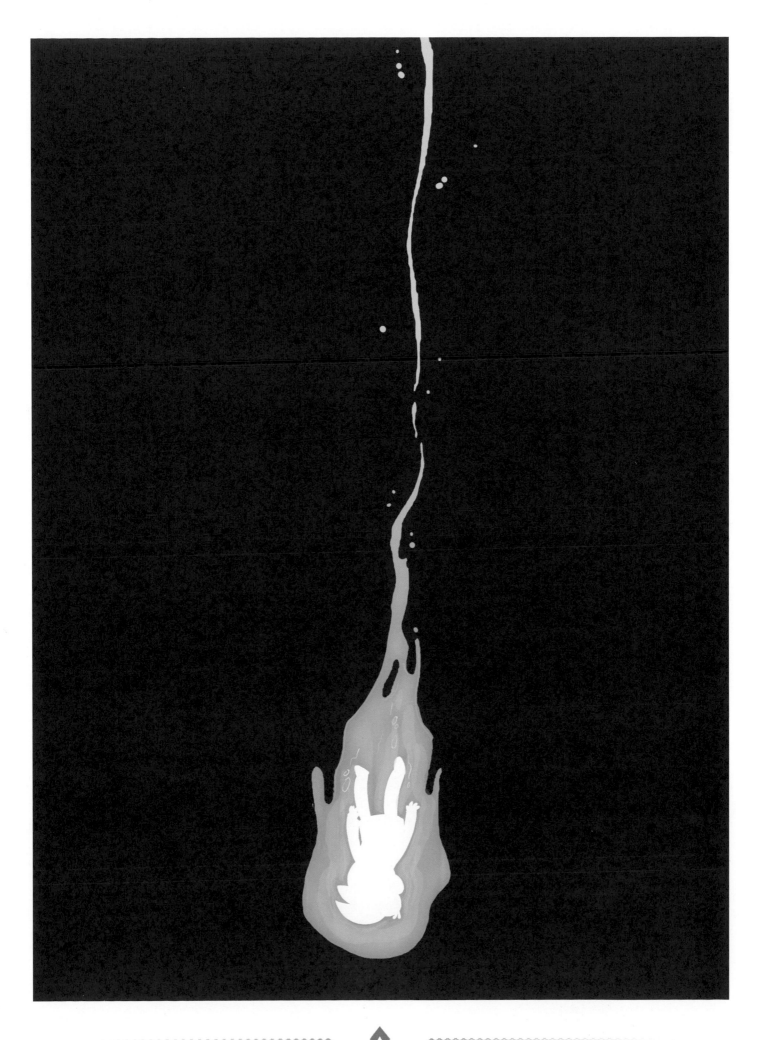

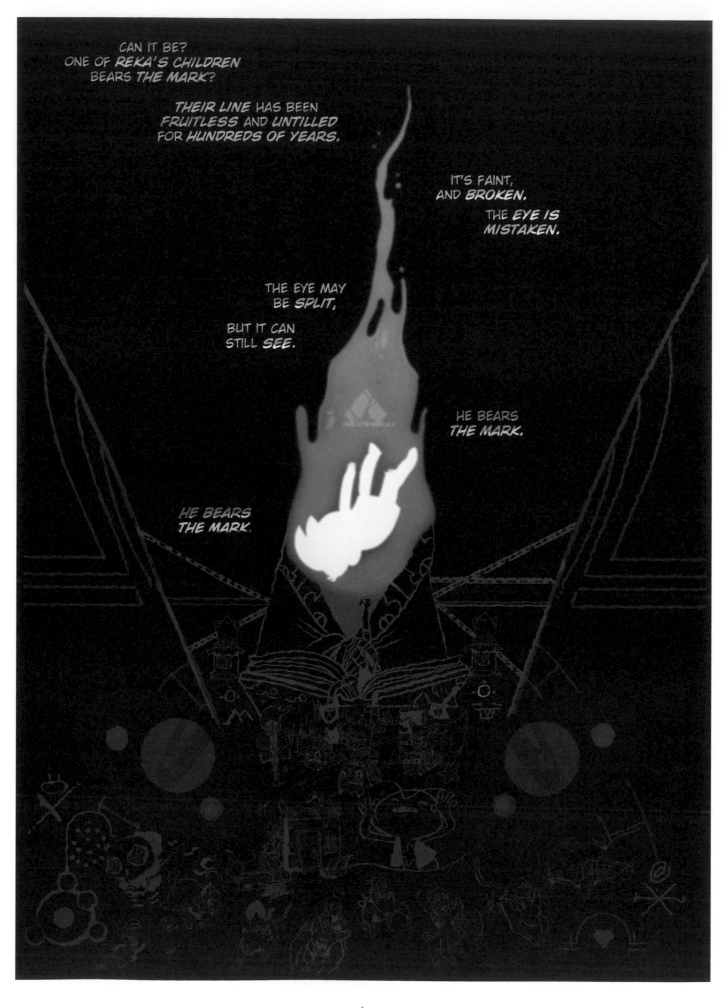

CAN IT BE?
ONE OF **REKA'S CHILDREN**
BEARS **THE MARK?**

THEIR LINE HAS BEEN
FRUITLESS AND **UNTILLED**
FOR **HUNDREDS OF YEARS.**

IT'S FAINT,
AND **BROKEN.**

THE **EYE IS
MISTAKEN.**

THE EYE MAY
BE **SPLIT,**

BUT IT CAN
STILL **SEE.**

HE BEARS
THE MARK.

HE BEARS
THE MARK.

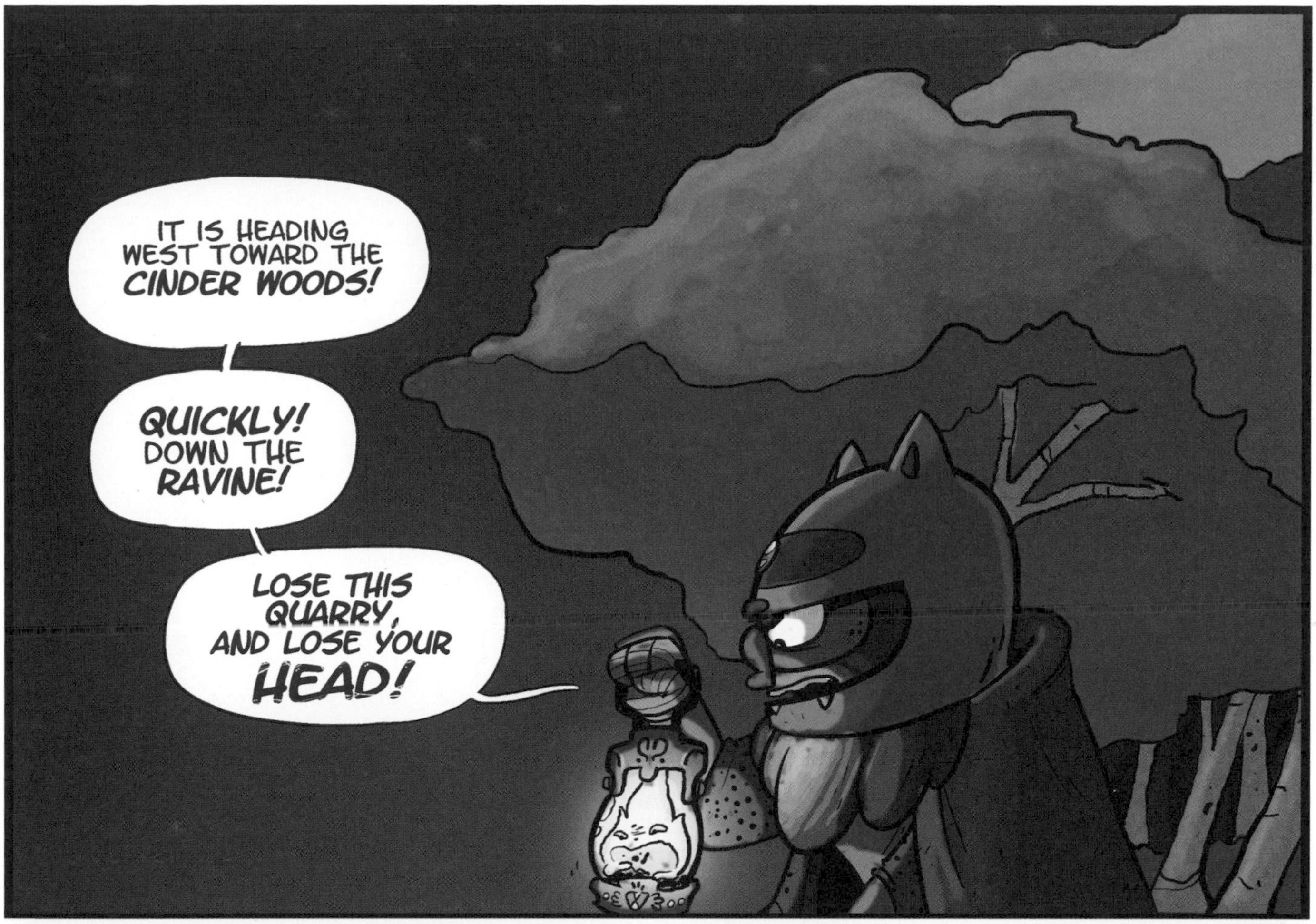
IT IS HEADING WEST TOWARD THE CINDER WOODS!
QUICKLY! DOWN THE RAVINE!
LOSE THIS QUARRY, AND LOSE YOUR HEAD!

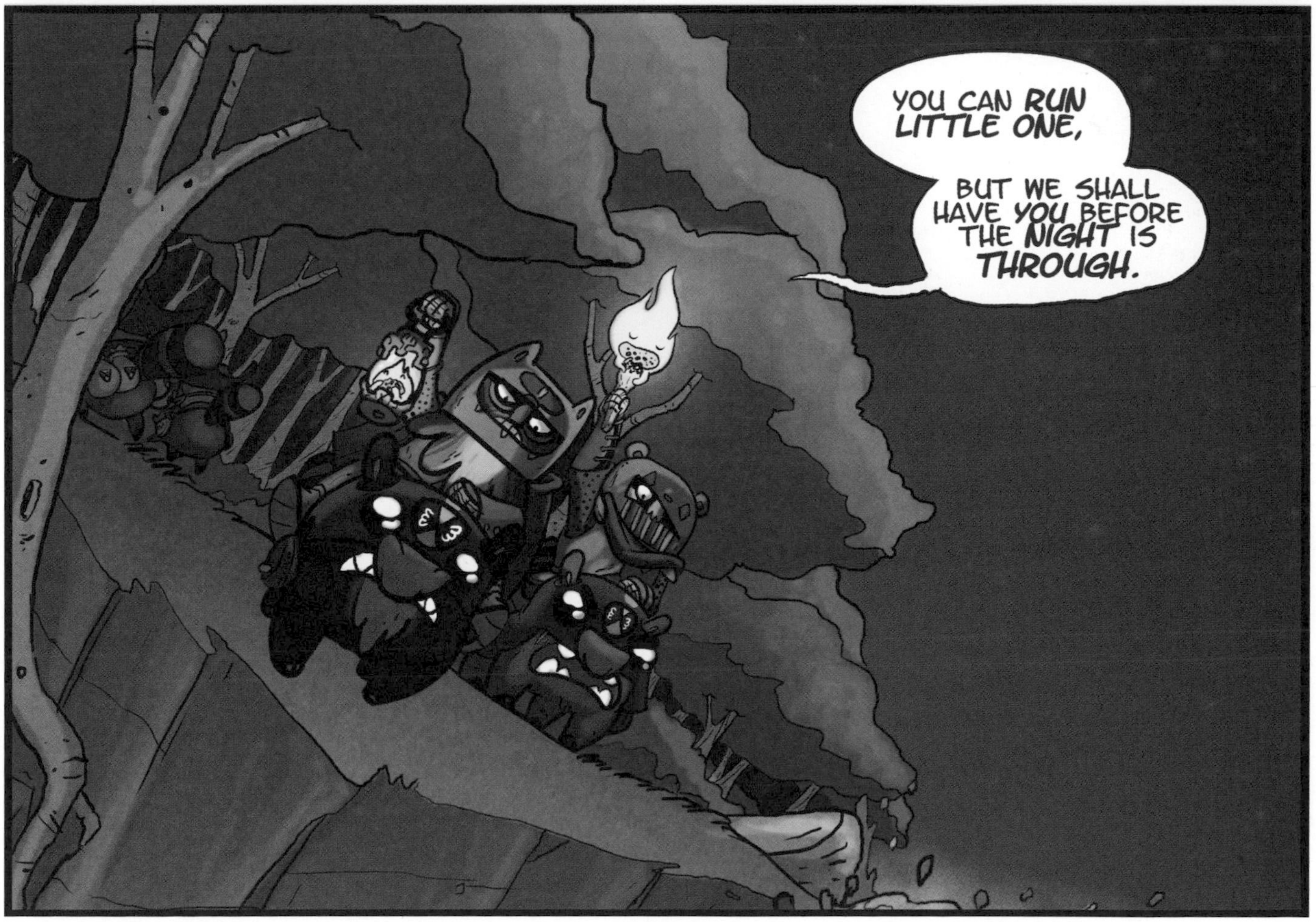
YOU CAN RUN LITTLE ONE,
BUT WE SHALL HAVE YOU BEFORE THE NIGHT IS THROUGH.

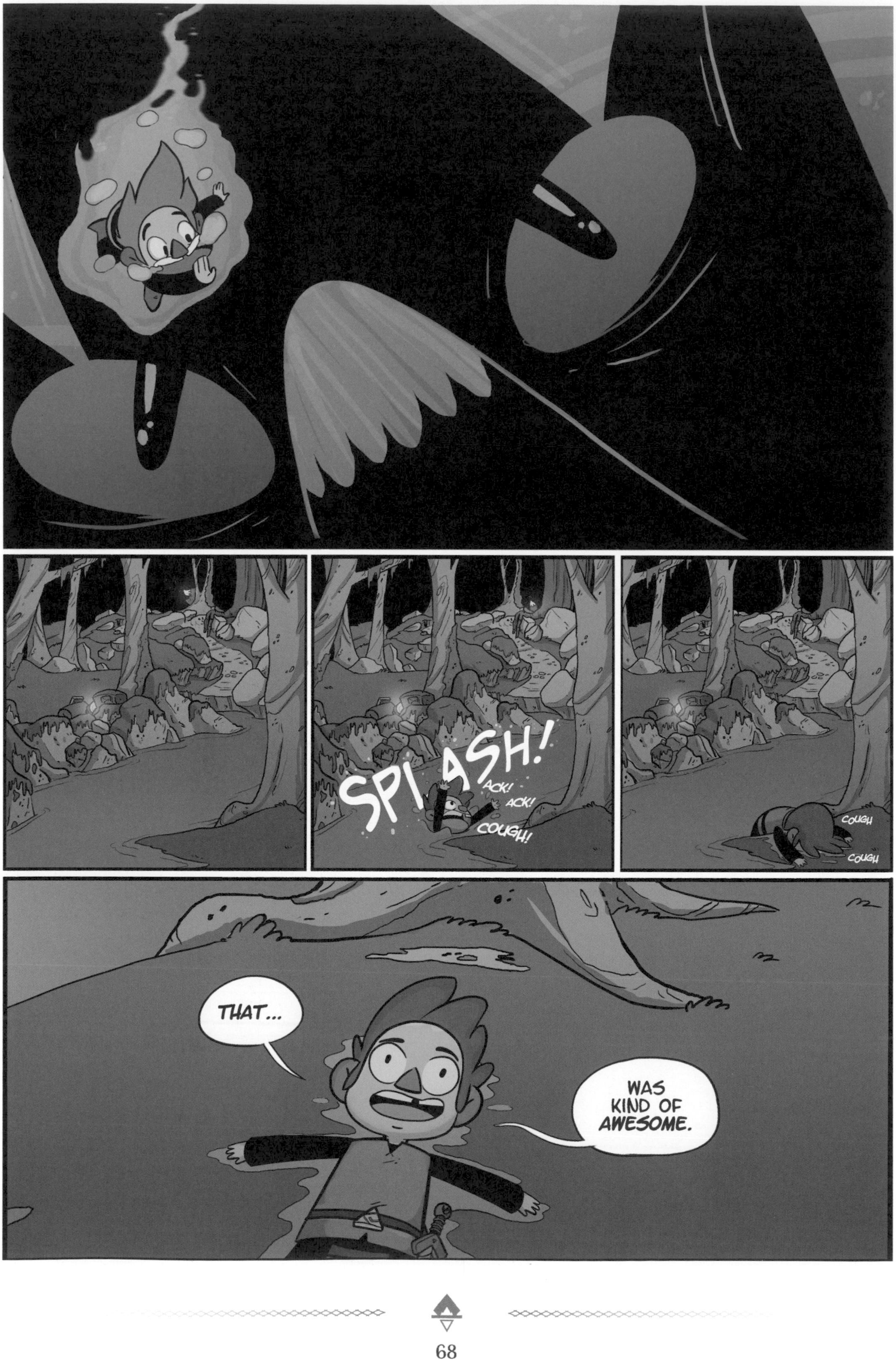
SPLASH!
ACK!
ACK!
COUGH!
COUGH
COUGH
THAT...
WAS KIND OF AWESOME.

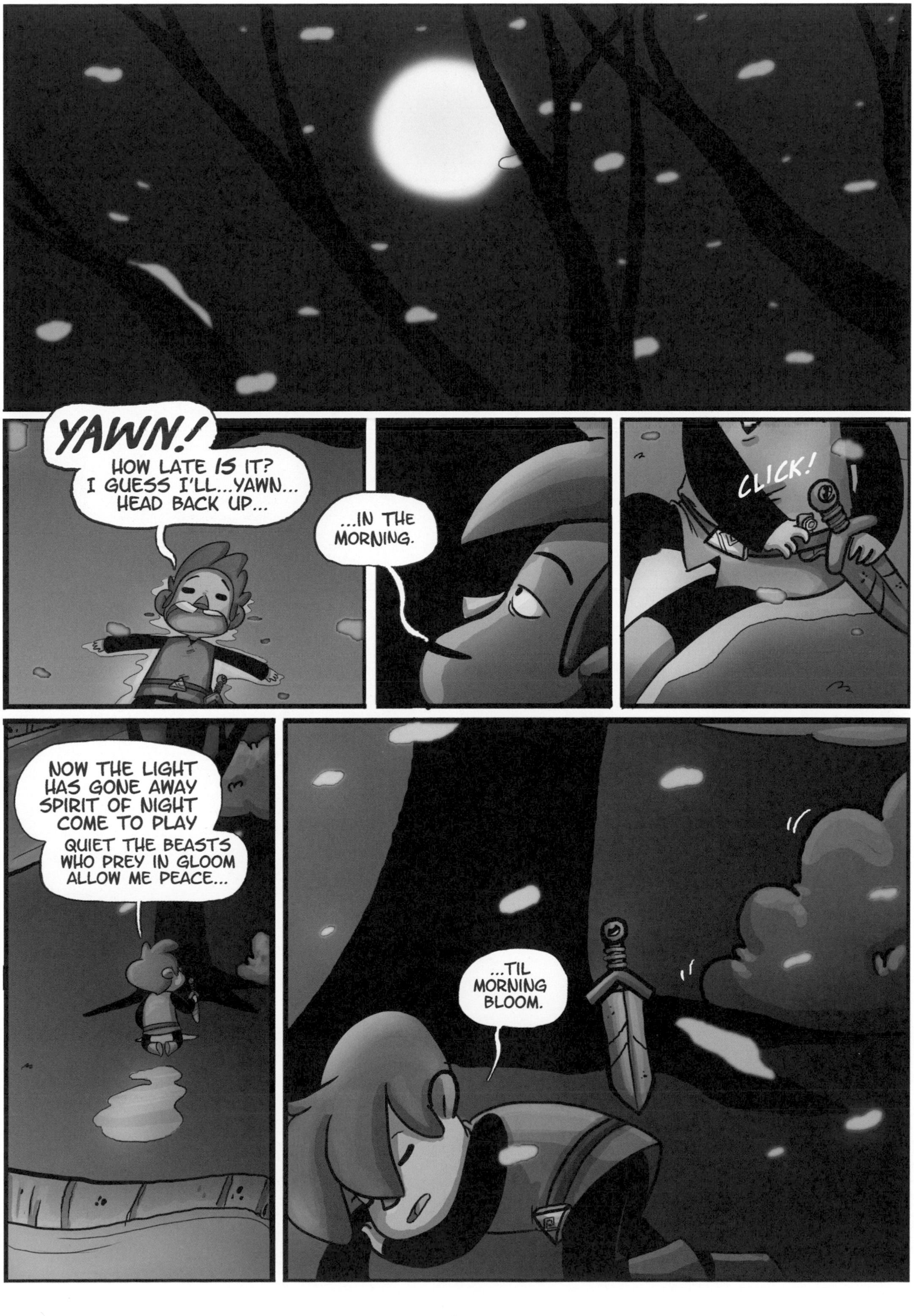
YAWN!
HOW LATE IS IT? I GUESS I'LL...YAWN... HEAD BACK UP...
...IN THE MORNING.
CLICK!
NOW THE LIGHT HAS GONE AWAY SPIRIT OF NIGHT COME TO PLAY
QUIET THE BEASTS WHO PREY IN GLOOM ALLOW ME PEACE...
...TIL MORNING BLOOM.

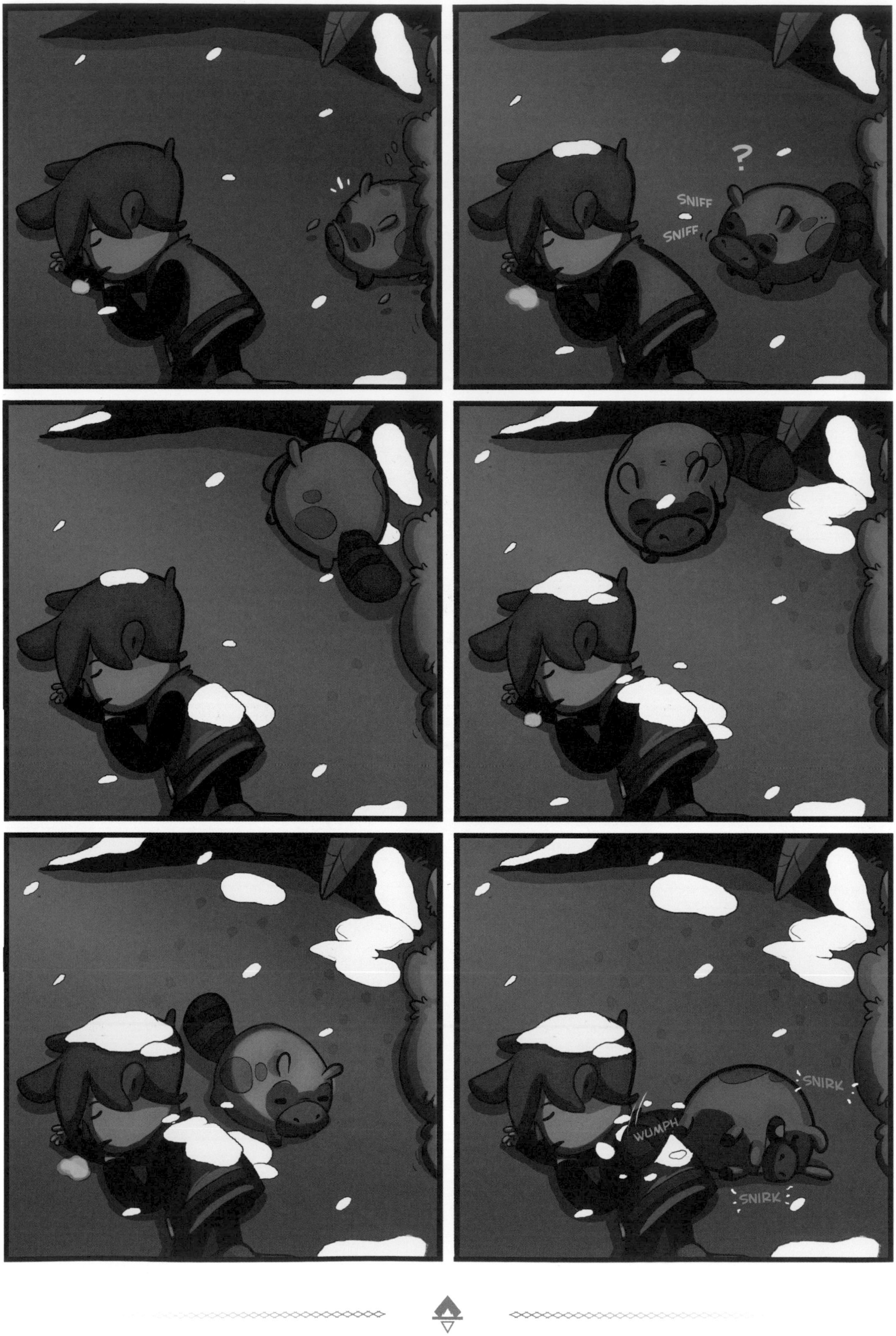
?
SNIFF
SNIFF
WUMPH
SNIRK
SNIRK

CHAPTER 5

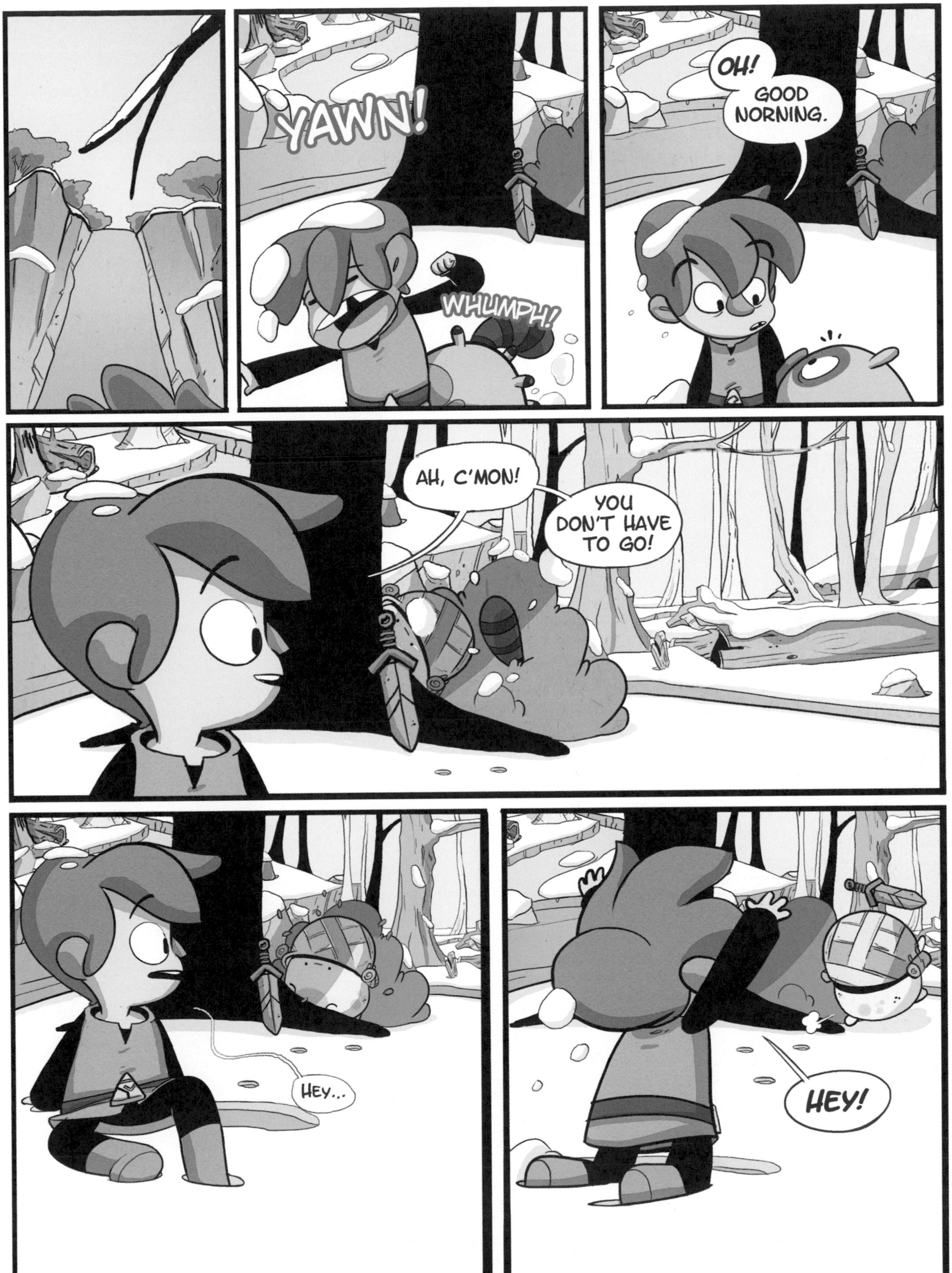
YAWN!
WHUMPH!
OH! GOOD NORNING.
AH, C'MON!
YOU DON'T HAVE TO GO!
HEY...
HEY!

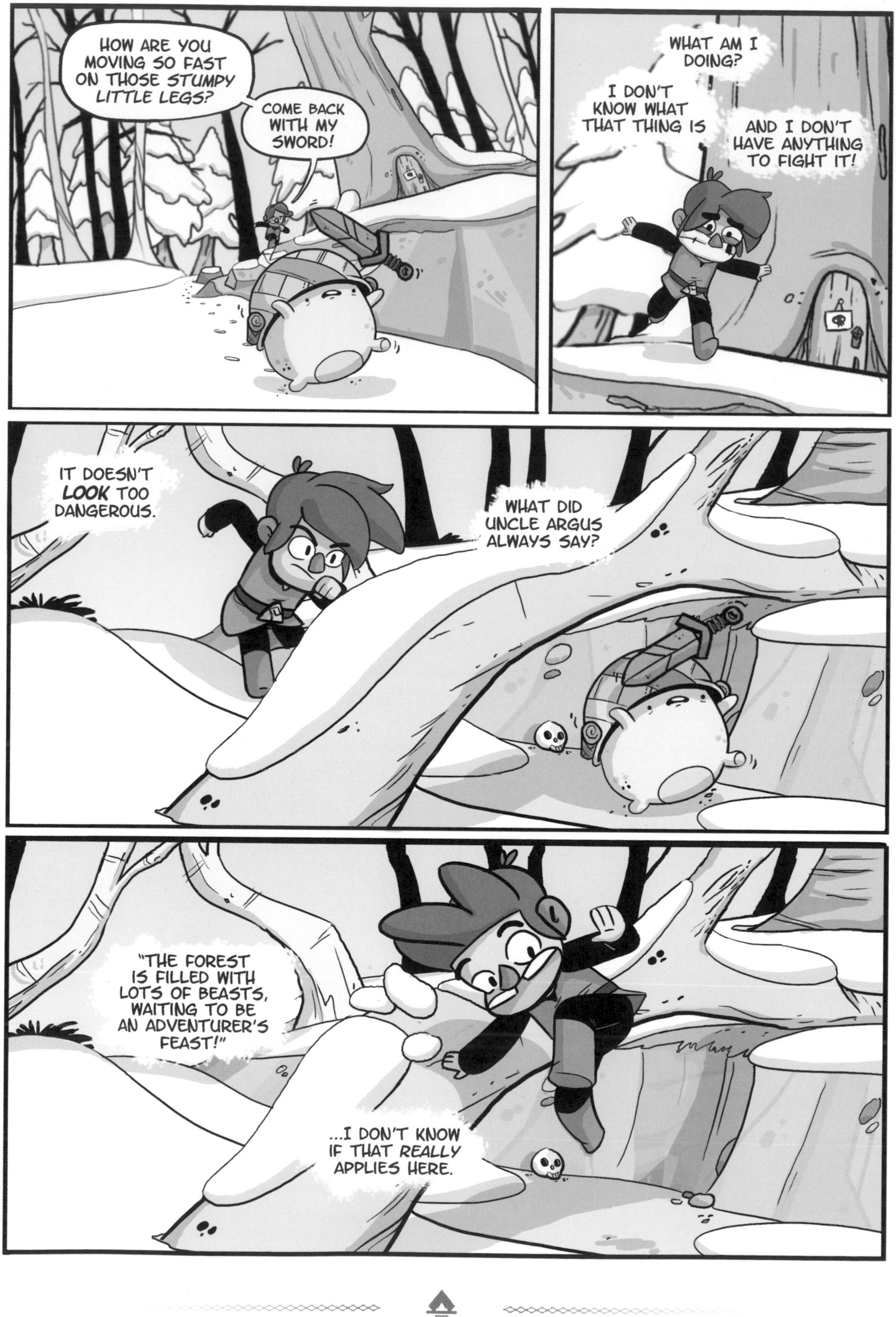
HOW ARE YOU MOVING SO FAST ON THOSE STUMPY LITTLE LEGS?
COME BACK WITH MY SWORD!
WHAT AM I DOING?
I DON'T KNOW WHAT THAT THING IS
AND I DON'T HAVE ANYTHING TO FIGHT IT!
IT DOESN'T LOOK TOO DANGEROUS.
WHAT DID UNCLE ARGUS ALWAYS SAY?
"THE FOREST IS FILLED WITH LOTS OF BEASTS, WAITING TO BE AN ADVENTURER'S FEAST!"
...I DON'T KNOW IF THAT REALLY APPLIES HERE.

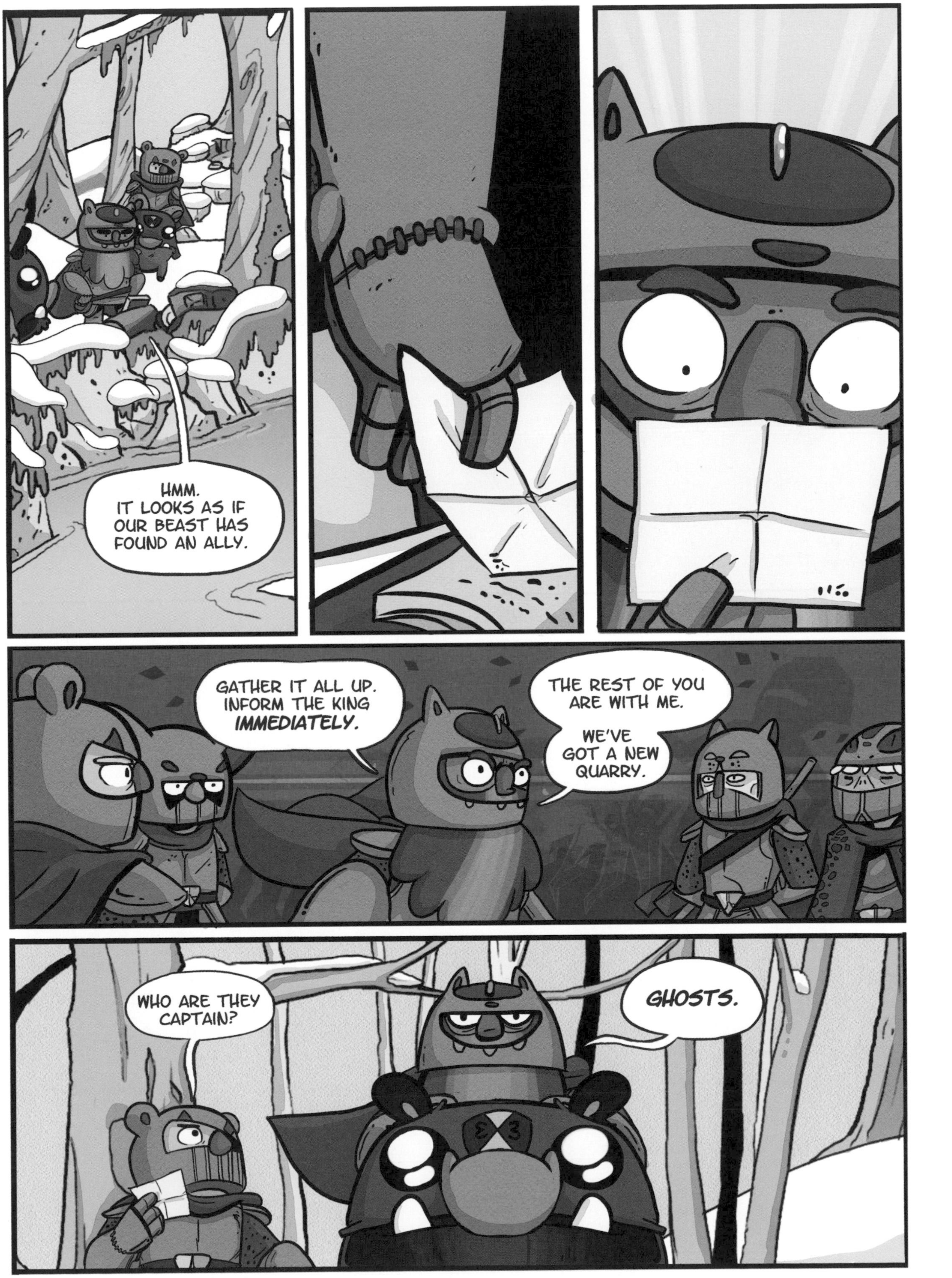
HMM.
IT LOOKS AS IF OUR BEAST HAS FOUND AN ALLY.
GATHER IT ALL UP. INFORM THE KING *IMMEDIATELY.*
THE REST OF YOU ARE WITH ME.
WE'VE GOT A NEW QUARRY.
WHO ARE THEY CAPTAIN?
GHOSTS.

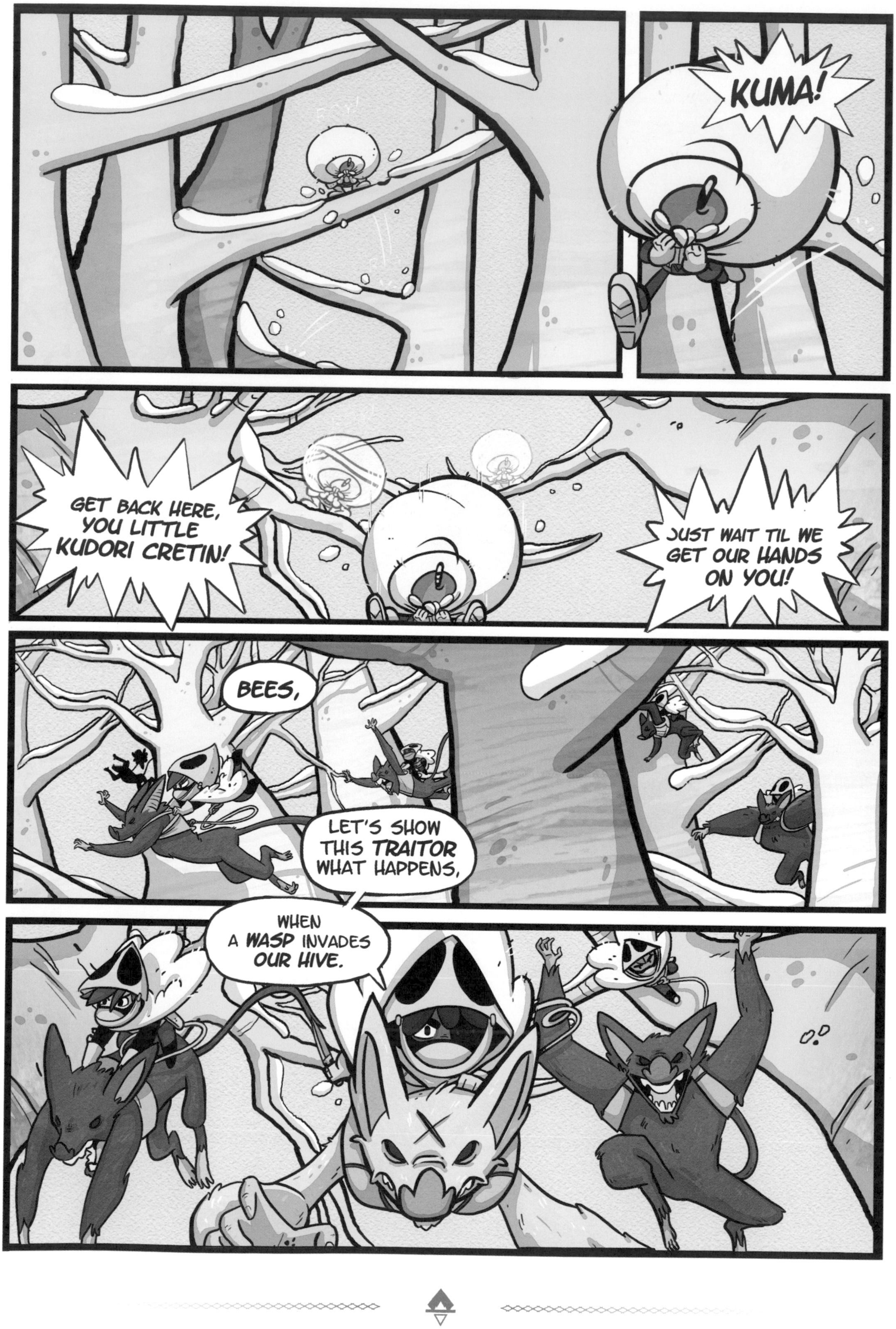
KUMA!
GET BACK HERE, YOU LITTLE KUDORI CRETIN!
JUST WAIT TIL WE GET OUR HANDS ON YOU!
BEES,
LET'S SHOW THIS TRAITOR WHAT HAPPENS,
WHEN A WASP INVADES OUR HIVE.

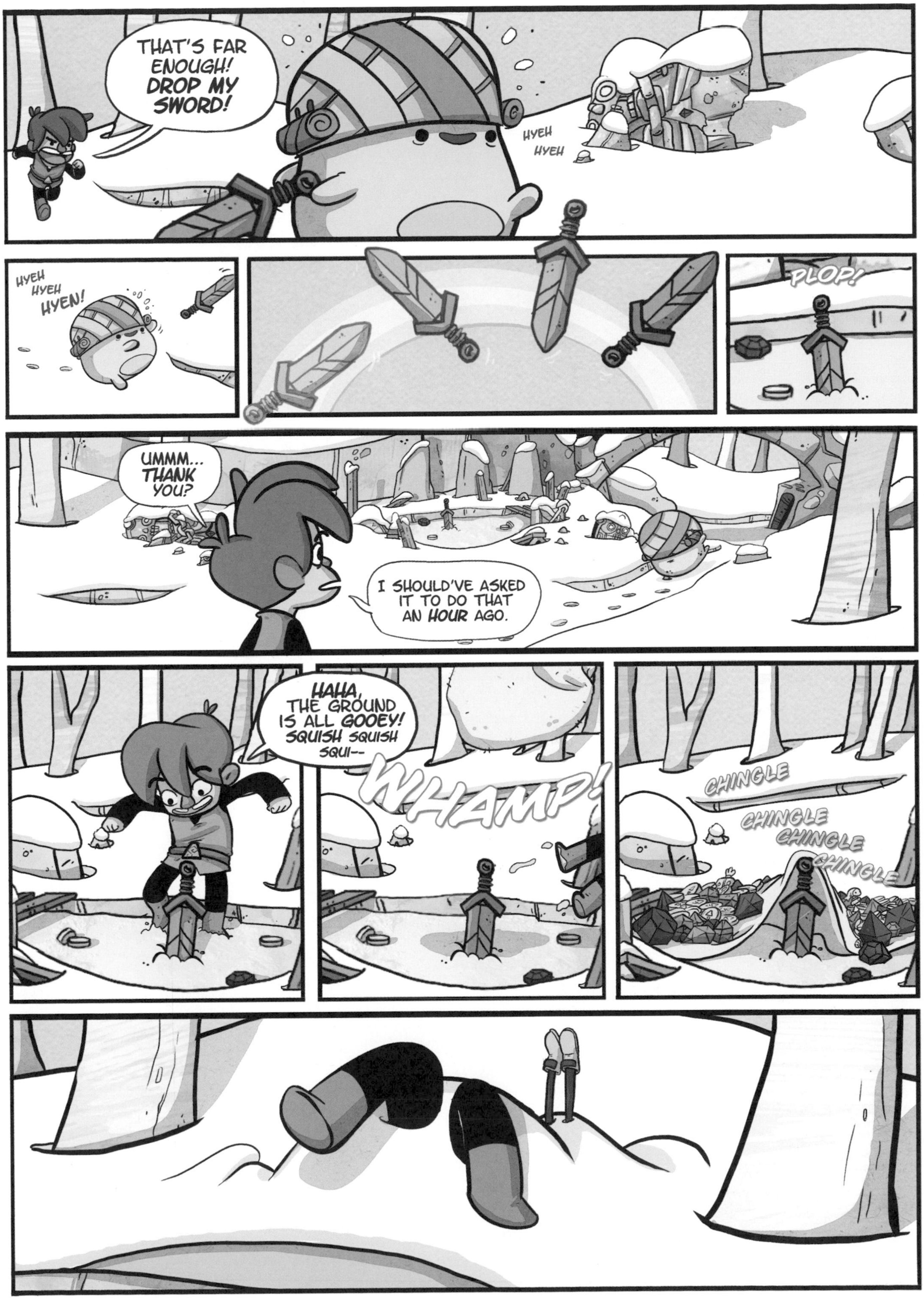
THAT'S FAR ENOUGH! DROP MY SWORD!
HYEH HYEH
HYEH HYEH HYEH!
PLOP!
UMMM... THANK YOU?
I SHOULD'VE ASKED IT TO DO THAT AN HOUR AGO.
HAHA, THE GROUND IS ALL GOOEY! SQUISH SQUISH SQUI--
WHAMP!
CHINGLE
CHINGLE
CHINGLE
CHINGLE

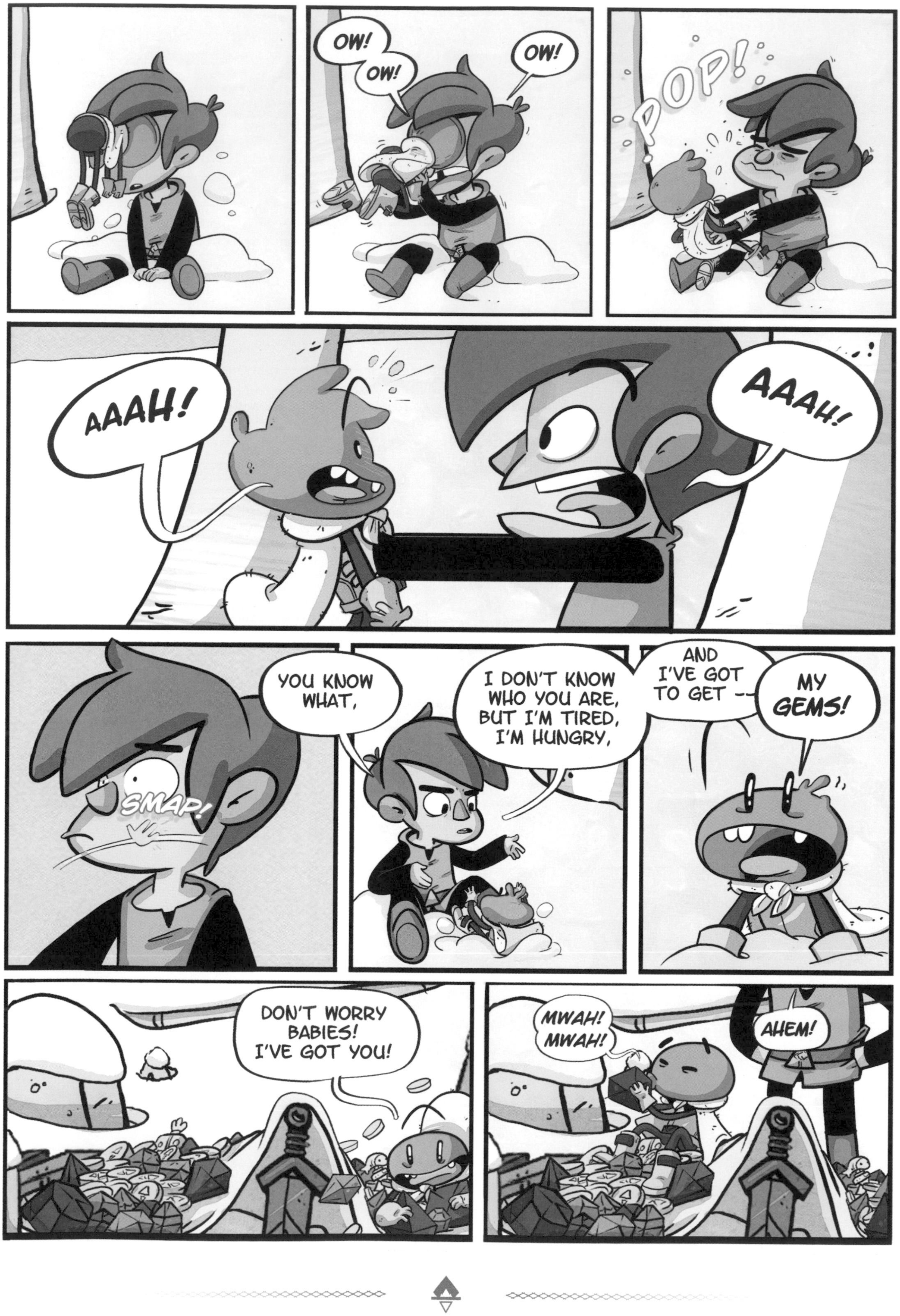
OW!
OW!
OW!
POP!
AAAH!
AAAH!
SMAP!
YOU KNOW WHAT,
I DON'T KNOW WHO YOU ARE, BUT I'M TIRED, I'M HUNGRY,
AND I'VE GOT TO GET --
MY GEMS!
DON'T WORRY BABIES! I'VE GOT YOU!
MWAH! MWAH!
AHEM!

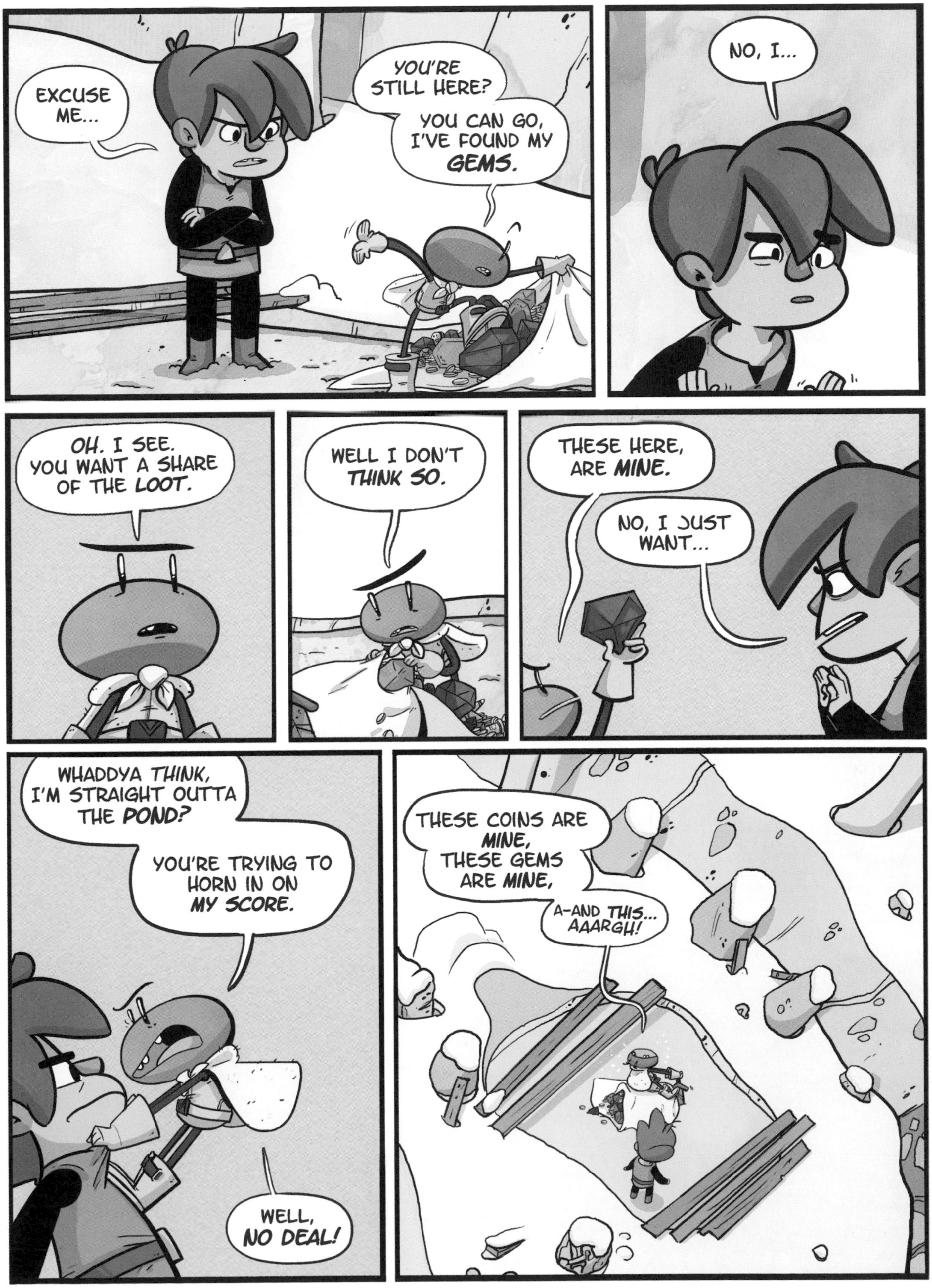
EXCUSE ME...
YOU'RE STILL HERE?
YOU CAN GO, I'VE FOUND MY GEMS.
NO, I...
OH. I SEE. YOU WANT A SHARE OF THE LOOT.
WELL I DON'T THINK SO.
THESE HERE, ARE MINE.
NO, I JUST WANT...
WHADDYA THINK, I'M STRAIGHT OUTTA THE POND?
YOU'RE TRYING TO HORN IN ON MY SCORE.
WELL, NO DEAL!
THESE COINS ARE MINE, THESE GEMS ARE MINE,
A-AND THIS... AAARGH!

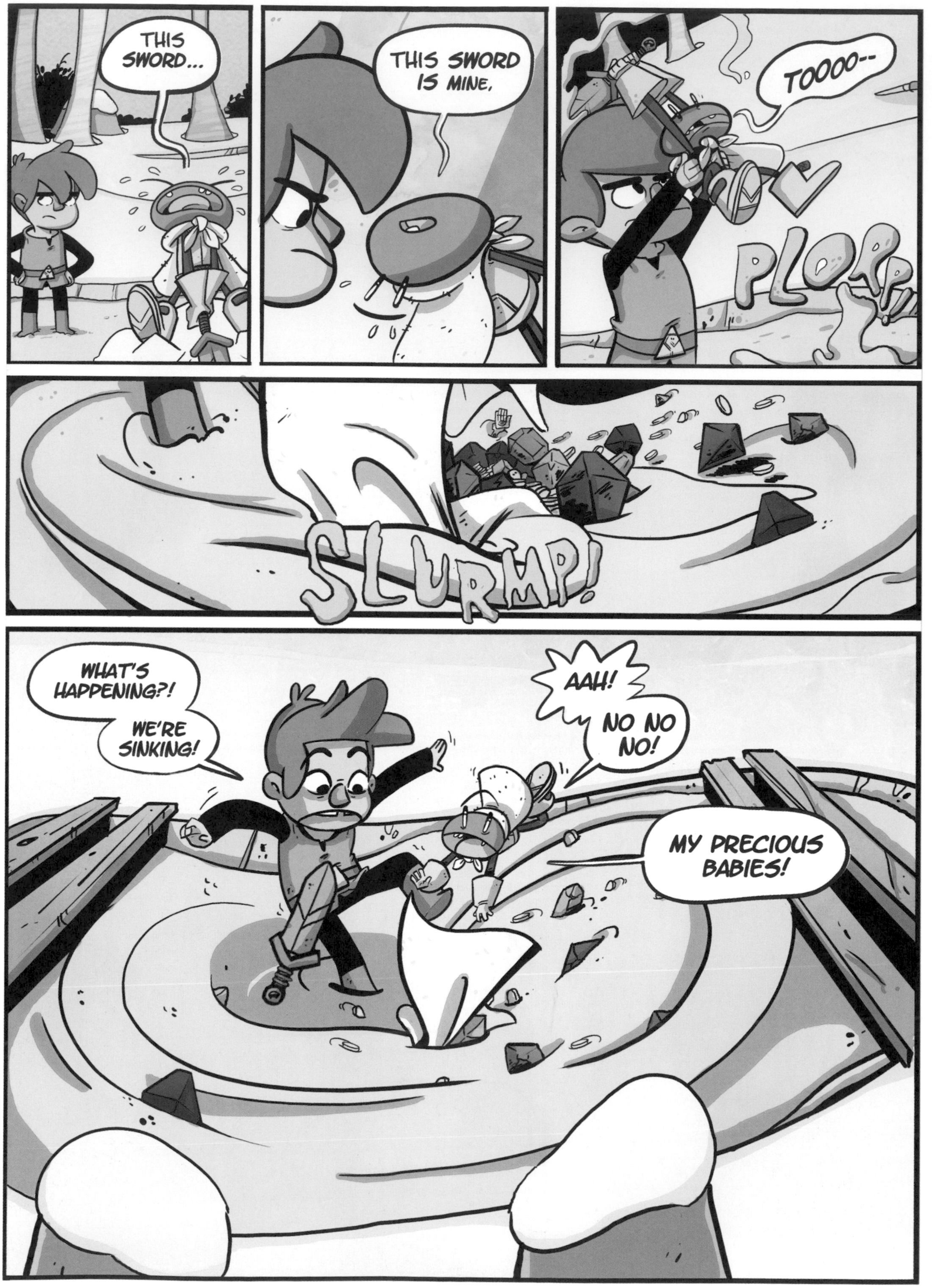
THIS SWORD...
THIS SWORD IS MINE.
TOOOO--
PLORP
SLURMP!
WHAT'S HAPPENING?!
WE'RE SINKING!
AAH!
NO NO NO!
MY PRECIOUS BABIES!

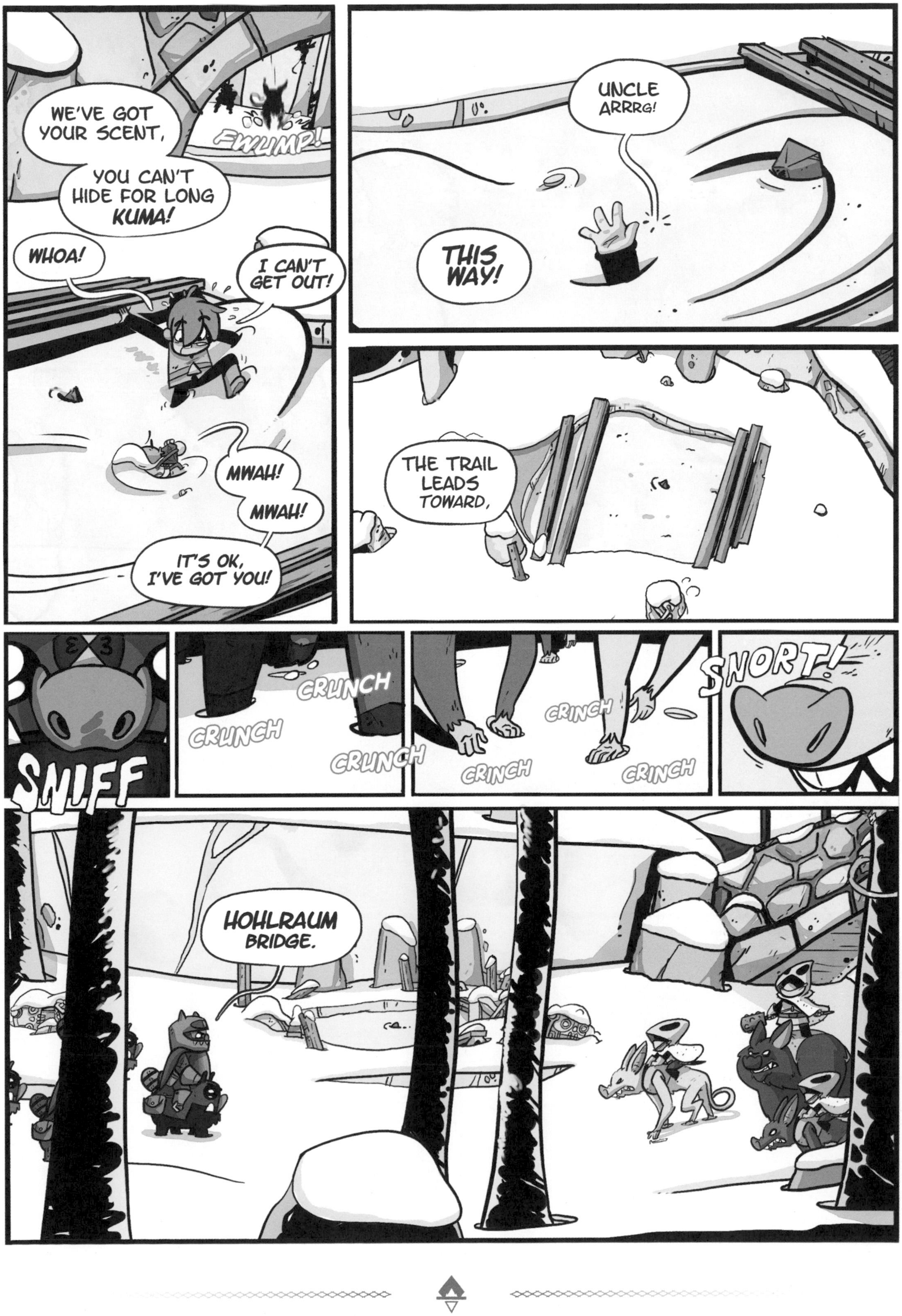
WE'VE GOT YOUR SCENT,
FWUMP!
YOU CAN'T HIDE FOR LONG KUMA!
WHOA!
I CAN'T GET OUT!
MWAH!
MWAH!
IT'S OK, I'VE GOT YOU!
UNCLE ARRRG!
THIS WAY!
THE TRAIL LEADS TOWARD,
SNIFF
CRUNCH
CRUNCH
CRUNCH
CRINCH
CRINCH
CRINCH
SNORT!
HOHLRAUM BRIDGE.

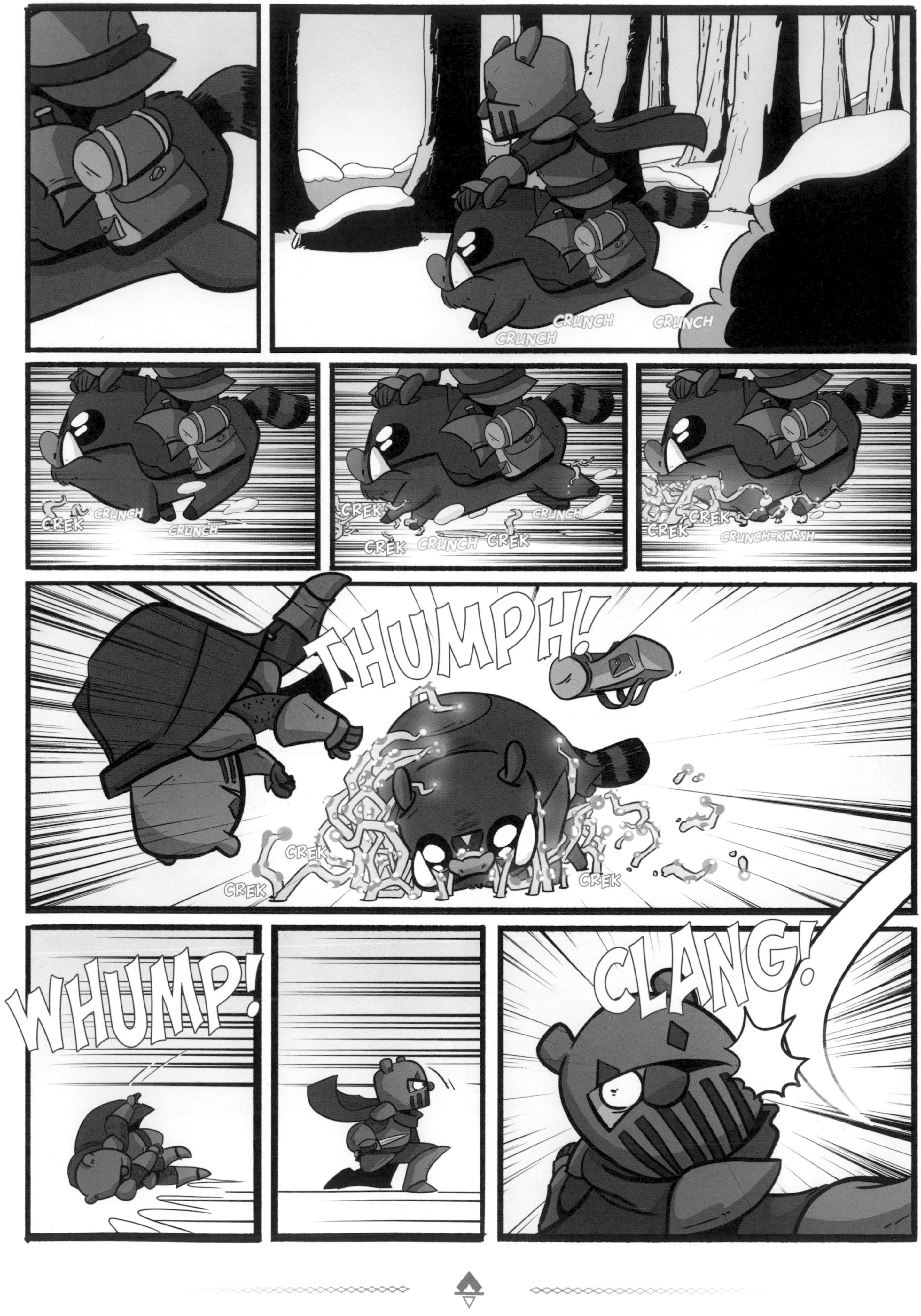
CRUNCH
CRUNCH
CRUNCH
CREK
CRUNCH
CRUNCH
CREK
CREK
CRUNCH
CREK
CRUNCH
CREK
CREK
CRUNCH-KRRSH
THUMPH!
CREK
CREK
CREK
WHUMP!
CLANG!

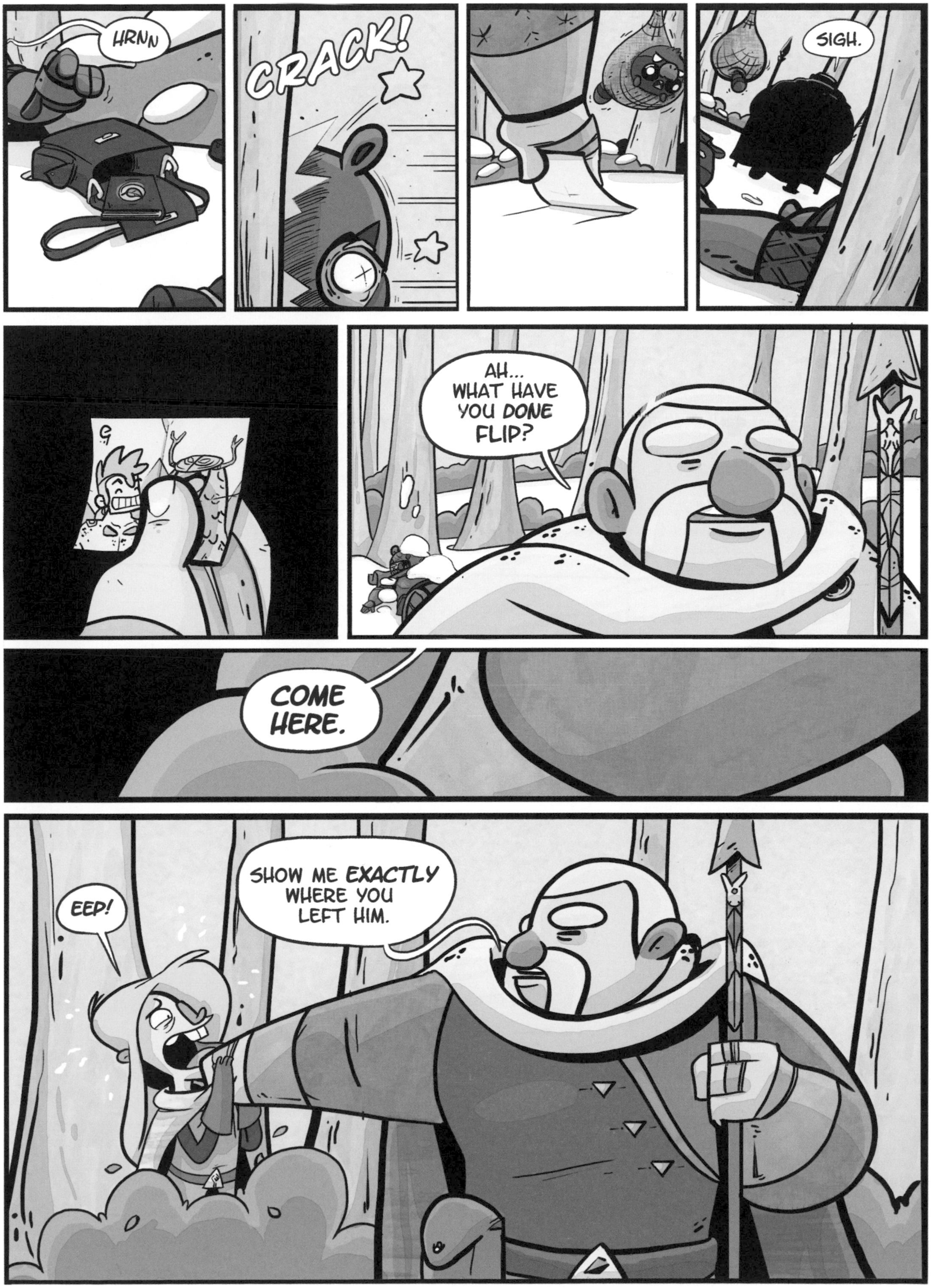
HRNN
CRACK!
SIGH.
AH... WHAT HAVE YOU DONE FLIP?
COME HERE.
EEP!
SHOW ME EXACTLY WHERE YOU LEFT HIM.

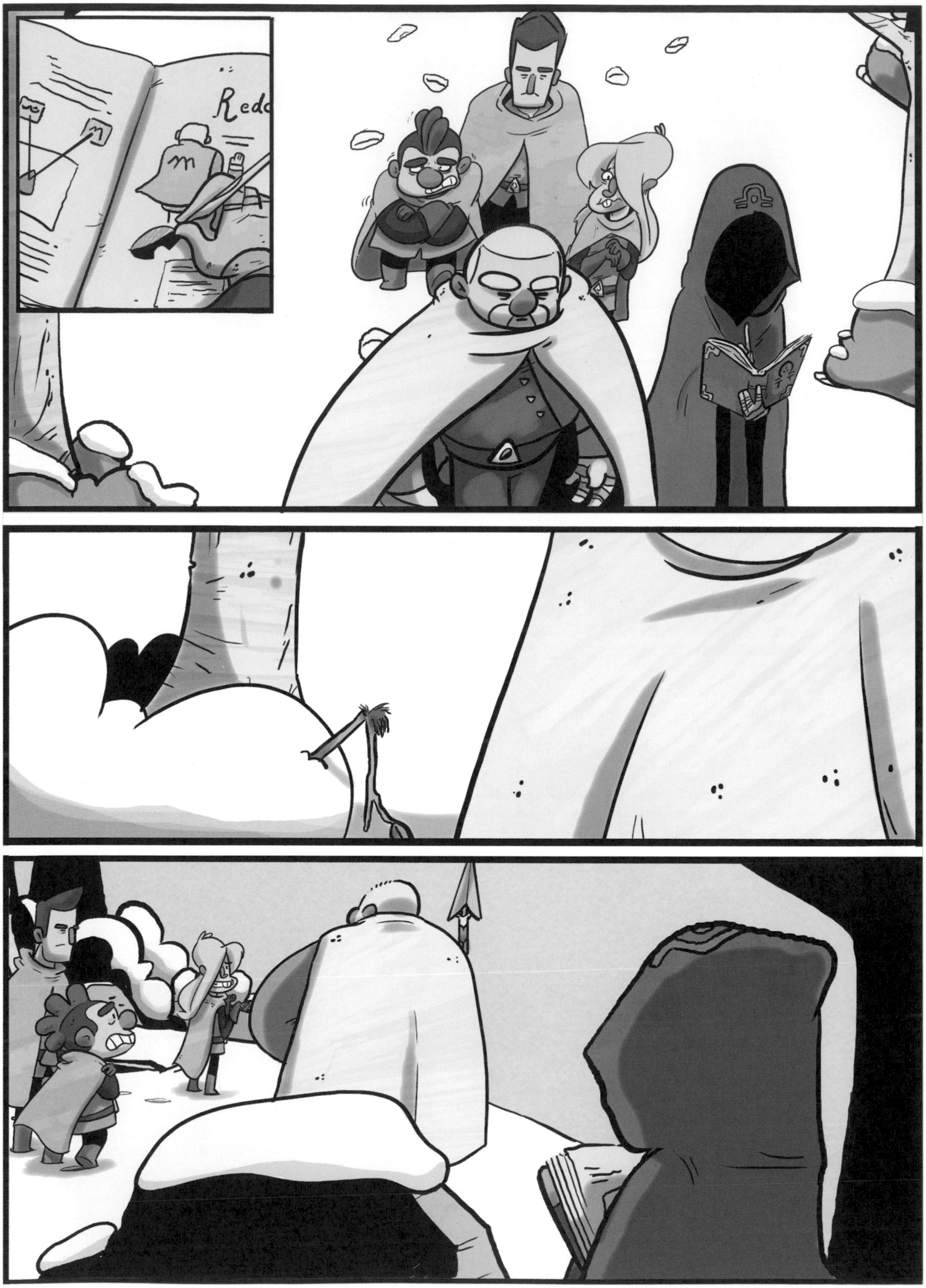

CHAPTER 6

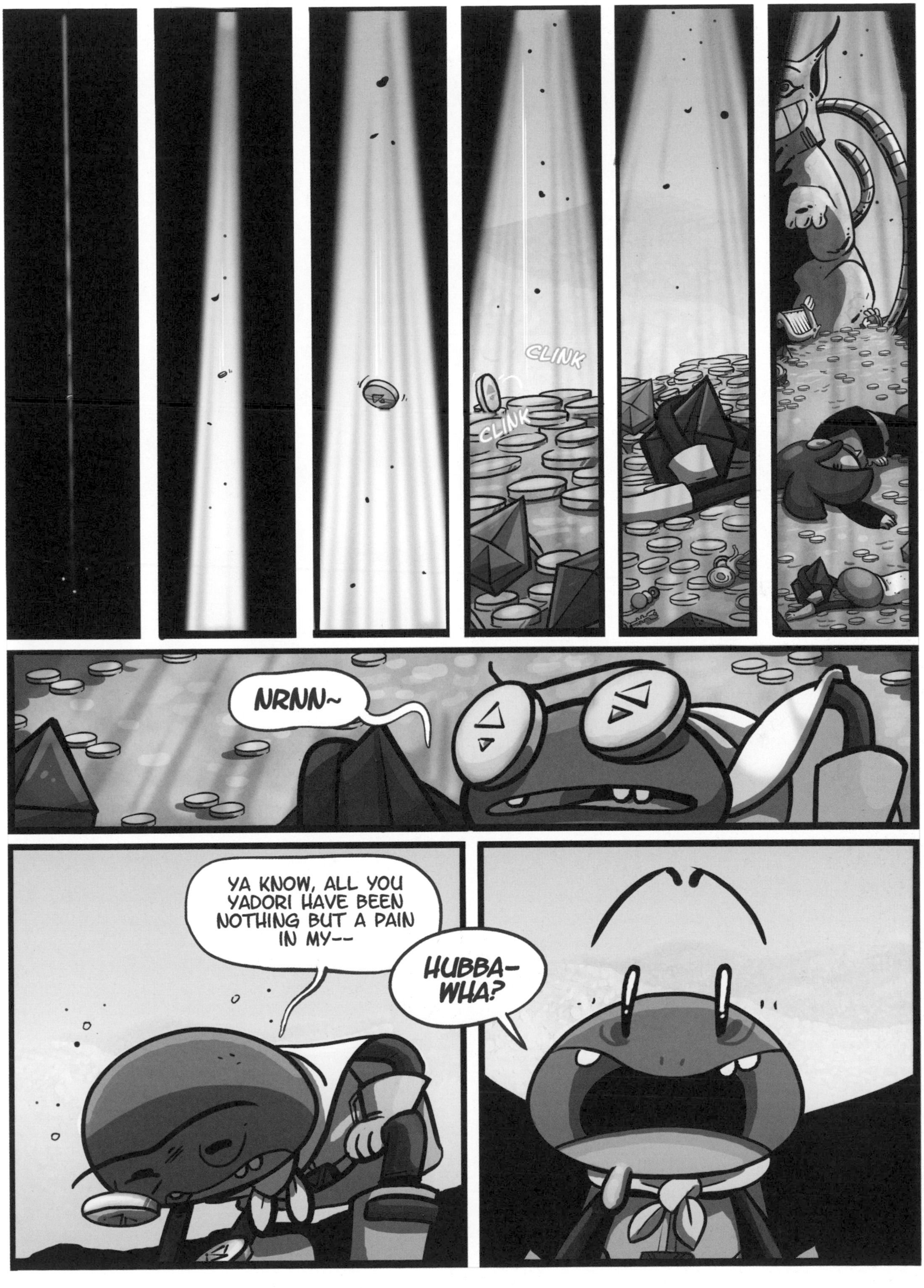
CLINK
CLINK
NRNN~
YA KNOW, ALL YOU YADORI HAVE BEEN NOTHING BUT A PAIN IN MY--
HUBBA-WHA?

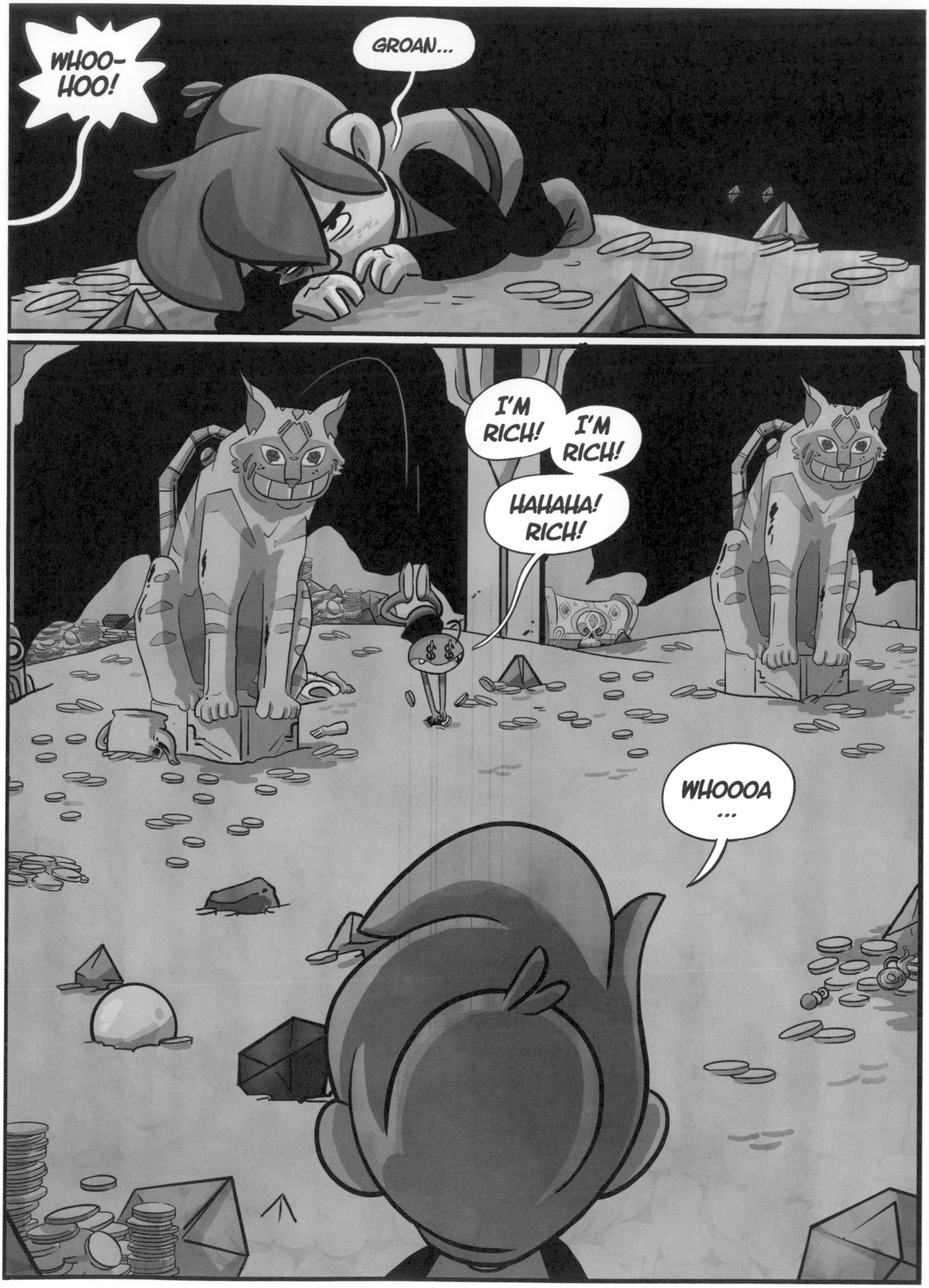
WHOO-
HOO!
GROAN...
I'M RICH!
I'M RICH!
HAHAHA! RICH!
WHOOOA
...

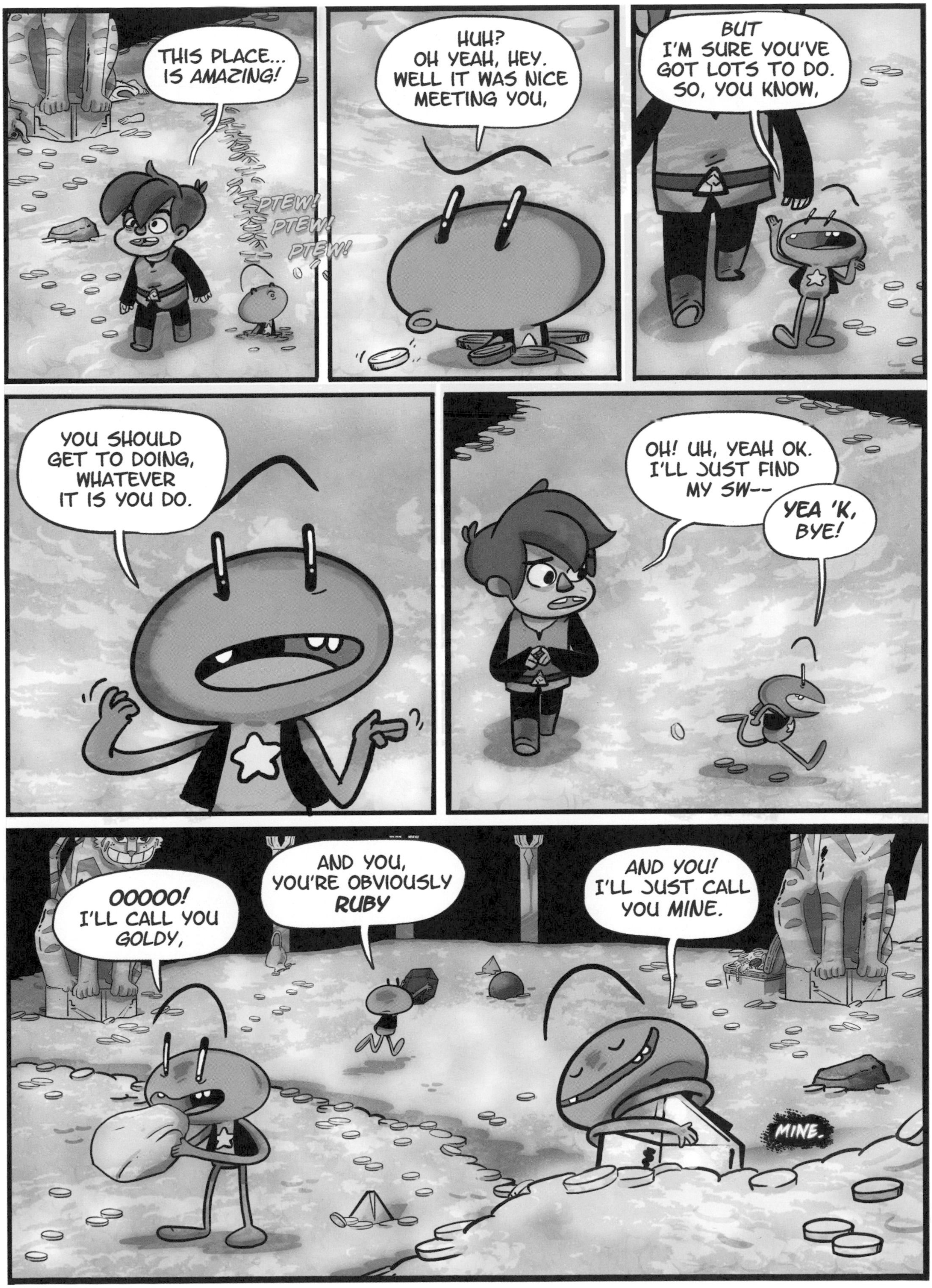
THIS PLACE... IS AMAZING!
PTEW! PTEW! PTEW!
HUH? OH YEAH, HEY. WELL IT WAS NICE MEETING YOU,
BUT I'M SURE YOU'VE GOT LOTS TO DO. SO, YOU KNOW,
YOU SHOULD GET TO DOING, WHATEVER IT IS YOU DO.
OH! UH, YEAH OK. I'LL JUST FIND MY SW--
YEA 'K, BYE!
OOOOO! I'LL CALL YOU GOLDY,
AND YOU, YOU'RE OBVIOUSLY RUBY
AND YOU! I'LL JUST CALL YOU MINE.
MINE.

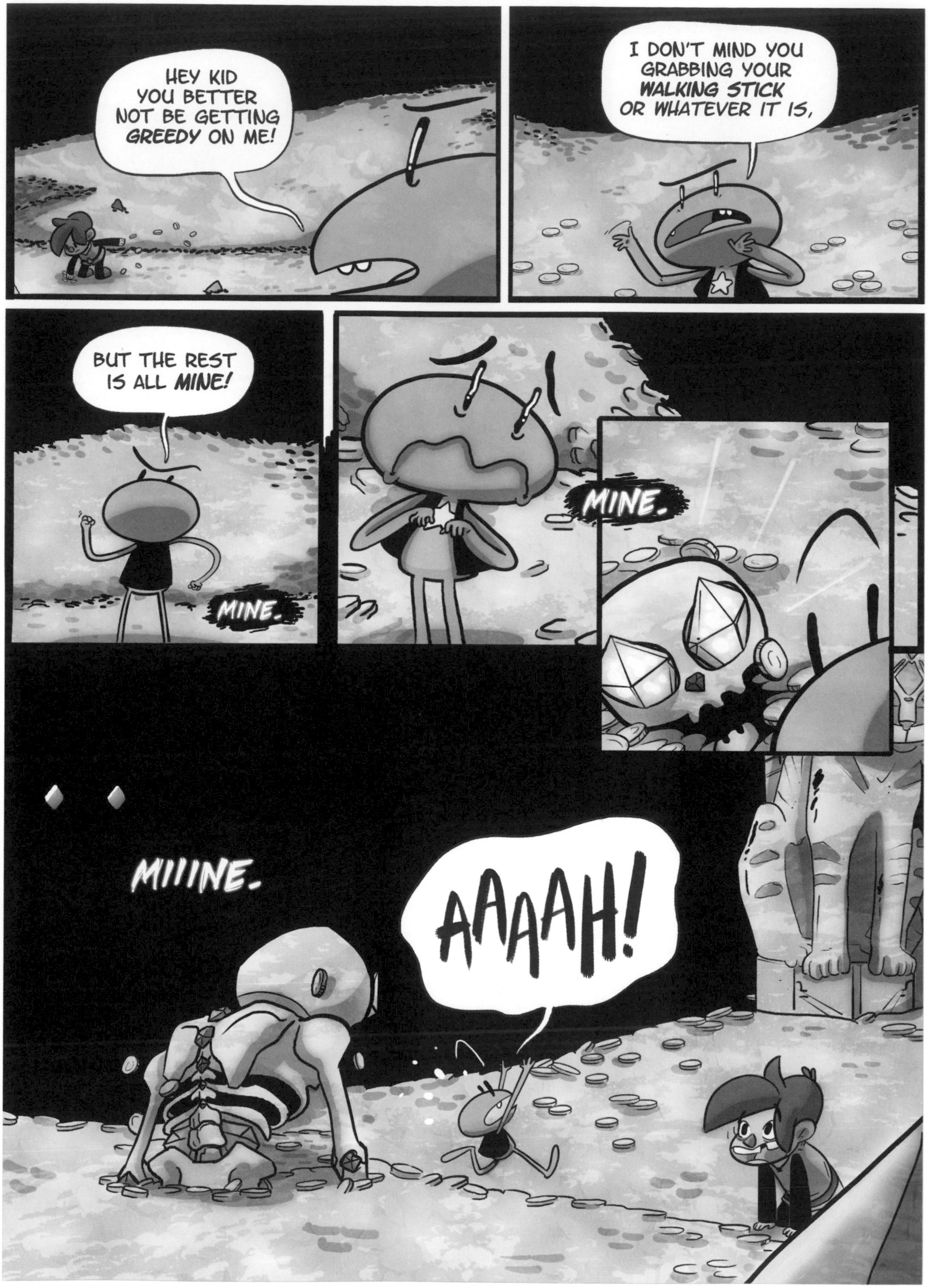
HEY KID YOU BETTER NOT BE GETTING GREEDY ON ME!
I DON'T MIND YOU GRABBING YOUR WALKING STICK OR WHATEVER IT IS,
BUT THE REST IS ALL MINE!
MINE.
MINE.
MIIINE.
AAAAH!

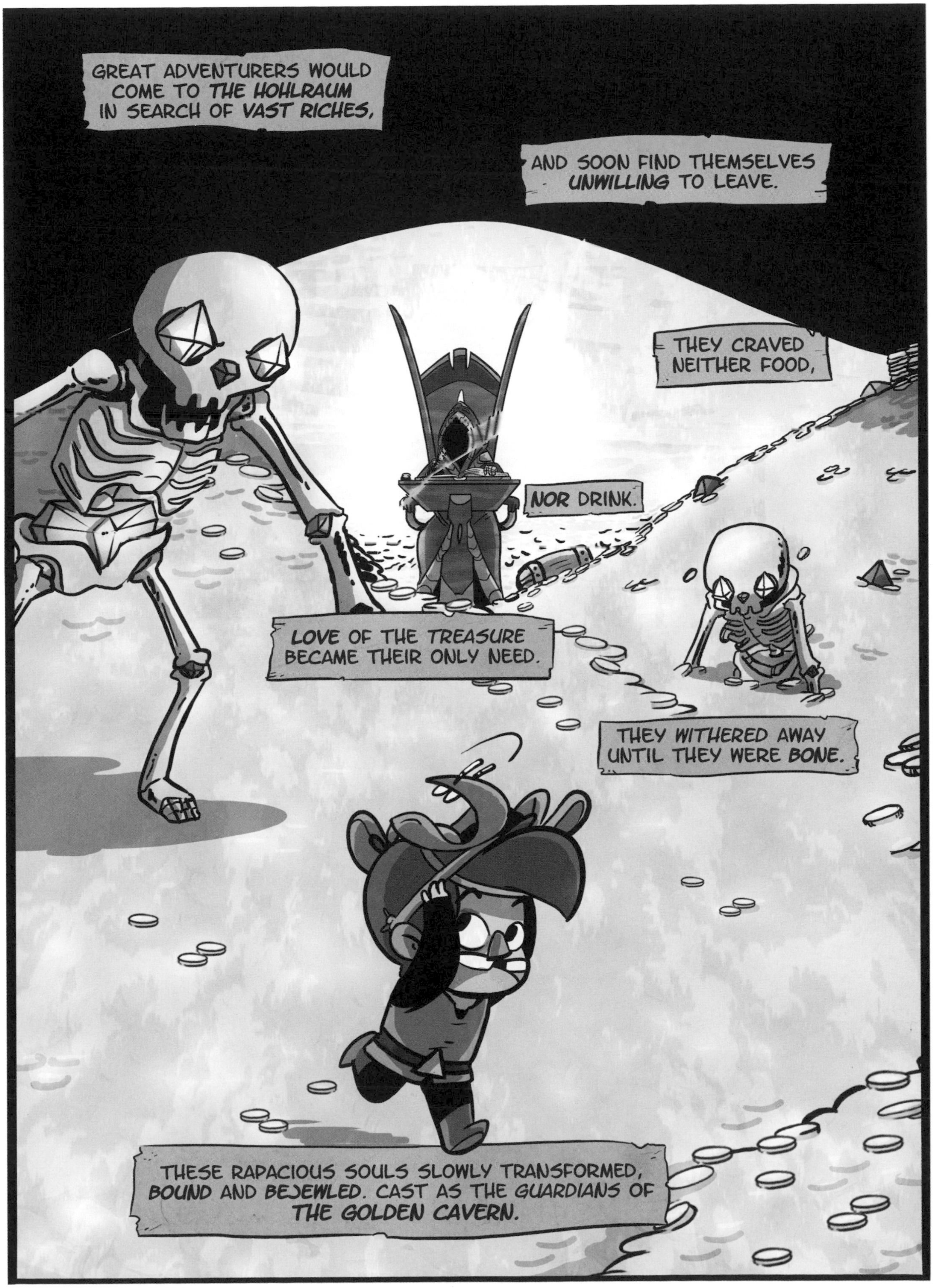
GREAT ADVENTURERS WOULD COME TO THE HOHLRAUM IN SEARCH OF VAST RICHES,
AND SOON FIND THEMSELVES UNWILLING TO LEAVE.
THEY CRAVED NEITHER FOOD,
NOR DRINK.
LOVE OF THE TREASURE BECAME THEIR ONLY NEED.
THEY WITHERED AWAY UNTIL THEY WERE BONE.
THESE RAPACIOUS SOULS SLOWLY TRANSFORMED, BOUND AND BEJEWLED. CAST AS THE GUARDIANS OF THE GOLDEN CAVERN.

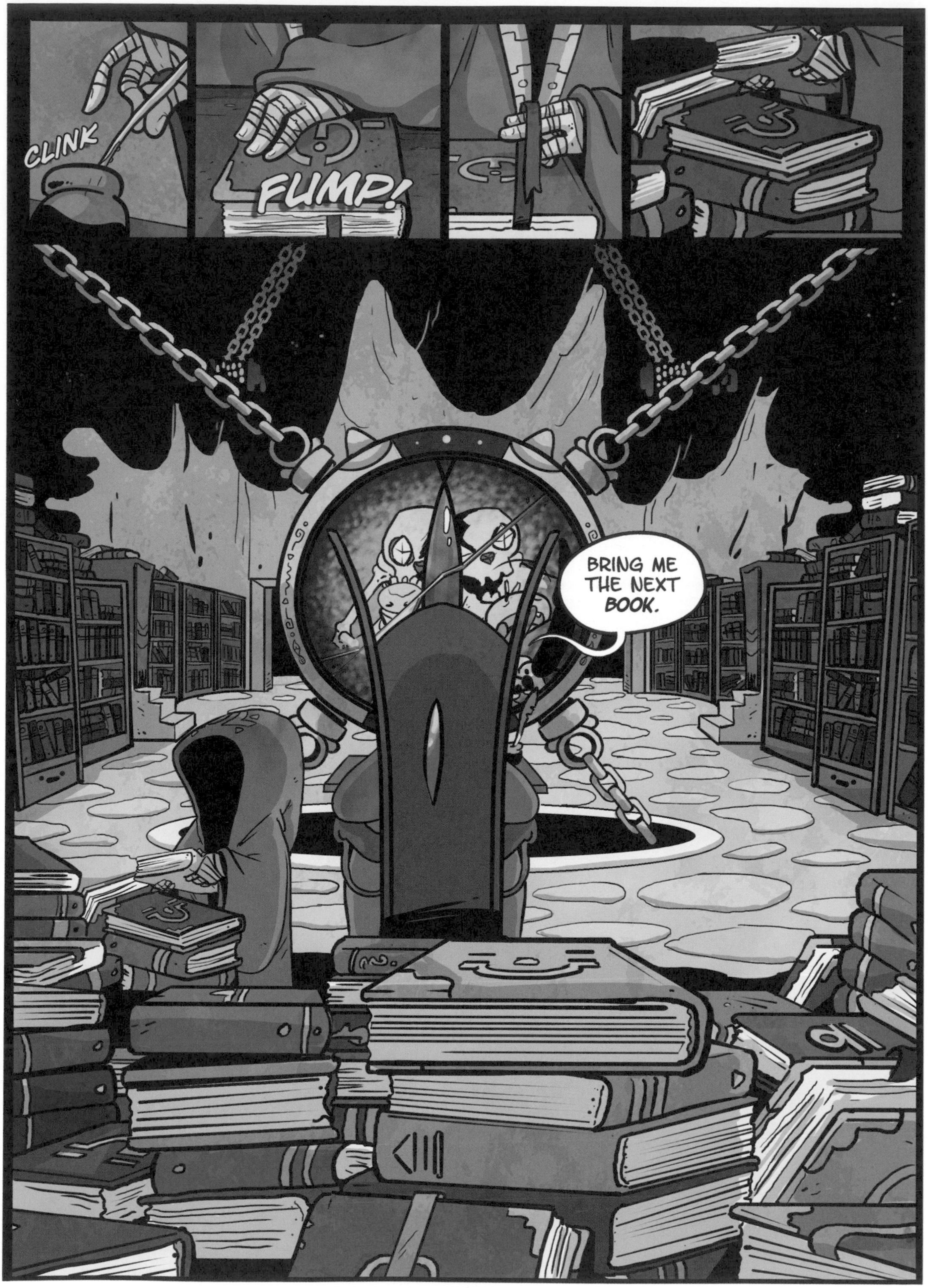
CLINK
FUMP!
BRING ME THE NEXT BOOK.

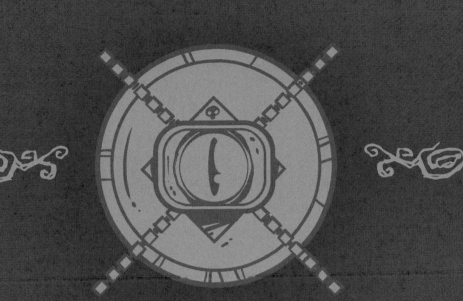

• • •

WATCHER'S
FIELD GUIDE
XIII

◆ ◆ ◆

 A BRIEF ADDENDUM OF
RECORDED MONSTERS
AND OBSERVATIONS.

PICOON

Roughly similar in size to a wild boar, the Picoon has the relatively hairless body of a pig with the striped and bushy tail of a raccoon when young. These placid, often timid creatures are highly intelligent and natural problem solvers. As they age, they grow hairier (almost woolly) and their tails grow stumpy in comparison, often cropped. Their thick, short tusks grow more prominent over time, a firm indicator of their age.

"Out in the forest, you're hard-pressed to find a more clever and suitable mount. Doesn't hurt that they're cute little things when they're young, either."

~ Knitzel, Redori Tracker

TERROR GUARD

The Terror Guard are often revered as a thing of legend, as fearsome for the tales of their horrifying skill and battle prowess as their association with Kramos - the King of Corpses. They are the elite of the elite for those who persist after their life has left them, horrifyingly powerful and thought to be unkillable. The most fearsome trait of the Terror Guard, however, is their gaze. Able to freeze the heart of even the most hardened adventurer, many a battle has been lost before sword has been drawn but for the chance meeting of their horrible gaze.

"Oh-ho-ho, the Terror Guard? I'm not inclined to believe they even exist. Why, if they exist, then Kramos himself would have to be real, and if that were true I… Well, best not to dwell on such chilling thoughts, mmm?"

~ Frel, inept Kudori Sage

GNOT

It is well known amongst those to frequent the forest that a gnot is "gnot" to be trifled with. They are diminutive, but quick and crafty, with natural camouflage that acts as a degree of armor. Disguising themselves as hollowed out tree stumps, their thorny arms and upper body look to be covered in compacted peat moss that can act as an irritant akin to poison ivy. They are solitary creatures by nature, with squat noses shaped like smushed leaves set on squat heads with bulbous squinted eyes, they grow over time to fit the size of their stump. On rare occasions, they can gather together as a pack to bring down larger threats to their native pockets of forest.

"Only thing harder to spot in the wood, than me, is a Gnot nest. Never had a worse rash than the time I sat straight on top of one. Thought I'd never sit again, and of course the others never let me hear the end of it."

~ Marel, Redori Stalker

Picoon

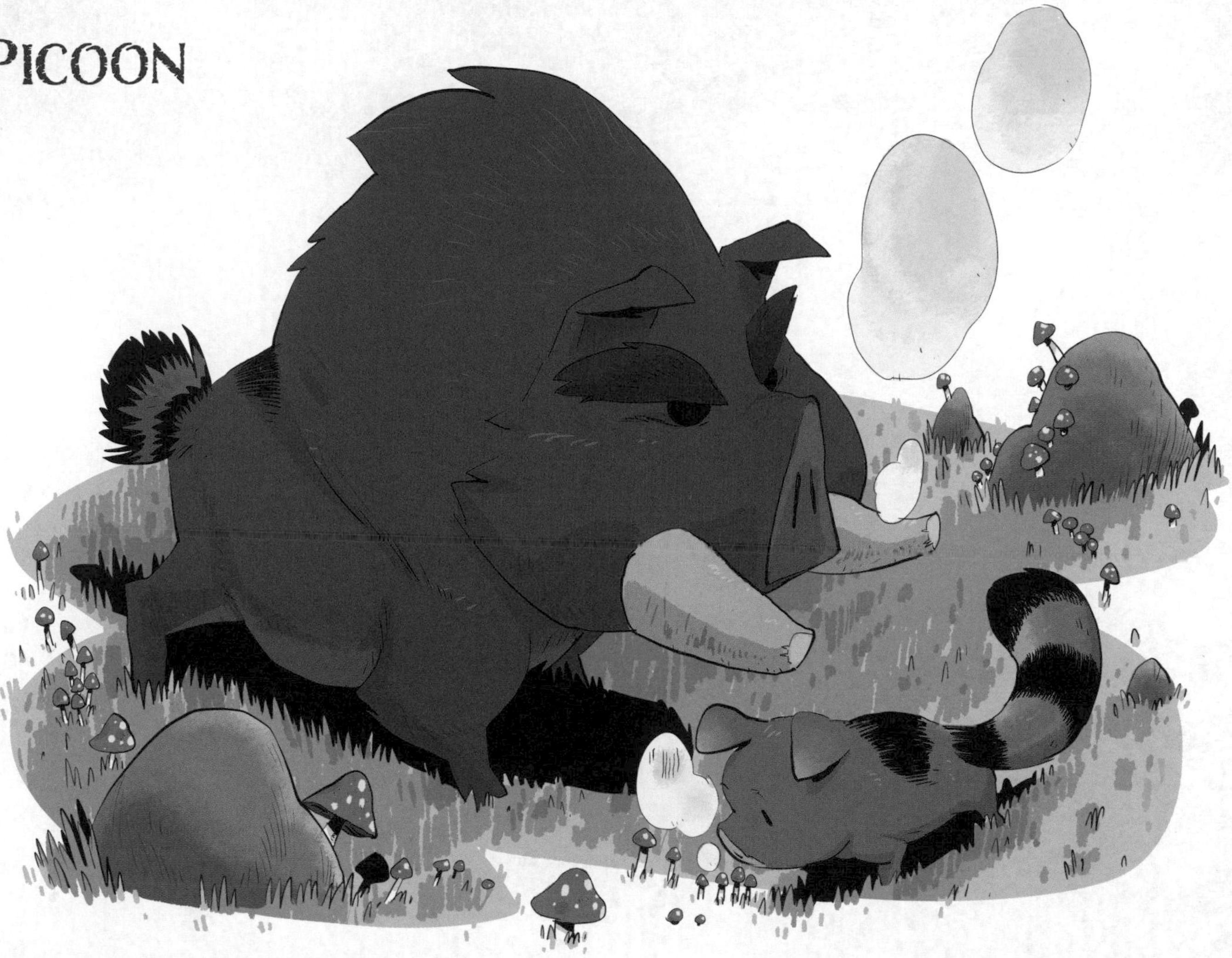

Terror Guard

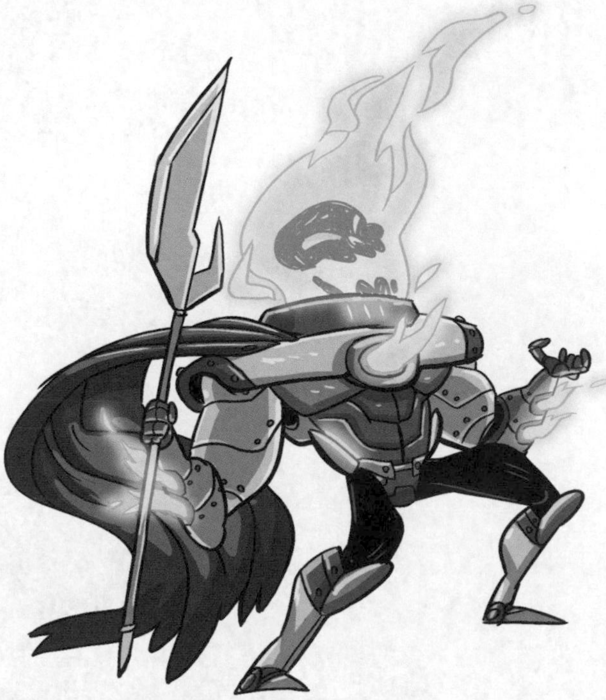

Gnot

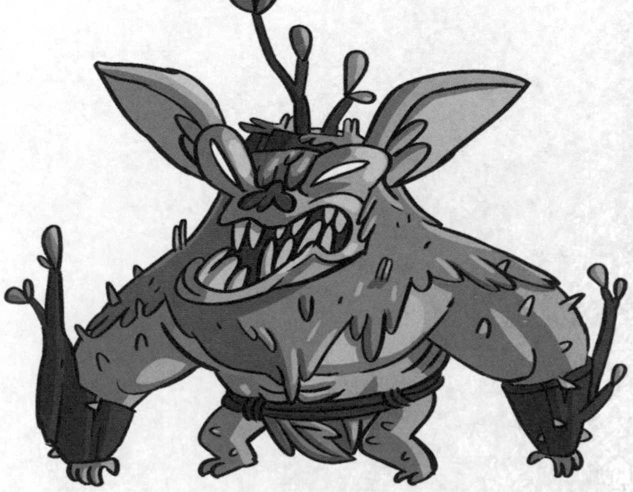

Bone Bobbin

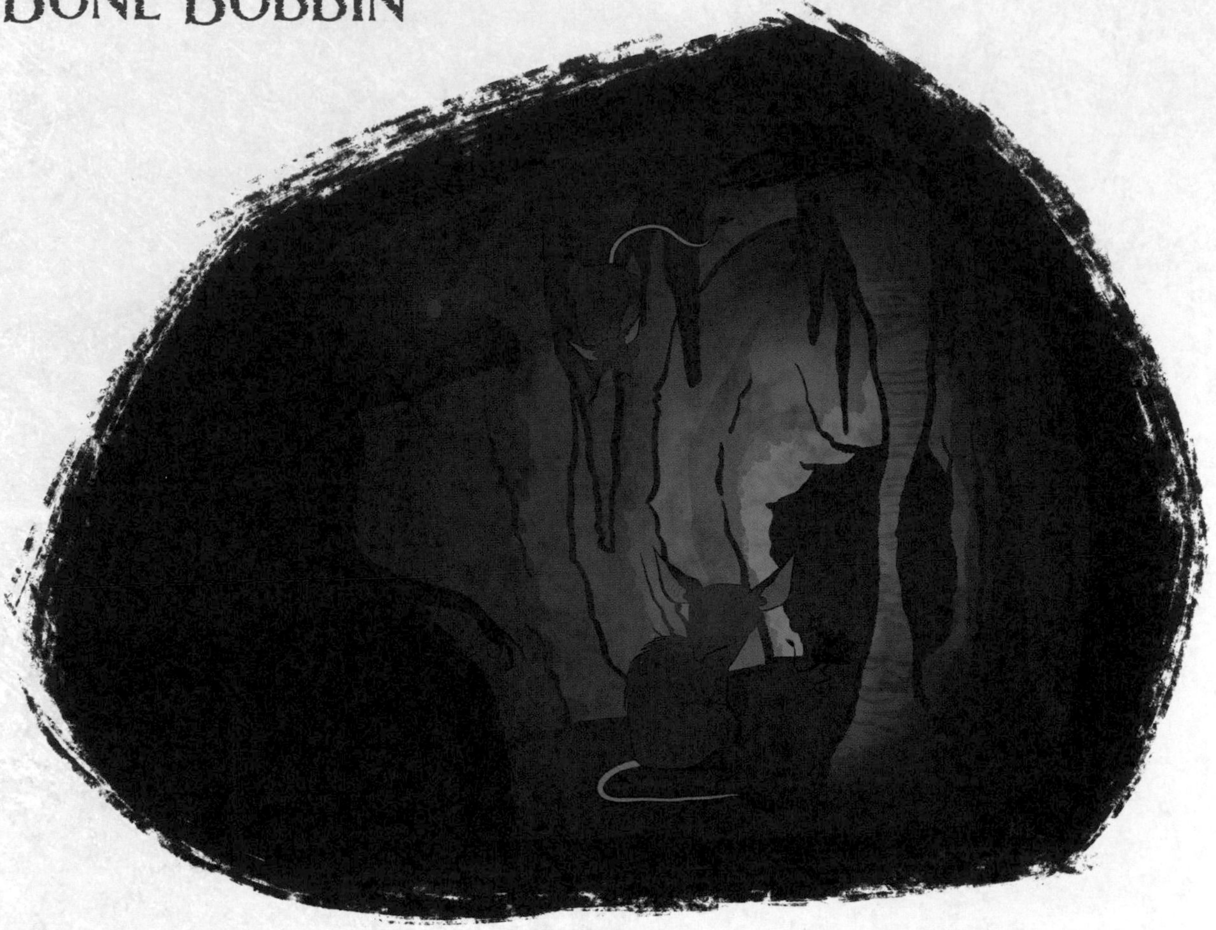

Sootch

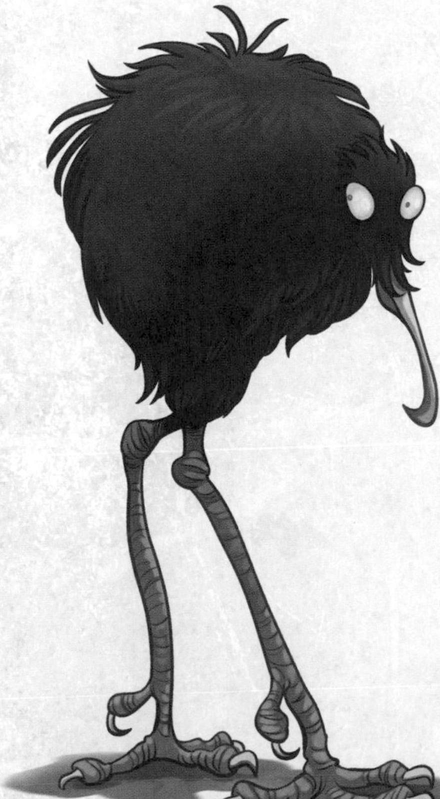

HupClaw

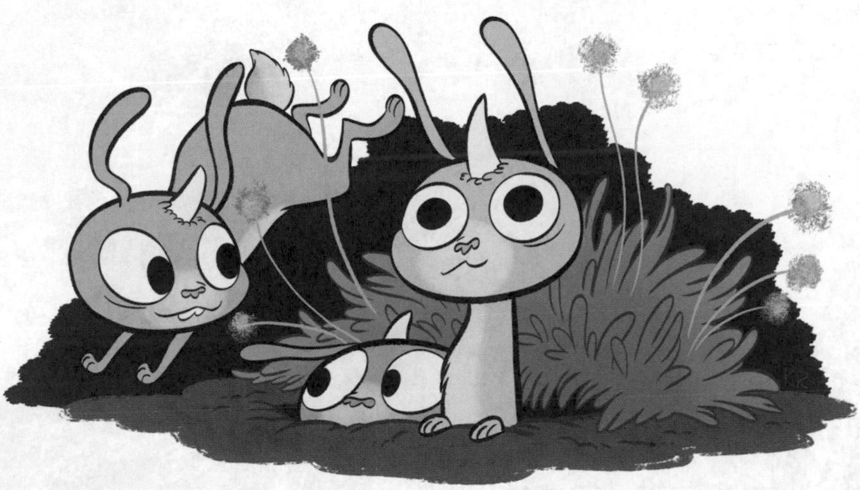

Bone Bobbin

With a keen sense of smell and incredibly acute vision in the dark, the dark blue rat-like bone bobbin is known to infest crypts and tunnels. While even the most soft and subtle of candlelight seems to disorient and pacify them, they are voracious and aggressive in the dark, with one bone bobbin often acting as a scout for hordes of a thousand or more nearby. They can often be seen by the glint of their glowing crimson eyes, or by the scars left behind by their deadly sharp claws. They have long, rubbery tails as long as their actual bodies, as well as rows of jagged flat teeth capable of pulverizing bone.

"Don't let th' size fool ya. If ya drop yer blade near a bobbin nest an' ya think: "Oh, this'll jus' take a wee moment ta snatch it back up" - Don't. S'already gone, an' ya stand ta lose even more."

~ Hook-hand Kip, Redori Fisherman

Sootch

No larger than the common sparrow or finch, Sootch are flightless little birds that prefer hot and arid biomes, such as the mesas of Airia. Sootch have lanky and disproportionate legs, as well as long, narrow beaks that give them an almost silly appearance, which (along with their shy nature) makes them an ideal target for predators. To cope with this perpetual threat, Sootch travel in large flocks, huddled together. Recently, small flocks of Sootch have been discovered in the Cinder Wood, more aggressive and territorial than their mountain cousins.

"Sootch? Seemed harmless enough, even in their li'l flocks, 'til they turned up in th' Cinder Wood. Somethin' about 'em was different, in the Wood. Mean li'l peckers, territorial li'l snots. Pests."

~ Ranos, Captain of the Yadori Guard (Fifth Division)

Hupclaw

Typically found in moderate litters of 8 to 9, Hupclaw live in interconnecting burrows that form a complex web of underground warrens. They are often found in habitats that support their primary diet of plants and insects, such as meadows, forests, and woodlands. Hupclaw appear to be some mix of rabbit and cat, roughly the size of both, but marked with a single small horn just above their nose. Their powerful hind legs make them swift and agile, and superb jumpers.

"As a young scholar, I had a beloved pet Hupclaw named Beaufort. He was endlessly cuddly, truly a wonderful familiar, but had a nasty habit of burrowing holes in the floor of my first laboratory."

~ Earthbinder Nurel, Kudori Elementalist

EVERLIVING

Fear and somber reverence surround the Everliving. It is said that when a member of the Yadori tribe reaches the height of their training, their body becomes ageless. Though their bodies do not, their minds age, and they grow increasingly aggressive and driven by instinct. They are sent away to the Terror Tombs to act as savage guardians: Gaunt skin stretched tight across bone, eyes sunken and vacant. As time struggles to ravage their ageless bodies, their skin turns ever more deeply purple and maroon. The older the Everliving, the darker the skin.

"Mother said not to look away. Grandfather was to be praised for his devotion and adherence to Yama's teachings. He was timeless now, like the mountains themselves. Still, the way his lip curled… The way his eyes just stared. I wept, despite myself."

~ Garrin, Yadori Armsmaster

THREAD

Thread are harvested primarily by traveling merchants for their beautiful silk, they are often crushed to make vibrantly colored pigments and inks as well. Forest-dwellers, they weave silken threads from branch to branch to catch smaller insects and morning dew. Though brightly colored and plentiful in the right regions, they are dangerously poisonous to eat.

"Some of the loveliest wares come from Thread silk, but you sure can't eat them, and their pigment doesn't make for great camouflage unless you're looking to entertain the children."

- Drumlin, Redori Tracker

BUSHELL IMP

Watch your belongings around a Bushell imp, the squat little compulsive thieves of the forest. In the presence of almost anything shiny or perceived as valuable the typically shy and weak beasts will be overcome with the urge to make off with their newfound treasure. More of a nuisance than any sort of legitimate threat, the plump little bean-shaped Bushell imp's first attempted theft is always some manner of armor for their squishy head: pots, pans, baskets, or whatever else they can get their hands on. Commonly, they are a pale shade of blue or green, but this can change from season to season.

"Squishy, stubby, little forest thieves. They can't help themselves around anything shiny, but they're not particularly fierce, and they're about as dangerous as a fat house cat."

~ Yadori Songsmith

EVERLIVING

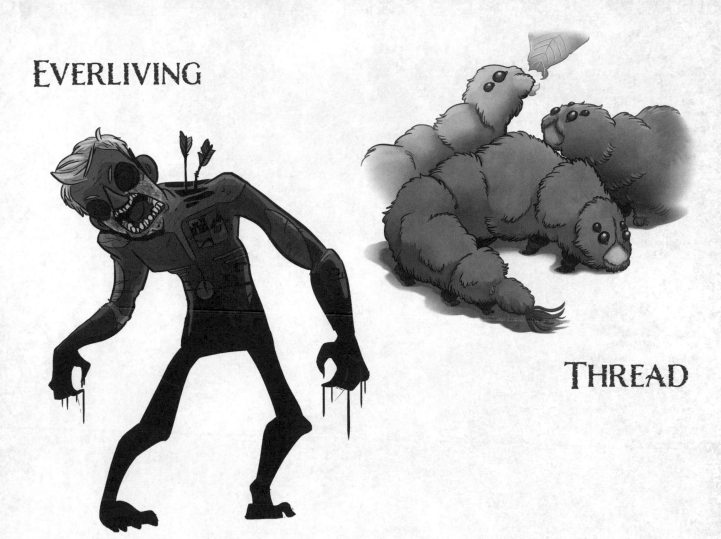

THREAD

BUSHELL IMP

MOGRIF

WICK

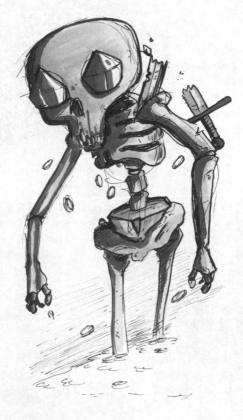

MOGRIF

As old as the land itself, the Mogrif have survived by hiding in plain sight. So long as the general size remains constant, the Mogrif can shape-shift to disguise their nature. In their true form, they appear to be red lizard-like humanoids with pale green eyes, pointy ears, and snub, bulbous beaks. With razor sharp claws to shred their prey, the dangerous and opportunistic Mogrif will keep its true self hidden until the ideal time to strike appears. Mimicking fur and hair is difficult for them, however, and they are primarily known to take the form of Yadori travelers and other (mostly) hairless animals.

"Never trust a Mogrif. They're older than dirt, and can't be trusted for even a second. They could be anyone, at any time, so.. I guess you shouldn't trust anyone. I mean, I'm no Mogrif, but how can you be sure? My head hurts."

~ Torlimus, Yadori Crusader

WICK

The lost halls of Hohlraum are a thing of legend, overflowing with glistening gold and glittering jewels. So great is the allure of this hoard that those who stumble upon it are rare to bring themselves to part from it. Neither food nor drink can tear them from their prize, until their greed and covetous nature slowly transform them into watchful, silent guardians of the golden cavern. Rotting away until they are little more than golden skeletons littered with gems, they warn intruders to leave their riches with a single ominous word: "Mine."

"Woe be to those who lust for coin,
whose sickness drives them to purloin.
Their greed would not be overcome,
the restless dead of lost Hohlraum."

~ Yates, High Songsmith of King's Keep

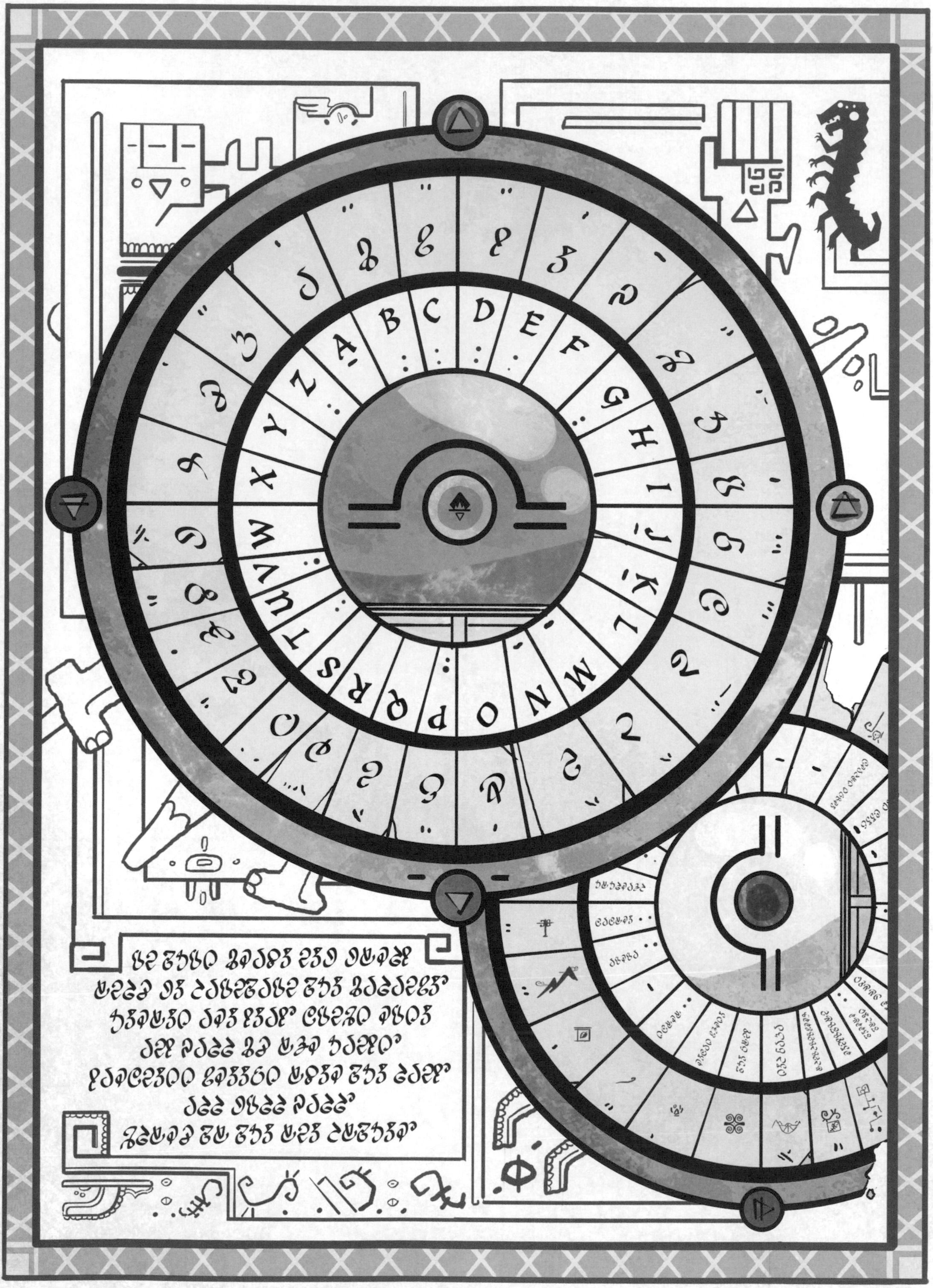
A B C D E F G H I J K L M N O P Q R S T U V W X Y Z

TENKO KING

>><< CONCEPT ART GALLERY >><<

The following pages of concept art feature characters and designs from my sketchbook. Shown throughout this section are initial concepts for the Redori and Kudori environments plus original sketches that make up the unique Tenko King world.

Enjoy!

-TAVIS

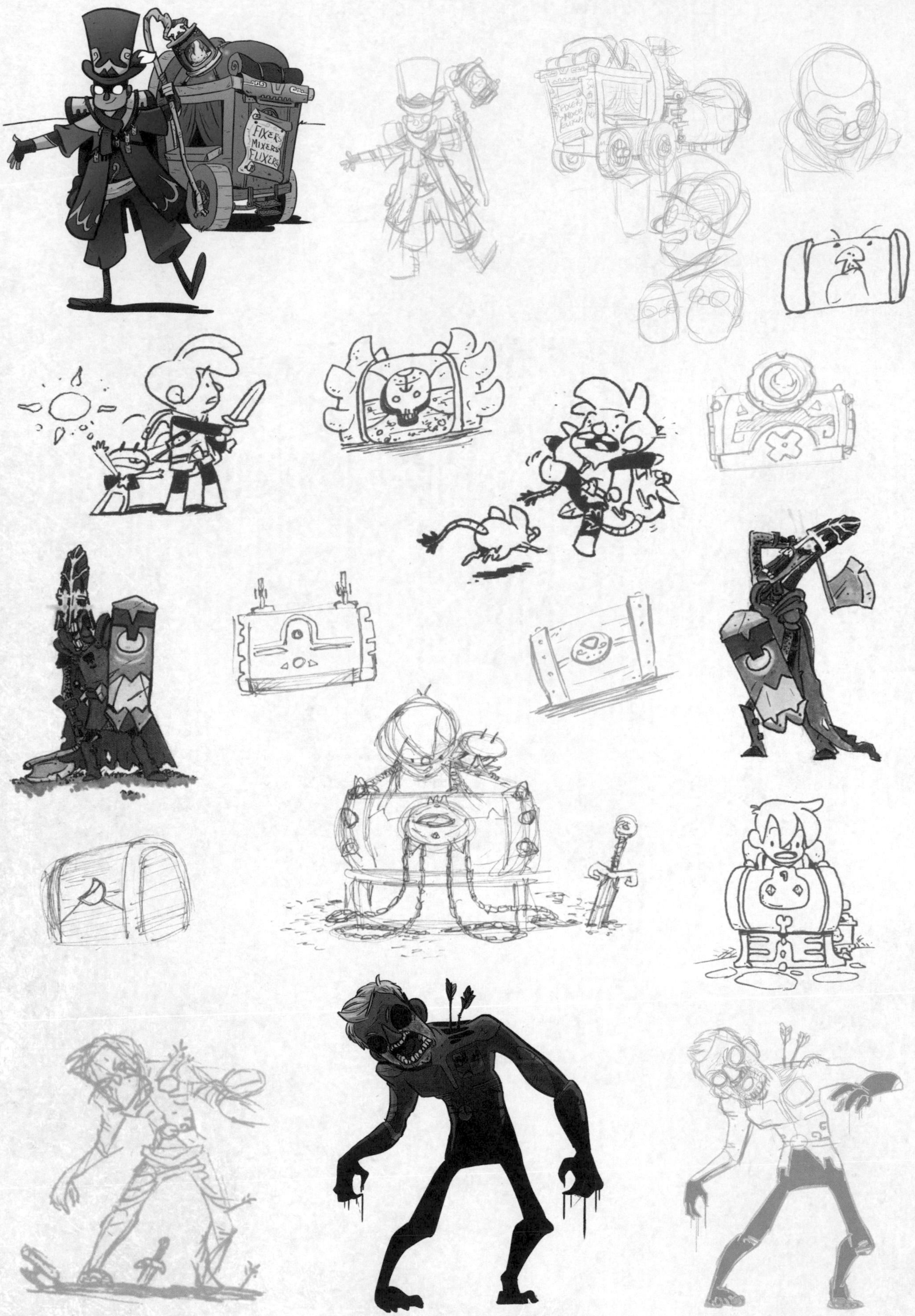
FIXERS
MIXERS
FLUXERS

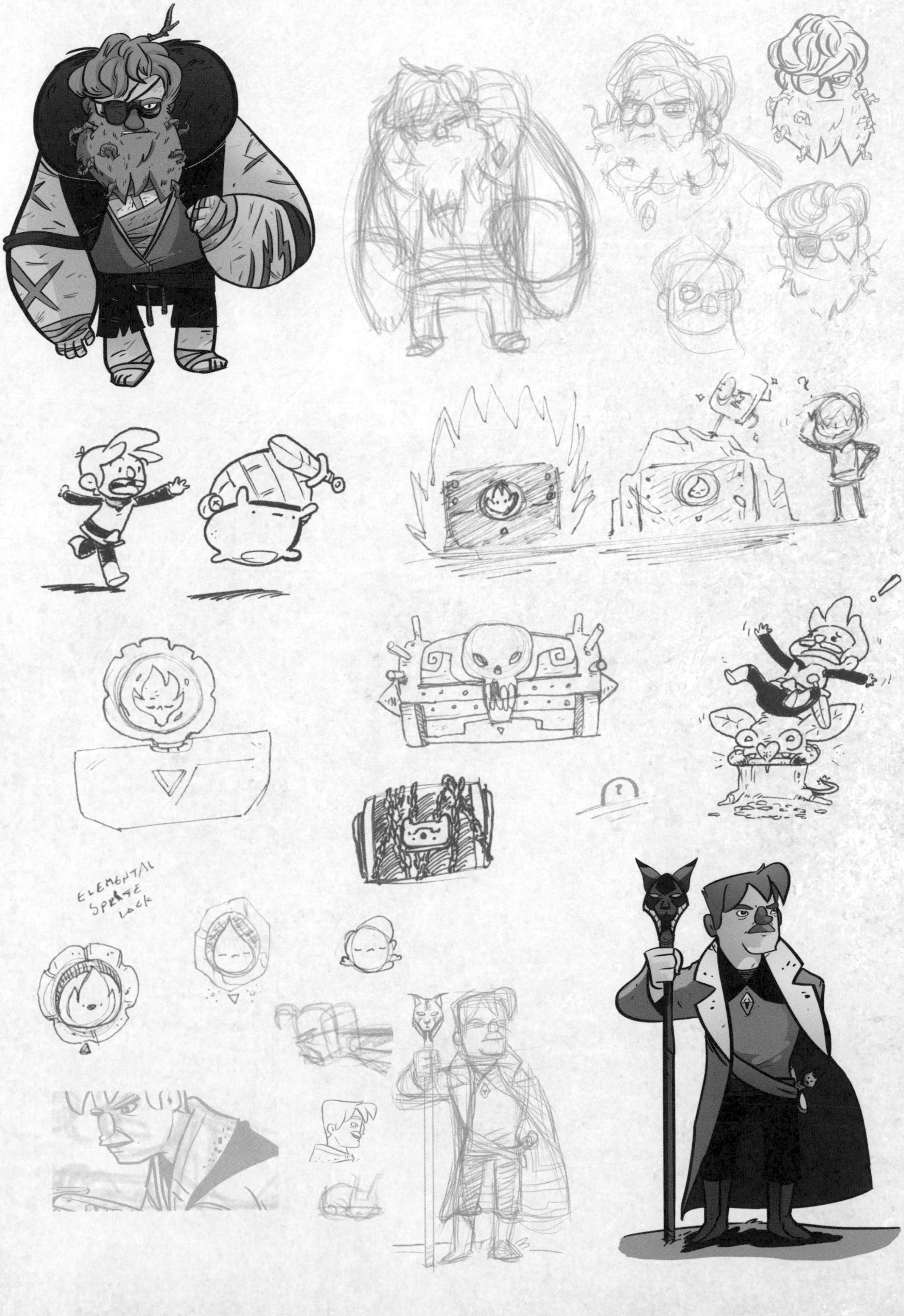
ELEMENTAL
SPRITE
LOCK

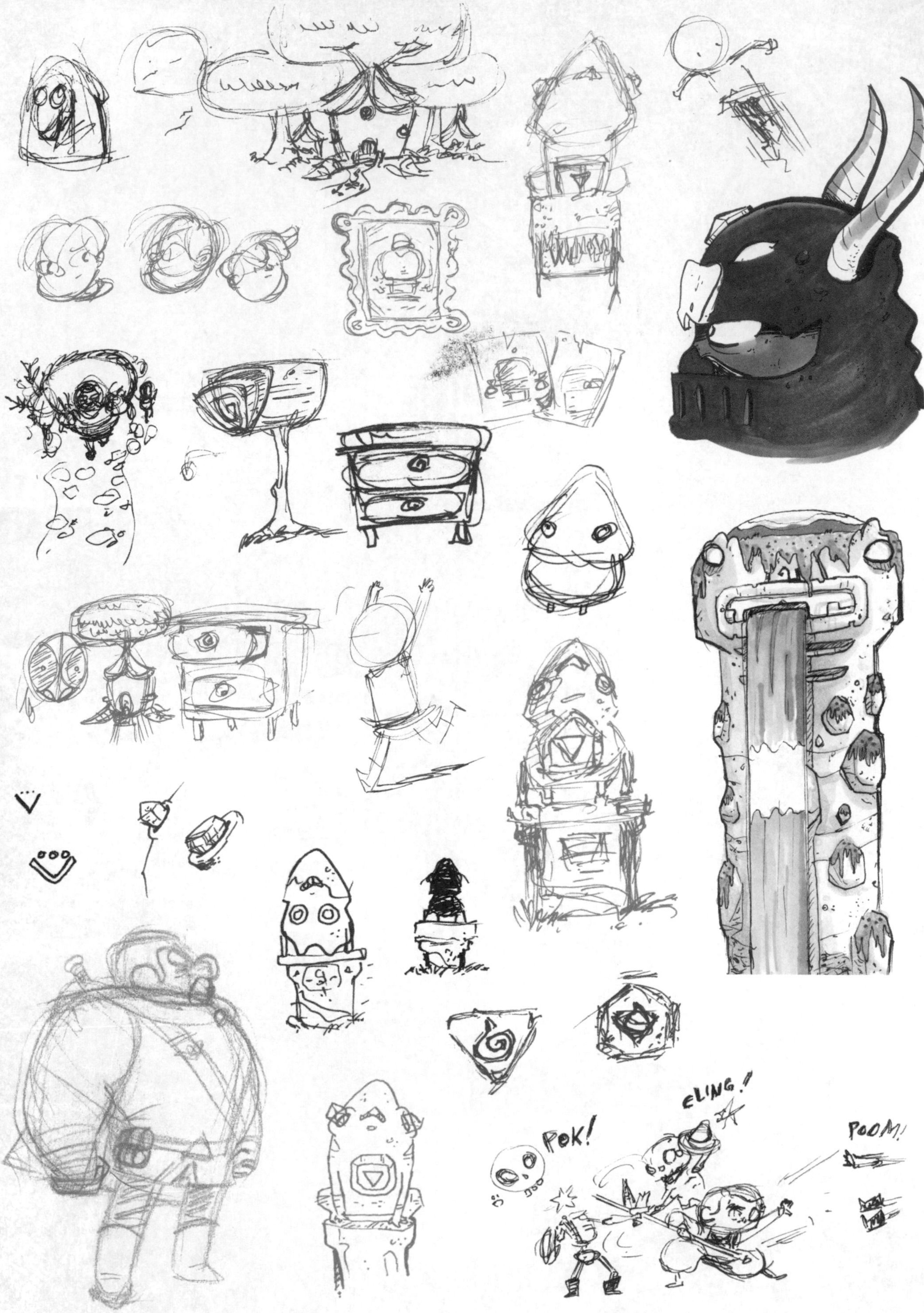
POK!
CLING!
POOM!

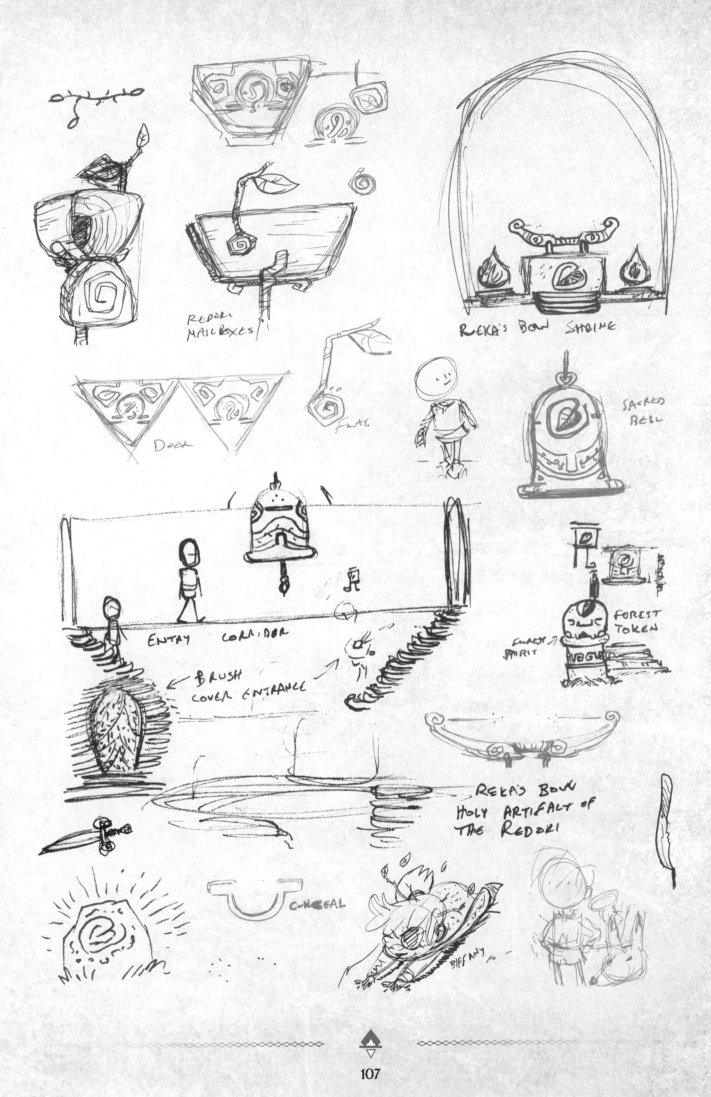

REDORI MAILBOXES

RUEKA'S BOW SHRINE

DOOR

SEAL

SACRED BELL

ENTRY CORRIDOR

BRUSH COVER ENTRANCE

FOREST TOKEN

FOREST SPIRIT

REKA'S BOW HOLY ARTIFACT OF THE REDORI

CONCEAL

BIFFANY

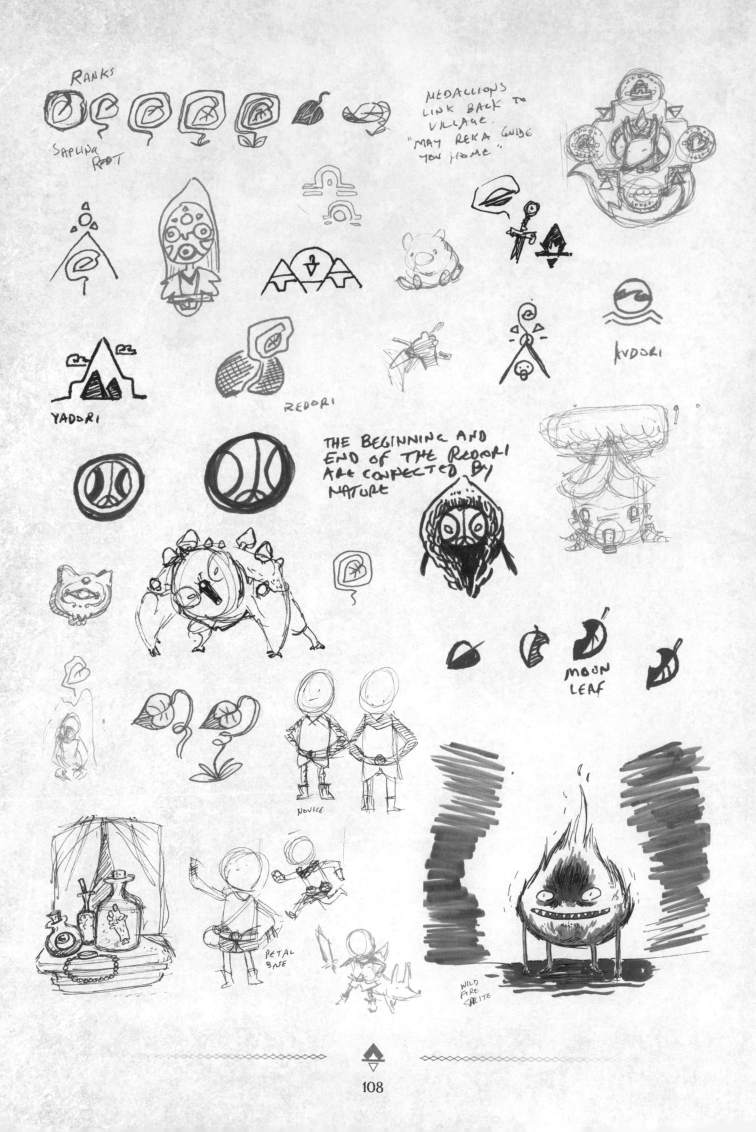

RANKS

SAPLING ROOT

MEDALLIONS
LINK BACK TO
VILLAGE.
"MAY REKA GUIDE
YOU HOME"

KUDORI

YADORI

REDORI

THE BEGINNING AND
END OF THE REDORI
ARE CONNECTED BY
NATURE

MOON
LEAF

NOVICE

PETAL
BNE

WILD
FIRE
SPRITE

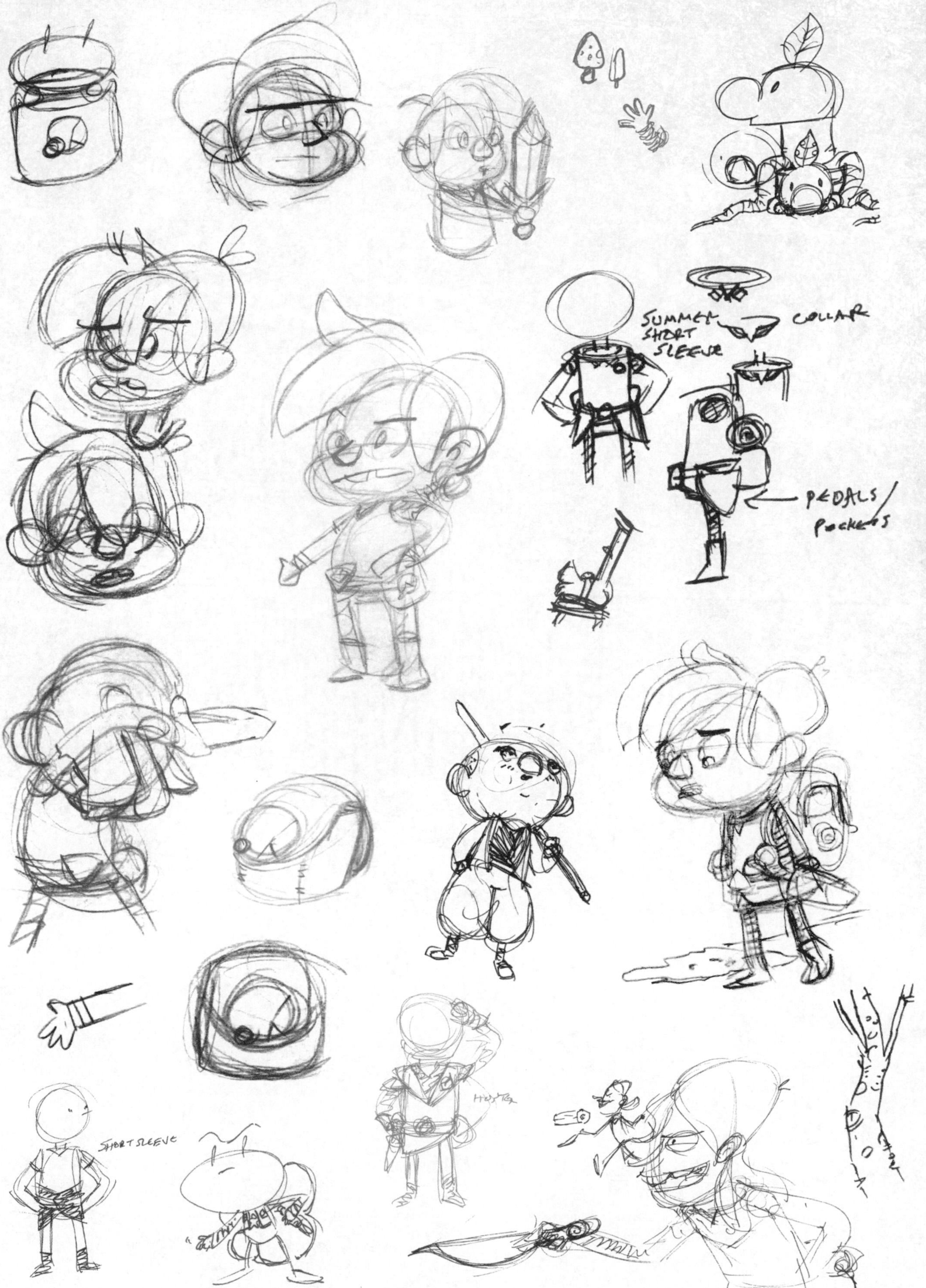
SUMMER SHORT SLEEVE
COLLAR
PEDALS / POCKETS
SHORT SLEEVE

DEDICATED TO MY SON, JONAS.

LIFE IS HARD, AND AMAZING, AND SCARY, AND WONDERFUL. YOU HAVE THE GREATEST HEART I KNOW. STAY KIND WHEN LIFE IS HARD, AND HUMBLE WHEN IT'S AMAZING. BE STRONG WHEN LIFE IS SCARY, AND NEVER LOSE YOUR SENSE OF WONDER.

There's a million people to thank, because I did not take this journey alone. The amazing fans who have supported this project and continue to support this project, my family for understanding the long nights and hard work, friends who have helped keep me sane or helped me bounce ideas around, and everyone who made this book what it is.

I hope my kids can look at this hard work and see the joy of creating something. That working hard at something you're passionate about hardly seems like work.

Thank you to my amazing wife and love of my life, Megan Maiden.

Thank you to my parents for their unending support and years and years of sketchbooks.

Thank you to my brother for being my sparring partner, and for years of headlocks and knife fights.

Thank you to Team Toonhound (Scott Kurtz, Cory Casoni, Steve Hamaker, Keith Wood, Brad Guigar, and Dylan Meconis) for the support, guidance, and friendship.

Thank you Katie J. Rice, Anthony Holden, and Derek Hunter not only for adding your own personal touches to the book, but also for inspiring me to be better.

Thank you to Myke Prohaska for the encouragement, excitement, and adding an extra bit of flavor to the Tenko King world.

Thank you to Sam Sykes who never stopped believing in me. I hope he leaves the air conditioning vents some day.

ART CONTRIBUTIONS:
Scott Kurtz, Steve Hamaker, Katie Rice, Derek Hunter, Anthony Holden

WRITING CONTRIBUTION:
Myke Prohaska

BOOK DESIGNED BY:
Keith Wood

TAVIS MAIDEN was activated in 1981 and spent much of
that time in the desert. In addition to comics and cartooning he
has had a number of obsessions, ranging from ping pong to pro
wrestling (and he just now decided that it would be awesome to
combine the two). His wife and children are the raddest people
in the world, and are unendingly supportive. Tavis has worked
with PVP, Table Titans, Penny Arcade, Wizards of the Coast,
BOOM!, Dynamite comics and more. It is strange for Tavis to
talk about himself in the third person, he usually saves that for
bids at world domination.

TWITTER.COM/TAVISMAIDEN · TAVISMAIDEN.TUMBLR.COM

MONSTERS, PIRATES, MAGIC, AND MORE!

TENKO KING

THE ADVENTURE CONTINUES IN VOLUME 2!